A.J. COATES

The Extinct Company

Book One in The Extinct Company Series

First published by Turkana Press 2021

First edition

ISBN: 9798500060990

*This book was professionally typeset on Reedsy.
Find out more at reedsy.com*

This book is dedicated to the memory of Yasmin – nurse, army officer, chef, gardener, seamstress, wine connoisseur, mother, wife, confidant, friend, a woman full of generosity, panache and humor and my excellent sister.

Contents

Acknowledgement

I would like to thank my wife Beth for her unflinching encouragement, help, and expertise every day. My children for being my first listeners and readers of my work and for giving me continuous positive feedback. My sister Yasmin, for both financial and moral support, I am sorry she is no longer with us to read my finished novel.

Thanks to my parents-in-law, Johnny and Elaine Mizell, for their faith in my abilities and for supporting us while I took time to write.

Hanneke Hoorn Coates, my mother, for always supporting my wild expeditions across the globe, including this desk based one.

Thanks to Jo Lane, my editor, for her wisdom, expertise and encouragement, also to Rafael Andres for creating such an amazing book cover.

Prologue Hue City, Vietnam, 1968.

Sergeant Gibson was covered in blood and bits of ancient wall that had been blasted down on top of him. He was exhausted, thirsty, and his whole team was now lying dead in the holes in the wall where they had sought cover. The Viet Cong had ceased fire and were walking silently forwards, pushing the bodies of the US soldiers with their sandals to see if they were still alive. They were heading towards Gibson. He sat there with a grenade in his battered hands. It was all he had left and he was going to destroy as many of the bastards as he could when he went.

A slapping noise broke the silence, the unmistakable note of a high velocity round hitting flesh.

One of the VC collapsed in a heap, then another, and another, as if some invisible wind was knocking them down. Within seconds Gibson was alone, the VC reduced to a collection of black pajamas lying on the ground.

Suddenly, from nowhere, a large, black hand reached forward and gently pulled the grenade from Gibson's grasp. "Good afternoon Sergeant, you look like you need a cup of tea." The hand belonged to a tall, athletic young soldier dressed in clean, grey-colored fatigues. His other hand held an elegant .375 Purdey hunting rifle with a silencer screwed into the barrel.

"I am Private Kitts." He spoke in an aristocratic voice that was better suited to an afternoon grouse shoot in the Highlands of Scotland than a battlefield in South Asia.

Private Kitts pulled a thermos from an embossed leather cylinder from his pack. He eased the lid from the top of the container and poured, handing a cup to Gibson who took it with a blank expression that turned to a smile. It was the best thing he had ever tasted in his entire life. Gibson closed his eyes in pleasure as the smokey, sweet warmth filled his mouth.

"Lapsang Souchong. Perfect after a hard battle, don't you think?"

Sergeant Gibson was starting to wonder if his grenade had in fact gone off and if he was now in heaven. Admittedly, he was rather surprised to find that angels were large black guys with fancy British accents. Private Kitts smiled broadly, raised his eyebrows and the thermos.

"Top up?"

Then he riffled through his pack again and brought out a small leather case. He undid the strap to reveal a neat silver box with a crest on the front, which he opened and proffered to Gibson.

"Marmite sandwich?"

1

Lokichogio, Kenya

Paloma Stuart sat in the co-pilot's seat of the single engine Caravan, swatting flies and swearing. She and the pilot, Wilson Namunyak, had landed in this most Northern Kenya airport to bring supplies for the refugee camp three hours ago. Paloma needed to get some more hours flying the Caravan before she could become Captain. Once they had supervised the unloading of their plane, Wilson announced he had a 'quick mission' and disappeared.

Sweat trickled down her back as small children heckled her from the rusty fence at the edge of the airfield. "Give me ten-dollar, pretty lady," they sang in unison.

To her relief, Wilson's handsome form finally appeared on the entry ladder. He was cradling a bumpy plastic sack.

"Captain Wilson, what the hell have you got?"

"Miss Stuart, I promised those kids last week that I'd buy a few dolls they made."

Wilson pushed back the edge of the sack to reveal a scratched, waxy face with wobbly blue eyes, the rest of its body clearly cobbled together from the broken body parts of other dolls: the effect was decidedly alarming. Wilson raised his eyebrows and shut the bag tightly, as if to prevent its escape.

"You sure those things aren't filled with drugs? What on earth are you going to do with them? Surely you aren't going to give them to your children?"

Wilson chuckled, clearly amused at her squeamishness. "I like my trainee pilots to have the pressure of carrying multiple passengers," he said drily. "Didn't you have dolls when you were a little girl, Miss Stuart?"

"I had one. We named it Moaning Myrtle. It made a sort of strangled sobbing noise when you put it on its back."

They had gone through the preflight checks, flipping switches and checking gauges. Paloma pushed a couple more buttons, and the prop turned twice and then coughed into life with a tremendous roar.

They adjusted their headsets to cut down the noise.

"Lokichogio Tower, this is Five Yankee Oscar Charlie Delta requesting permission to taxi for takeoff." Shifting her finger off the transmit button, Paloma continued her story. "My brother decided Moaning Myrtle contained a horcrux and that it had to be destroyed."

The ground unit pulled away the wheel chocks, gave the thumbs up, and Wilson guided the plane forward. The pitch of the engine increased.

"Alistair filled Moaning Myrtle with petrol, put a lighted candle on her chest and then he shot holes in her until she burst into a ball of fire," she said, laughing at the memory.

Paloma pressed the button that connected her with the tower. "Permission to take off. Destination Wilson airport, Nairobi. Two souls on board."

At the head of the runway the Caravan rocked like a stallion preparing for a charge.

Paloma pushed the throttle, released the brakes, and they blazed down the runway. The empty plane quickly lifted off the ground and Paloma pulled her up and around onto their course, heading in a graceful curve.

Wilson looked at her. She had a huge grin on her face and she stuck her tongue out at him.

"I literally do not know what you were talking about. Was that some kind of weird *Mzungu* language? Horewhatsits? Moaning Myrtle?"

"Oh my! Your kids have missed an important part of their education. I can't believe you are buying them freaky dolls and NOT Harry Potter books."

"Harry Potter boo... what the.." Wilson's voice through her headset cut short. Ragged holes were snapping a line through the underside of the wing towards the cockpit.

The plane lurched sideways and Wilson slumped against his harness. Holes blasted through the plexiglass and studded the top of the cockpit. A vicious wind whipped through the plane.

Paloma pulled hard on the controls, desperately pushing the aircraft sideways and then up and away from the gunfire that was peppering the fuselage. The frame of the plane howled in complaint as it reached the limits of force. She dragged the yoke back with brute force, pulling them skyward.

Wilson was motionless; crimson blood dripped from a corner of his mouth.

Paloma took a deep breath. She couldn't help him—the plane was bucking like a bronco and she needed both hands to control it. She hit the mike on the control yoke, "Mayday. Mayday. This is Five Yankee Oscar Charlie Delta coming from Loki en route to Wilson. We've been hit by ground fire. Pilot is hit and seriously wounded. We are falling apart. Give me somewhere safe to land—I'm not sure how long we can stay airborne."

Then the engine belched a thick cloud of black smoke and stopped, its comforting roar replaced by screaming wind as the nose dipped down.

"Mayday. Mayday. We're going down. My position is 36 North 6-6-

3-3-8-8 East 4-5-2-5-6-8.''

Paloma scanned the empty savannah ahead, searching for somewhere to land. She glanced at the large Garmin GPS screen and saw, to her horror, that in her panic, she had done a 180-degree turn and was heading back toward their attackers. The Lokichogio road was snaking under her. No trees. Paloma lined it up under the plane. The Caravan was a tough aircraft, capable of landing in very short distances when the engine was working.

She took a deep breath, her hands wet with sweat.

"You can do it. Relax. Concentrate. Set her down like a bird on a branch," Wilson's voice came over the intercom.

"Wilson! Wilson? Where are you hit? I can't let go!"

"I am just leaking slightly. You concentrate on landing, like I showed you."

The ground was coming up fast. Paloma maneuvered the plane like a bird until it hit the dirt hard in an enormous ball of dust and bounced. Smacking down again and speeding on down the track, stones clattered against the bottom of the fuselage like a rally car at full tilt.

She applied the brakes gradually, worried about bursting a tire on the rough road. The craft bumped along the road with violence, eventually easing as it ran out of steam. Coming to a halt at last, silence and heat greeted them through the broken windows.

Paloma unclipped her harness then reached across to do Wilson's.

"Know why I'm called Wilson, don't you?"

"No." The sheer terror she had just experienced was replaced with relief that he was still talking.

"I was born in a plane en route to Wilson airport."

"Ha, good job it wasn't Lokichogio!"

Wilson chuckled. Then an expression that only a Maasai Warrior could compose crossed his face.

"Wilson, what—"

"Paloma. Listen to me. Carefully. Don't ask questions. This is an order from your Captain. In the case behind my seat you'll find a Heckler Kock MP5. You know how to use it. See that cloud of dust on the track ahead? That is a pickup full of armed men coming to kill us. Get out of the plane and get into the ditch on the side of the road. When the pickup reaches 200m shoot at the front tires. When you hit one the car will flip. Don't hesitate. Get up and run towards it. Use the ditch. Shoot anything that moves. Keep shooting until they stop moving. Now, go."

"But, what about–"

"Go, go, go!" His voice was weak but resolute.

Paloma grabbed the heavy case and jumped onto the hot murram track from the door at the back of the plane. She could see the pickup: a wobbly mirage on the heat of the road. As she ran across to the ditch, she could hear Wilson calmly using the radio.

"Mayday. Mayday this is Five Yankee Oscar Charlie Delta. We are on the ground and coming under imminent attack. Send armed support immediately."

She threw herself into the ditch, pulled the weapon out of the case, cocked it, switched it to single shot and flicked off the safety.

Through the red dot scope she pulled a bead on the fast-approaching vehicle. Her hands were steady, her breathing calm. As the pickup crossed the 200m line, she squeezed off two shots in rapid succession.

The Toyota appeared to do a neat, slow-motion cartwheel. Bodies, weapons, and what appeared to be a goat, flew out of the cargo bed.

Paloma forced herself into a flat sprint before the hunk of metal stopped rolling, closing the last 100m between them in seconds. A bloody figure clothed in dirty bedsheets was pulling himself out of the place where the windscreen used to be. In his hands was an AK47 submachine gun.

Two neat shots cracked out from her MP5. The dirty sheets crumpled and the AK clattered on the buckled bonnet.

5

Micro seconds later, the air tore apart with a rip of bullets and the explosion of automatic fire as the surrounding earth disintegrated into dust. Paloma buried her face in the ground, shots zinging around her until she heard the click of an empty mag. She looked up just in time to see the wild charge of a remarkably skinny man, dressed in way-too-big military fatigues, screaming towards her. Two more neat shots rang out from her weapon and the man dropped in a heap on the ground. A black and white shape moved out from behind the remains of the car, and Paloma swung her weapon into position.

"Blaaaah, blah..." The 'flying goat' trotted nonchalantly over to a thorn bush and started grazing.

Paloma stepped cautiously towards the wreckage, kicking weapons away from bodies as she moved. Nothing else stirred. All the men were dead. Hurrying back to the bullet-ridden plane, she climbed back into the cabin. Wilson had pressed wound dressing onto his leg and bits of wrapping from the first aid kit littered the cabin.

Wilson smiled thinly as Paloma hurried down the aisle.

"Well done, Miss Stuart, excellent landing and excellent shooting. That will be all for today's lesson."

"Wilson, what the hell is going on?"

Wilson paused. He looked into Paloma's dusty face and green eyes before speaking.

"You must not repeat this, but you have earned the right to hear it. I work uncover for INTERPOL, the international Criminal Police Organization. We came to believe the dolls are a critical element in a smuggling ring. Some of our most wanted criminals seem to be connected to them. We don't know what they are smuggling. The ones I collected are empty, but this is where their journey starts. I am sorry; I really didn't expect anyone to react so strongly to me buying some empty dolls. I put you in great danger."

"Well, we survived. But what makes you think they are being used in a smuggling operation?"

Wilson closed his eyes, and Paloma could see he was in great pain.

Rummaging through the first aid kit and she pulled out a sachet of pain killers and gave them to Wilson along with her water bottle.

He swallowed gratefully, then answered, "This is going to sound strange, but it piqued our suspicion when our agent in Mombasa noticed a bunch of retirees on cruise ships carrying them. We look out for stuff that doesn't look normal."

"Yeah, that is weird. Why don't you just get some older operative from INTERPOL to go on a cruise?"

As she spoke, Paloma was making a better job of the dressing Wilson had crudely applied. Her hands were shaking; talking to him was calming her down.

In the distance came the heavy *whomp, whomp* of helicopters.

"Paloma, you need to leave the aircraft. I'll be fine. Get out and hide. I don't know who this is, but they certainly responded quickly to our distress call. Go. Go!"

Grabbing her weapon, she rushed out of the plane, Wilson urging her all the way. She dropped back into the cover of the ditch, tucking under a scrubby thorn bush. Within seconds, two fat Puma choppers with Kenyan army markings circled the scene and dropped onto the ground, disgorging a phalanx of heavily armed troops who fanned out—weapons at the ready—in a reassuring and professional choreography.

Paloma stood up, relieved.

A tall officer walked towards Paloma with a slightly admiring grin on his face.

"Captain Githanga, Kenyan Army. Are you finished here, Miss?"

Paloma wiped the dirt from her face, brushed her hair out of her eyes, and stood up. She handed him the MP5.

"Yes, yes, thank you. Captain Wilson, though. Wilson's the pilot,

7

he's in the cockpit. He's been hit."

"My combat medics are already with him. He's in expert hands. Once they stabilize him, we'll get him back to Nairobi and in hospital."

Hot tears of relief made tracks through the dust on her face as she walked beside the Captain. Strong arms reached down and pulled her into the bowels of the helicopter. Someone handed her a metal mug full of hot masala chai and she collapsed onto the canvas bench in the cargo area. Both doors were open and through one they lifted Wilson strapped to a stretcher. He looked over at her and shouted over the din of the engine,

"I was born in a plane, but sure as hell had no intention of dying in one! Good job, Miss Stuart. I owe you a beer."

They left the doors open with soldiers scanning the ground with their barrels as the beast lifted off the ground and set course back to Nairobi.

2

Pipeline Road, Panama

Alistair Gordon Stuart swung his legs out of the Land Rover Defender. His jungle boots hit the thick mud and he grabbed the worn but cared for Stihl chainsaw from the back of the car. He surveyed the fallen tree across the track with the eye of an expert and walked towards it, flexing his arms to loosen them up.

After an hour of crashing his car through the overgrown track, he was glad of an excuse to step out of the vehicle and stretch his legs. Thick drops of rain found their way through the canopy of trees, making streaks in the mud splattered sides of Land Rover. As the rain touched the ground, hot, damp air rose towards him in a cocktail of monkey droppings and crushed leaves.

The track was the famous Pipeline Road, built by American combat engineers in the 1930s to service an oil pipeline that crossed the narrow isthmus of Panama. It ran parallel to the Canal and provided land-based insurance against the bombing of the waterway.

The chainsaw roared into life on a second pull, blotting out the soft sounds of wind and rain. Alistair started carving out neat sections of tree trunks and branches across the track. They fell into the wet mud at his feet as he worked.

After half an hour, the tree lay in the road like a neatly sliced sausage. He killed the motor and reached for his water.

Suddenly, the sky blackened as if someone had spilt a bottle of ink in the heavens above. Wind battered the trees, gyrating them violently and ripped small branches and leaves, tossing them to the ground. The rain came down so thickly Alistair felt like he was standing under a blood-warm waterfall. Bigger branches came crashing down in alarming cracks, pulling tendrils of lianas with them as they fell.

Alistair looked around for a place to make a safe camp. Driving on down the track would be a battle. In the next kilometer there was a slope that even in the dry weather tested the Land Rover and his driving skills. He grabbed his machete from the dashboard and started cutting a path off the road with a powerful backhand, forehand stoke. He needed to find some decent trees to put up his shelter.

A tremendous clap shook the forest, followed by a flash of light that threw the complete scene into sharp relief.

There in front of him, tucked neatly into a slight rise in the ground and covered in vegetation, was what appeared to be a solid building. He cut his way towards it. All these years he must have driven and even walked right past it and never saw it.

It looked like an old bunker, solid concrete walls like ancient slabs of rock, growing out of the earth with narrow slits for windows. Round the side led a zigzag trench. Alistair was enjoying himself alone, discovering mysteries in the wild with the force of nature being thrown at him.

He went back to the car, putting his high-powered torch in his pocket, and then finished cutting his way to the trench at the side of the building. With his cotton bush shirt plastered to his back with rain, he felt a rising excitement. As he got closer, he could see the remains of a camouflage paint pattern on the walls. Water ran down open drains around the building as the storm increased in ferocity, stabbing the forest with vicious barbs of lightning. The trench led to what looked like a rear entrance, which was closed with a thick steel door. Grabbing a wheel-like handle, Alistair tried to spin it, heaving until it felt like the muscles in his back would pop open. The door was set deep into the walls, which looked like they were at least a meter thick. Clearly nobody had been here for decades. Small trees were attempting to grasp the concrete apron around the building and layers of leaf litter and fallen branches smothered the foundations.

He balanced on his left leg and punched out at the handle with a karate kick that would have felled a horse. His boot connected with the metal and the wheel spun, landing Alistair on his backside in surprise.

Grinning to himself, splayed out in the pouring rain, he effortlessly jumped back onto his feet with a flick. Spinning the handle until it stopped, he put his shoulder against the door and pushed.

3

The Bunker

T he door opened reluctantly, hinges screaming: metal on metal, rust on rust. Alistair's heart was pounding as he swept his torch around the dark space.

The concrete box he had stepped into was a compressed version of outside. Thin slit windows punctured the thick walls at firing height. Musty ammonia filled his lungs. He shone the beam of his torch across rusty tables, an old desk and chairs upholstered in moldy orange vinyl. The beam flashed as it caught the eyes of bats who were chirping and stirring from their perches. His eyes narrowed as his torch illuminated a stainless-steel cabinet.

Bat guano stuck to Alistair's wet boots as he walked over to get a better look at the cabinet. Something about it looked out of place. As he ran the light along its empty shelves, a thick metal binder glinted in the light. It stood upright and alone. Alistair cocked his head and read the words stenciled on the spine: "SGT. GIBSON".

He reached up to grab the binder with his left hand, holding his torch steady with his right. It was stuck to the shelf. He clamped the torch between his teeth and tugged with both hands.

A metallic click freed the binder, and it hinged forwards. Then, the cabinet itself generated a noise like a wind-up toy. Alistair's mind clicked to a dusty village in Afghanistan as he leapt backwards and buried his face in the bat shit.

But there was no explosion.

Alistair rose from the floor and went back to inspect the cabinet. With a bit of force, it slid to one side, revealing a solid metal door. On the door was a faded military looking symbol. On a dark shield-like shape was a blood red animal skull with long curving horns. Piercing one eye and protruding from the top of the skull was an arrow.

Alistair spat the muck out of his mouth and wiped his lips on his wet sleeve. He snatched up the torch and stared at the door with the strange symbol.

At least he assumed it was a door; it had no handle and no hinges. He ran his fingers around the edges where the metal met the concrete. Nothing. He pushed. Solid and immobile. Stepping back, he traced the perimeter of the door with his torch. On the right side, set into a stainless-steel plate, was a single line of ten black buttons. Etched onto the plate were the numbers 1 to 10 and the words 'THE MAGIC SHOP.' Alistair pressed the buttons in a dozen combinations. They made satisfying clicking sounds, but nothing happened and the door stood resolutely shut.

4

Gamboa

Ten days later. 7am. Alistair sat at his favorite table under a Myrtle tree at the GAS57 pub, watching the tugs power their way through the brown water of the Panama Canal.

GAS57 was halfway up the famous canal in the village of Gamboa, an unchanged tropical paradise built by the Americans in the 1930s during the heyday of the old Canal Zone.

The pub sat on the site of the town's original gas station, building number 57, hence the name. The ground floor accommodated the pub. Its interior featured high ceilings, mismatched chairs, tables, and comfortable sofas. The floors above held apartments with deep overhanging roofs and wide, cool verandas. Alistair's apartment was in the roof's apex.

Paloma slid into a seat next to Alistair and closed her eyes. After arriving at midnight from Nairobi via Paris, she was enjoying soaking up the moist warm air, the distant bellows of howler monkeys and the sheer peace of the place. Paloma was wearing pajamas and Blundstone boots and sat cross-legged on the chair. She had been away nearly a year getting her flying hours up.

"God, it feels good to be home."

Alistair smiled affectionately. He adored his sister and was glad she was back in Panama safely. Although they had been chatting online, neither of them had spoken in person about what had happened in Kenya yet.

From the door of the pub stepped a tall, powerful looking man with skin like polished cocobolo wood. He was carrying a tray bearing fruit, bread, butter, a large jar of Marmite and a fine thermos. He was Dr. Kitts-Vincent, world's foremost tropical butterfly expert, skilled jungle craftsman and owner and operator of GAS57 Pub. Alistair and Paloma called him Dr. KV. KV was the Latin term used by British public school children for keeping lookout. Their father had introduced him that way when they were tiny children and it had stuck. As someone who had always watched out for them, the name suited him.

"Paloma, we have surely missed you. This hooligan has been completely out of control since you left."

Dr. Kitts-Vincent had the rich accent of someone who had been through the upper echelons of English public schools.

He sat down, and as he poured the tea, the unmistakable, smokey aroma of Lapsang Souchong tea filled the air. Dr. Kitts-Vincent had been their surrogate parent since their father had been killed when Alistair was sixteen and Paloma thirteen; that was over six years ago.

"Yuck, Marmite," Paloma wrinkled her little nose.

"Come on girl, it's a tradition."

They relaxed in the comfort of ritual and looked at Paloma expectantly, eager to hear about her recent ordeal.

"Last Thursday at around 9.30am Wilson and I oversaw the loading of the Caravan. Can you believe it nearly 1000kg of microwavable cake mix! Who has a microwave in a refugee camp? I'll tell you the whole thing just got crazier and crazier as the day went on."

Paloma told them the entire story: Wilson's dolls, the bullet holes in the plane and Wilson's injuries, the harrowing landing, the battle

15

with the guys in the pickup and their return to Nairobi with the Kenyan Army by helicopter. As promised, she didn't mention Wilson's role with INTERPOL.

"Wilson's fine. He'll be flying again a couple weeks and he has some more scars to show his children."

"Paloma, what happened to the dolls?" asked Dr. KV.

"The dolls, oh the dolls. I'm not sure. They were lying on the floor when I jumped out to hide when we heard the choppers. But I didn't go back to the plane after that. Why?"

"I have a feeling that either the dolls were important. Something in that plane was important." Dr. Kitts-Vincent paused and then continued his train of thought. "Whoever was shooting at the plane wanted to get it down and wanted to get rid of you and Wilson. How did Wilson know with such certainty that the approaching cloud of dust would be a pickup full of men who wanted to kill you? Why did he order you to kill anything that moved?"

"And what has the goat got to do with it?" chimed in Alistair, eyebrows raised.

Paloma punched him in the arm.

"Paloma, there is more to this story. Are you afraid to tell us something?"

"Seriously, Paloma. I think Dr. KV is right. Something is very fishy about the whole thing. I mean, random lads playing with their AKs don't shoot down a fast-moving plane flying at nearly 1000m."

"I promised Wilson not to tell." Paloma's mouth went into a determined straight line.

"Paloma, I realize you are now an adult, but your father asked me to look after you, and that doesn't stop when you reach eighteen. I believe you have inadvertently got yourself into something very dangerous. I admire your determination to keep your promise to Wilson, but you can trust us more than anyone in the world. We cannot protect you unless we know what might be a danger to you." Dr. KV spoke with gravity.

"Paloma, Dr. KV is right. Getting shot down and then attacked by armed men is pretty serious stuff."

Paloma looked at both of them. She realized she needed to talk about it. Taking a deep breath, she told them about Wilson's connection to INTERPOL and the suspected smuggling ring.

When she finished , the three of them sat lost in their own thoughts. They absentmindedly watched a skyscraper sized container ship glide past, attended by a bevy of tugs that were attached to it by seemingly impossibly small ropes.

"OK, my turn," Alistair said.

"You have a war story?" Dr. KV and Paloma chimed together in surprise.

"Well, sort of. It's someone else's and I only know the ending of the last chapter."

"Don't tell me you actually got a job and then got fired." Paloma raised her eyebrows.

"Very funny. Who do you think manages the estate in Scotland? Seriously, if this is what I think it is, it may even be worth something," Alistair retorted.

"Go on," Paloma said impatiently.

Alistair lowered the register of his voice and affected a salty sailor accent. "It was a dark and stormy night..." Paloma and Dr. KV both groaned.

Alistair grinned, then recounted his discovery of the bunker in the forest off Pipeline Road, SGT. GIBSON's file, the sliding cabinet and the hidden door marked with the mysterious symbol. He described the ten-digit keypad and his frustration at being unable to crack it.

When he finished, Paloma was wide eyed and open-mouthed.

Dr. KV, however, looked like he had seen a ghost. "OK, Alistair, take us there. But give me a moment, I must collect something from

17

my rooms." Dr. Kitts-Vincent hurried back to the pub, ignoring the remains of breakfast and surprising Alistair and Paloma.

"Wow, Alistair, Dr. KV looked a bit shaken. I've never seen that before. Didn't you mention the bunker to him before now?"

"No, I thought it would make a fun distraction for us all after your horrible experience." Alistair drained his coffee cup and ate the last piece of Marmite toast with a slightly perplexed look on his face.

5

THE MAGIC SHOP

They piled into Alistair's Defender, which was in a state of permanent expedition readiness. Paloma had on a very battered pair of combat trousers and a tank top with the words 'TOMB RAIDER' written across her chest. She pointed at the writing and gave the thumbs up to Alistair, who just shook his head and rolled his eyes.

"Boy, Alistair, don't you ever clean this rig out? It smells like a mushroom farm in here."

"Yeah, well, you just came from the desert. We have this thing here called 'humidity.'"

Dr. KV smiled as they sparred back and forth. He was used to it and had missed it.

As soon as they quit the tarmac and hit the dirt track of Pipeline Road, Dr. KV pulled a battered notebook from his shirt pocket and said gravely, "One of my greatest friends, Gibson, left me this in his will. I met him in Vietnam back in '68. He was a Sergeant in the US Special forces. Extraordinary chap and a renowned expert on tropical beetles. And this little notebook," he said, flipping it open to a labeled sketch, "is full of drawings of lovely bugs." Sunlight filtered through the canopy, flecking the pages as he thumbed through them. "Gibson was based here in Panama. His enthusiasm for this habitat is one reason I moved here for my research on butterflies. But this notebook of his has more than just bugs. There are cryptic notes that I've never been able to decipher, at least not until today. Look at this—" He raised the notebook between them, with his finger on a page: 'THE MAGIC SHOP 56-67'.

"Oh my God, that has to be the code for the door... surely!" Alistair's eyes fixed on the page; Paloma grabbed the steering wheel before they disappeared off the track.

"Alistair, eyes on the track, please."

"Sergeant Gibson was certainly a fascinating man, and whatever is beyond your door must somehow connect to him. Before you were born, Gibson, your father and I were great pals. All three of us loved the jungle. We bought the GAS57 pub together. Your father and I never learned exactly what Gibson did after he left the army, but we knew it was dangerous. He would only say it was for the good of the world. We knew he had some kind of base in the jungle here. He also used to disappear off on international missions, sometimes for months. One day he never returned."

"But how come you never told us about the lost bunker? You know how much fun Paloma and I have searching for old buildings in the jungle."

"It is a fair question, Alistair, and I should have guessed you would one day find it. To be really honest, I know what you and Paloma are like. If I had told you about Sergeant Gibson, and that he was involved in risky, international, 'save the world' missions and that he had a hidden base in the jungle, you two would spend night and day trying to find it. And then you would probably want to get involved. I was trying to protect you."

They slipped into the silence of their own thoughts. Alistair increased speed, skillfully navigating the muddy road and its old wooden bridges.

After twenty minutes, Paloma piped up, "Hey, when are Grandpa and Grandma coming through the canal on the cruise ship? Let's jump on board as they come through Gamboa."

"Paloma, you can't just jump on board a cruise ship halfway through a canal transit," Dr. KV pointed out.

"Well, the canal pilots do it all the time, plus I know the Captain of the ship was some kind of junior officer under Grandpa when he was a big cheese in the Navy. I'm sure he'll let us hop on board in Gamboa."

"Next Wednesday," Alistair replied. "And grandpa won't appreciate you calling him a 'big cheese'. He was actually an Admiral."

"Grandpa would be delighted to be called a 'big cheese', especially by his favorite granddaughter."

"Mmm Paloma, you're his only granddaughter."

"Exactly. So, I have special privileges when addressing him."

Their mother's father was a formidable character, one of the US Navy's first black Admirals and accustomed to commanding an entire US Navy fleet. But Paloma was right: she could do no wrong in his eyes. Especially once she passed her private pilot's license at 16. He had started his navy career as a pilot and had coached Paloma to fly.

"OK, this is it." Alistair pulled the Landy to a halt by the fallen tree he had cut up in the storm.

"I must have walked past here a hundred times hunting butterflies," said Dr. KV.

"Follow me. They did a brilliant job making it disappear. I only saw it because the lightening back-lit it."

Alistair led them through the thick undergrowth and into the zigzag trench. He stopped and pointed at a mound of tangled undergrowth.

Paloma and Dr. KV both blinked. It was as if they had just been shown a fantastic magic trick. There was, in fact, a door in front of them, barely discernible.

Alistair spun the handles and they entered the bunker.

"Phew—bat shit city." Paloma stuck out her tongue and screwed up her eyes.

"Just you wait, Miss Prissy," which Paloma was not, and Alistair knew it. He beckoned them over to the stainless-steel cupboard with his torch and pulled the folder marked 'Sgt. Gibson' with both hands. Dr. KV shook his head and smiled at seeing his friend's name.

The cabinet slid neatly to one side, just as Alistair had described.

"Hey, that's a cool symbol—wonder what it means." Paloma was rubbing the dirt off the horned symbol Alistair had seen earlier.

THE MAGIC SHOP"Dr. KV, the honors, please."

They were joking around, but their hearts were racing and their palms sweaty.

Dr. KV pressed the numbers, following the sequence in his friend's notebook; each one making a nice click as he did so.

From behind the wall came the sound of compressed air being released, and the door slid upwards. The odor of engine oil and EP 90 rushed at them in a dry gust, overpowering the cloying odor of the bat guano.

With palpable excitement, the three of them stepped across the threshold of the open door into the darkness. Paloma shrieked with delight and hopped from one foot to the other, her feet echoing on metal. As if by command, floodlights hummed on and whiteness illuminated the four walls of yet another concrete bunker. The green door behind them slid down, sealing them in.

They found themselves on a narrow steel walkway that circled the close, grey walls. An open stairway dropped down and none of them hesitated to descend. Each step revealed a better view of a vast warehouse space below. Rows and rows of military vehicles came into view, all unique. Some had tracks. Some had wheels. Some were armored and bristling with guns. All were painted in an array of military colors. From where they stood on the stairs high above, the scene looked like a childhood collection of army dinky toys that had been lovingly stored for some future child to play with. As they descended, the edges of the room came into perspective. Set against each wall were workbenches covered in tools, drills and cutting equipment, all carefully laid out.

In fact, it felt so much like a team had just stopped for lunch that Alistair called out, "Hello? Um—anybody there?" They looked at each other, faces full of fear and excitement.

"What *is* this place?" Paloma said what they were all thinking.

They descended to the warehouse floor, and the scene came into sharper focus. The scent of well-kept machinery mingled with a familiar government issue institutional smell was somehow reassuring.

Paloma walked forward and leaned against a Daimler armored car, patting it and grinning.

"This gentleman is one of the first four-wheel-drive vehicles with independent suspension and it is seriously cool!"

She had always been drawn to machinery. As a young girl, Paloma had cut out pictures of V8 engines and stuck them to the walls of her bedroom while her friends collected fluffy pink unicorns and dolphins.

"Hey, there are doors everywhere." Alistair and Dr. KV walked across to the nearest one marked 'CLINIC. LAB. OFFICE. MEETING'.

To the right was the same numbered keypad.

"Hang on, hang on—Sgt. Gibson—" Dr. KV was flicking through the pages of the notebook.

"Here—C.L.O.M: 1-9-4-5."

Alistair punched in the numbers, and the door slid up.

Together, they stepped across the threshold into a corridor. Fluorescent lights hummed on, and the door slid shut again.

"Perhaps it's overdue that we try this in reverse." Dr. KV punched the same numbers in the keypad on this side of the door.

It slid up.

"Ah. That's rather a relief."

Along the corridor were four doors. The CLINIC and LAB were on the left. The doors for the OFFICE and MEETING room were to the right.

Dr. KV quickly found the codes for each door. All were fully equipped according to their labels, 1970s government issue style: functional but comfortable. Though a fine layer of dust covered everything, the rooms were remarkably tidy.

"Not a single dud lightbulb. And feel the dry air? No mold. There must be a dehumidification system running. So where do you think the power is coming from?"

"My guess is that there is an underground electrical line attached to the grid," Dr. KV speculated.

Leaving the corridor, they crossed the big vehicle hall again. And, with the aid of Gibson's notebook, they entered a door marked 'MESS. DORMS. GYM. BATHROOM'.

Where the CLINIC, LAB and OFFICE rooms had felt generic and nondescript, the MESS had personality. At the far side was a bar that appeared to be well stocked. There was a pool table, a dartboard, and a boxy 1970s TV. Alistair and Dr. KV skirted the low tables and comfy chairs, drawn to a wall of indiscriminately displayed photos, flags, and bullet riddled bits of equipment, including a huge propeller from what looked like a Flying Fortress.

It was a wall of a hundred stories.

Dr. KV scanned the photos. His eyes rested on a group of men wearing tiger-stripe camo and jeans. They were standing in front of a Huey gunship, holding beers and laughing as if someone had just cracked a joke. Dr. KV tapped the figure in the middle, wearing aviator glasses and a handlebar mustache. "This is Sergeant Gibson."

They could almost feel his presence in the room.

Smiling at one another, they went back to the corridor to continue exploring.

The GYM was a hardcore martial arts studio. Worn leather punch bags orbited the central boxing ring alongside racks of free weights and stands of swords, stored pommels up.

Over the next few hours, the three climbed on vehicles, opened cupboards, and continued to find more doors to more rooms.

Dr. KV suggested they explore further in the direction of two massive doors: IN and OUT, clearly designed for vehicles to drive in one way and out the other.

The OUT door opened onto a corridor wide enough to accommodate the biggest vehicle in the collection. The walls and ceiling were made of familiar square metal corrugations reminiscent of shipping containers. On the right was a heavily reinforced door marked DOGS OF WAR.

Dr. KV quoted, "Cry 'Havoc!', and let slip the Dogs of War!"

"Shakespeare's Julius Caesar," Alistair responded. "This must be the Armory. Have you got the code, Marc Antony? I mean, Dr. KV?"

He flipped through the pages. "DOW 3-15-44," smiled Dr. KV. "Of course."

Alistair crouched down and ducked under the door before it was halfway up. He had spent his childhood drawing and making guns. By the time he was thirteen, he probably had the biggest library of weapons books of any boy in the world. Everything from a collection of historical drawings of The Earliest firearms all the way through to highly technical weapons manuals.

The lights flashed on, illuminating a massive armory that might have been an exhibit entitled 'Firearms of the 20th Century'. There was a water-cooled Vickers machine gun from WW1, a nest of AK47 submachine guns, snipers' rifles, handguns—everything. In the center of the room stood a worn machine table with hundreds of neatly labeled little drawers. The evocative smell of gun oil, cordite, and metal filled their nostrils.

Alistair surveyed the room, mouth open.

He darted around, picking up weapons, pausing occasionally, running his fingers over well-oiled barrels.

"Come and collect me in a month," he announced, holding a Thompson machine gun and eyeing the doors marked AMMO and FIRING RANGE.

Paloma grabbed his arm and led her brother back to the machine gun racks. "Later. Let's see where the OUT door spits us. Dr. KV is right, it's time to get a bearing on the exit."

Walking backwards, Alistair allowed himself to be dragged away by his sister.

"Did you see the FN SLR? That's one of my favorites," he raved.

"Yes, dear, that's nice."

Back in the shipping container tunnel they marched side by side towards the distant doors marked OUT.

Dr. KV punched the keypad. Orange sunlight, humidity, and birdcall washed over them. As the door closed shut, they turned to see it transform into a mound of earth and vines.

Their boots sloshed as they followed the track leading from the doorway; disguised as a stream bed, the track was invisible. It flowed into and became one of a thousand indeterminate, muddy tracks that crisscrossed the forest. Eventually they intersected Pipeline Road but no one could have retraced the path to the exit of THE MAGIC SHOP.

They knew where they were and trudged back to the Landy.

It was getting dark.

"We'll head home and come back tomorrow," Dr. KV announced. He still had the authority of a surrogate parent and although both of them wanted to explore more, they remained silent.

6

The Unicorn Quest

A s they had hoped, The Admiral had pulled strings. And, as the Unicorn Quest cruise ship tied off on two buoys on the side of the Panama Canal to overnight next to Gamboa, Alistair and Paloma had paddled across in their grey kayaks and gained entry through the 'play door' where guests launched for water activities. They had packed their evening clothes in waterproof bags.

A junior officer was waiting and led them to their grandparents' palatial 'cabin' which was really a suite.

Although Alistair and Paloma were now adults, their grandparents showered them with questions about food, boyfriends, girlfriends, health, and money. Questions that were a comfortable, affectionate ritual which provided Alistair and Paloma an excellent opportunity to tease each other in front of an appreciative audience.

After drinks and dinner—fresh lobster with salad served by a silent, white-gloved crew—they told their grandparents about their find in the jungle, swearing them to secrecy.

Paloma then recounted being shot down in Kenya. She started her story after takeoff, skipping the details of Wilson's 'quick mission and their cargo. The Admiral beamed with pride. Although he never talked about it, they knew he'd been shot down several times over enemy territory and escaped to fight again.

"I want to tell you two about something fishy going on in this ship," he started.

"Oh Bill, honestly, I am sure they don't want to hear your mad ideas," their grandmother said. "He's bored and thinks he still works for the government." Georgina Rowena was shaking her head. She, too, was a formidable character. She had met Bill at the public library in Savannah when he was still a young student. They had fallen madly in love on their first encounter.

This liaison with a black man in 1950s Southern America was considered a sin, and she had been subjected to vicious attacks from her family, her friends, and all of Chatham County. After marrying, he had risen through the ranks of the navy and she absorbed the abuses that accompanied unmitigated jealousy from other navy wives without flinching.

"Go on, Grandpa," Paloma begged. Alistair exchanged looks with their grandmother.

He began. His voice was deep, measured and used to being listened to. It still had a hint of the South.

"You haven't seen most of our fellow shipmates but you can probably imagine them: retired, well heeled, slightly soft, and dangerous—if you get between them and the buffet. Many of them don't actually have a home. They mosey from cruise to cruise, traveling the world. We know the types and we encounter them every year, though Grandma and I generally socialize more with the crew. But this year they seem different. I can't quite put my finger on it. They are spending more money, buying champagne, things like that. Usually, these types are well-known for sticking to what their 'plan' provides, what they get for free. Otherwise, they'll run out of funds before they finish their innings, if you understand what I mean."

They nodded.

"The other thing is, they chat and gossip rather loudly—they're all half deaf. So, we can't help picking up quite a lot of conversation. Sounds like they all started their cruises in Mombasa. That's strange. Normally they start in a US port so they can simply transfer all their belongings from one ship to another. But these people flew from the US to Mombasa on a private charter—why on earth would they do that? I got to talking to one fellow, and he told me about how he and a bunch of other passengers had travelled up through the Suez and across the Med on a series of different ships owned by the same company as this one, the Unicorn Line. And the way he was talking, the group sticks together. And here they are going through the Panama Canal, headed for the west coast to San Francisco."

Paloma interjected, "Maybe they are just a bunch of old friends that want to travel together."

"Well, that's what I thought. But I've been listening. And they had clearly not met before this trip." He leaned forward in his chair. "Now here is the weird part. I have discovered, through my extensive and much-objected-to research," throwing a look at their grandmother, "that our fellow passengers are carrying some very creepy looking dolls that seemed to be—"

"Made up of mismatched doll parts?" Paloma finished.

He sat up straight. "How did you know that? Is it some kind of weird trend retirees are following? Did we miss the memo?"

"You see Bill, utter nonsense, just—" but her voice trailed off when she saw Alistair and Paloma's expressions.

"I didn't give you all the details when I told you about being shot down. Wilson was late coming to the plane because he had a small 'mission' to make. When he got on board, he was carrying half a dozen dolls, similar to the ones you're describing." Paloma's skin was turning pale. "They shot us down within seven minutes of those dolls being

29

brought on the plane. I don't think those guys were after us—I think they were after the dolls."

"Made up of random parts... means... maybe there is something inside the dolls," Alistair said. "We have to get one."

"But you can't just take one, they would notice, and there's a part to this story I missed out." The Admiral had moved to the edge of his seat. "There are about a dozen very fit-looking men and women on board this ship and I'm certain—from 50 years' experience—they are highly trained ex-military types. And, they have bulges under their jackets."

"If this is all part of the same story, that means someone's hired some serious babysitters," Alistair said.

"So, do you think this is some kind of smuggling operation?" asked Paloma.

"Exactly, my excellent granddaughter. Exactly."

The Admiral looked pleased with himself and gave their grandmother an 'I told you so' grin. She looked furious.

"So, let us get this straight. If this is smuggling—which it very well may be and it has already provoked the attempted murder of our granddaughter—we should immediately contact the US Embassy. Bill you still know the Ambassador in Panama . And then we will get off this ship as fast as we can."

They all looked like kids who had just had their ball taken away.

It was The Admiral who spoke up first. "She's right, as usual. This is not something we should get mixed up in—especially you two. Now, Alistair, Paloma, off you go. Let me call the Ambassador."

"But Grandpa, what about you guys? Aren't you in danger?" Paloma pleaded.

"Don't you worry about us. We are tougher than you think and I am certainly not getting in a kayak tonight. I can see your apartment from here and from there you can see our rooms. So, we will monitor each other." The Admiral looked at Alistair and Paloma and then winked at his wife.

Within half an hour, they were in Alistair's canal-side apartment, peering through the Leica scope mounted on a tripod in the sitting room. Indeed, they could see their grandparents' suite on the enormous cruise ship. Their grandmother was pouring a drink, and The Admiral was speaking on the phone.

A few minutes later, The Admiral called the apartment with 'The Plan'.

Alistair relayed the plan to Paloma "Our first job is to build a doll like the one you saw on the plane. Then we will switch ours with one from the ship and see what's so special inside. Meanwhile, we will try to get the names of everyone with a doll on board. Don't worry about Grandma and Grandpa. The embassy will send a couple of 'technical crew members' onboard the ship—undercover CIA operatives—to protect them and to cause some 'engine problems' for the next twenty-four-hours. This will give us time to make and switch the doll. And Grandpa said it's probably better if Grandma is not completely—ahem—aware of what's happening."

7

Cerro Patacon

Alistair and Paloma got up early and dressed in overalls and rubber boots and then headed out to Cerro Patacon, the growing mountain of rubbish and junk just outside Panama city. Vultures and seagulls could be seen spiraling up as they approached. Even with the car's AC on full blast, it was the stench that hit first.

Inside the dump they found Ronnie, an old friend of their dad's who turned up at G57 Pub every now and again. Ronnie was so large he could hardly walk. He had an infectious grin and was adored as the patrician of a sprawling family who all seemed to work for him. One of his many 'cousins' followed him around carrying a folding chair which they would slip under him every time he stood still, wheezing and then lowering himself on to the complaining chair. Today Ronnie was holding court in the broken bike section. His nieces were working nearby like four exotic butterflies, fluttering around Ronnie and giggling.

Paloma had to clear her throat several times to get Alistair to focus on the man they had come to see, his eyes dreamily tracking the butterflies. Ronnie followed his gaze and roared with laughter, clearly proud of his nieces.

"Maybe," he said in Spanish, "if you speak to them politely, they will help us."

Alistair blushed to the tops of his ears, causing Ronnie's face— a knot of oiled wood—to crack with delight.

"We are looking for broken dolls, sort of this big." Alistair held up his hands. The girls smiled at each other, and he went even redder. He wasn't sure if they were laughing at his request for broken dolls or at his Spanish accent. He had learned his Spanish from his much-loved Nanny, Carmen, who came from Colon where the accent was a very distinct dialect. The same, in fact, as Ronnie's.

Paloma rolled her eyes and described what they were looking for in more detail.

Ronnie clapped his hands together, and the girls disappeared to search.

Ronnie didn't ask what the dolls were for and treated the request with the same gravity as he did any request to retrieve things from the dump. It was how he reigned supreme over the vast empire of rotting paraphernalia that folks threw out.

They exchanged pleasantries for ten minutes until the girls appeared clutching little bodies of broken dolls which, from a distance, looked like crowds of mini people piled in heaps on their arms.

Paloma sorted them into two piles 'keep' or 'reject' and they loaded the 'keep' pile into the Landy.

Alistair gave Ronnie a 'present' of cash, which he refused multiple times until Alistair suggested he buy something nice for 'the girls,' one of whom was now returning Alistair's dreamy stares with her own almond eyes. She had an air of authority and intelligence about her that appealed to Alistair. That, and the fact that she was extremely beautiful. She moved like a dancer.

On Paloma's third "OK, let's go", Alistair tore himself away.

They got in the car and headed for Gamboa.

Taking their spot under their Myrtle tree at G57, Dr. KV spotted them through the open pub window and trotted out to join them. A few feet from their table, he made a dramatic 'about face' turn and disappeared back inside the pub. He returned in a haze of mist, dowsing them both in a cloud of Lysol spray.

"Phewee—how is Ronnie?"

Alistair reached into his bag for a sample of doll limbs.

Dr. Kitts-Vincent did not flinch. "There is someone here I want you to meet."

They looked around. The only person in sight was an elderly lady sitting in the window, knitting.

"Dr. KV, we have exactly—" Alistair looked at his watch, "—7 hours to create this doll, sneak on board and switch it for one that someone, and we don't know who yet, already has on board"

"That is why you need Misha."

He smiled at the lady in the window and nodded. She put away her knitting and approached them in the garden.

"Good Morning, my name is Misha," she said with a thick Russian accent.

Dr. KV explained, "Misha is an old friend of mine; she has retired in Panama. I believe what we are getting into is bigger and more dangerous than you can imagine. I know I can't stop you, but I can try to protect you by helping you. Misha was the Director of Cyber security in the 1960s for the KGB. In fact, you could say, she was the world's first hacker. Misha."

Misha smiled a 'thank you,' to Dr. KV and continued in her Russian accent. "For your doll to work we have to track it, stream live video from it, and, it must be impossible to detect."

She pulled an iPad from her large handbag.

"I have been looking at the dolls that passengers have on the ship and selected a few that I think we could copy with what you have salvaged."

Alistair and Paloma looked awestruck. On her screen were scores of live cams from cabins in the ship and all of them had a doll somewhere in the screen.

"Everyone, everywhere, is being watched all the time," she said by way of explanation. "You just have to find out who is doing the watching. The rest is easy. Shall we get to work?"

8

The Doll

After three hours they had built their doll based on one belonging to a 'Mr. and Mrs. Kelly' in cabin 727. Cabin 727 was just down the hall from their grandparents' suite. So, if needed, Alistair, who was going alone, had a convenient escape.

Misha drank vodka from a tiny glass as she finished tucking a tracking device and two micro-cameras into the doll on her lap.

Alistair changed into a ship steward's uniform that Dr. KV had 'borrowed'.

He was going to paddle across and enter through the same gate they had used earlier as soon as darkness fell.

They were all feeling very nervous. Misha gave them each a shot of vodka and said, "And now we name de baby."

"Fergus," said Alistair

"Fergus?!" repeated Paloma, looking inside the doll's rather ragged outfit. "It can't be 'Fergus'—wrong equipment," holding up the smock to show.

They all laughed, relaxing a bit.

"How about 'Athena', the Egyptian goddess of wisdom, war and useful arts?"

They agreed and put the doll in a waterproof backpack for its kayak journey.

Misha gave Alistair an earpiece that he tucked invisibly inside his ear. After checking all their communication systems, Alistair and Paloma set off towards his kayak they had hidden under the railway bridge beside the canal edge.

Darkness was falling quickly as he settled himself in. Paloma gave him a shove and the black kayak glided out into the lapping water.

"Be careful. It's a jungle out there," she said.

He returned her smile, shook his head, and dug his paddle into the water. Paloma watched him until he disappeared silently in the direction of the enormous cruise ship. She stood on the shadowy bank with her arms folded across her chest; her smile fading.

He bumped against the hull of the ship and softly tapped on the door as instructed. It slid open, revealing the petite face of a young woman in an officer's uniform. Her hair was pulled back in a tight pigtail which was covered by a baseball cap. She motioned him to climb aboard, which he did, pulling his kayak into the ship.

She pushed a trolley full of soft, clean towels towards him. He grabbed it and stuffed the backpack between the towels.

She pointed her chin towards the elevator door and said, "Siete."

She handed him an ID Card on a strap. It had his face on it above the details of his new persona, 'Steven Smith. Cabin Steward'.

He smiled at her and said, "Gracias," but she didn't smile back.

He swiped his ID on the panel at the side of the set of doors labeled 'service elevator,' punched the number 7 and waited. The doors hissed open. The girl turned and left without a second glance.

As the doors slid open on the seventh floor, he stepped into another world.

Misha had downloaded a floor plan before he had left and he had done his best to memorize it: ship's stewards should look like they know where they're going.

He walked purposefully towards Cabin 727, pushing his cart before him.

Misha's Russian accent filled his head, confusing him for a second before he remembered the earpiece.

"All clear, Mr. and Mrs. Kelly have just left for dinner."

He stepped in front of the door, gave three sharp raps, and paused a few seconds.

He swiped his card over the door pad and heard an automated click. Turning the handle, he walked in with his trolley.

"Fresh Towels, Mr. and Mrs. Kelly," he announced, partly to tell Misha and partly to calm his nerves.

He scanned the room and saw four dolls sitting up on the writing desk, including the one they had copied. They had done a good job.

He grabbed the doll and put it in his trolley, pulling the fake one, 'Athena', from the pack. He shoved her into place on the desk.

Just as he had stuffed the real one inside his pack, he sensed someone behind him. He spun around.

A stunning young woman was standing in front of him with wet hair wrapped in a towel. She pulled earphones out of her ears and stood with her hands on her hips, head cocked to one side.

"And what have we got here?" she peered down at his ID. "Hello—Steven?" Somehow, he didn't look like a Steven. "I'm Sandy."

Alistair went bright red, his throat went dry, and he muttered, "Um—fresh towels."

"Wow, Steven, this is quick service. Why, I have only just got this one wet." She had a Texas accent.

"Um, I knocked, but nobody answered," Alistair tried.

She nodded, enjoying his embarrassment.

"Not sure what my parents would say, finding you alone here with me—and just a towel between us."

"I, emm, think I should be going."

"But Steven, I haven't gotten my fresh towels yet."

She walked towards her bedroom, throwing the wet towel behind her as she pulled the door shut.

His earpiece spoke again. "Alistair, Mrs. Kelly is coming back. Hide. She's probably just forgotten something— there is no way of going back into the hallway—if she sees you, she'll know you are not her room steward."

"O bloody hell," Alistair said to himself, looking for an escape.

He had to risk it. He aimed the trolley for Sandy's door. As he burst in, she was just pulling on a robe made of lace and silk. She beamed. "You know the reason I am on this godforsaken tub is because of my 'behavior' with boys at school..."

Alistair cut her off with a "shush", finger on his lips, "Your mum's coming back."

Sandy blanched and grabbed an oversized 'TEXAS A&M' sweatshirt.

"So? Sorry, what exactly are you doing here, why are you hiding from my mom, more to the point why should I hide you from my mom?" she whispered.

They heard the front door opening, someone rummaging through a drawer and then rushing out again.

"How did you know she was coming?"

"I have a Russian in my ear—I'm sorry, I can't explain, it's—it's really complicated," Alistair replied impishly.

"Ehh despite appearances," said Sandy, one of those people who was so beautiful that people couldn't help staring, "I am actually at the very top of my class at Texas A&M."

"I'm sorry I didn't mean it like that. I am sure you are very smart as well, I mean you are very smart full stop— and then gorgeous on top of that. I mean, looks aren't everything—I mean—" he was bright red again.

She was smiling kindly this time. "You are gorgeous yourself but I'm not so sure if you are that smart, especially when it comes to handling towels—and you still haven't told me why you are hiding from my mum. Although boys often seem to want to hide from her."

At that moment they felt the main engines start up.

"I've got to go. I can't stay on the ship."

"Oh, so you mean you are not a towel steward after all?" said Sandy, smiling with the same questioning look she had started with, head tilted to one side.

"Thank you, Sandy. You have been brilliant, you could have easily given me up. I am sorry I can't explain why I am here."

"Do pop in any time," she said in a superb British accent. She lifted his chin and kissed him lightly on his cheek.

Glowing, he walked to the main door, opening it a crack to see if anyone was in the hallway.

Sandy nodded at him as he stepped out, pushing his trolley with a spring in his step.

As he headed towards the service lift, three men came out of a room on his right. In the center was a tanned, good looking character that reminded him of photos he'd seen of a young Ernest Hemingway. He was wearing a linen suit and tan shoes and walked with the air of a man on a mission. Two men in gray, right hands inside jacket pockets flanked him. They processed Alistair with their eyes.

The man that looked like Ernest Hemingway demanded, "Steward, what are you doing here? I haven't seen you on this level before."

His sidekicks moved their right hands a fraction closer to what Alistair knew were pistols inside their jackets.

"Towels for The Admiral, sir. My friend who is normally their steward has a, um, slight stomach problem, so I said I would bring them for him."

Alistair smiled ingratiatingly and stepped across the corridor to his grandfather's cabin door, and knocked.

He could feel the ship underneath him rumble as the engines wound themselves up to speed.

The door in front of him opened and The Admiral's face appeared with a look of annoyance.

"Good evening sir, I have the fresh towels you requested."

"Ah, ah, oh yes." He held the door open and Alistair pushed the towel trolley through.

The three men hadn't moved. The Admiral closed the door behind Alistair.

"Did you get it?"

Alistair pulled the waterproof bag from between the towels to show his grandfather.

"Good job, well done. I can't wait to see what's inside this doll."

"Grandpa, I have to leave. Now."

"How are you going to do that? We're already moving—just wait in our rooms until we get to the locks on the Gatun side. You can slip out when the pilot comes on board."

"I can't. Those men saw me come in with towels and they are waiting for me to come out. I'll have to get past them somehow. They are already suspicious. I'll take the service elevator down and then jump and swim for it."

"Bill, who's there?" Alistair's grandmother's voice came from their bedroom.

"Nothing dear, just the steward with the towels," The Admiral called to the other room, then said quietly to Alistair, "How are you going to get past those thugs?"

"How about you have a good old chat to distract them—let me tell you my life story type thing?" Alistair knew this was the kind of small talk his grandfather particularly loathed. There was a pause.

"OK. I am ready," said The Admiral, steeling himself as if he were going to battle once more.

They stepped out into the hallway, Alistair turning smartly left towards the service elevator. His grandfather walked right, arms outstretched. "Soooo, we are neighbors on this magical voyage of discovery. My name is Bill from Annapolis. Where are you folks from?"

Alistair heard him waffling on as the elevator doors slid open. He stepped in, pulling in the trolley, and parked it to block the way. Just as it was sliding closed, one sidekick started towards him and put his foot between the closing doors.

"Very sorry sir, this is a service elevator. Guest elevators are over there," said Alistair, pointing towards the other side of the hall and gently pushed the man's foot out with the trolley. The doors slid shut, and the lift descended.

They opened again at the 'play gate' level. The girl in the baseball cap was waiting for him and he swung the waterproof pack onto his back, pulling the straps tight.

The girl unlatched the play gate door and said in Spanish, "Jump as far as you can so you don't get sucked back by the propellors."

They could hear the loud roar of the water churning below; it was terrifying.

Just then there were footsteps clanging down the steel stairs.

"Quick, hide behind here," the girl continued. She indicated a steel locker full of life jackets.

She then began sorting through a pile of chains on the floor, her back to the stairs.

As the footsteps hit the bottom rung, she glanced around nonchalantly.

"Sorry, Sir, this is a restricted area."

The man, one of the sidekicks from deck seven, drew a pistol out of his pocket, a fat nasty looking Glock, and pointed it at her back.

"Where's that steward? I know he came down 'ere," he said with a cockney accent, nodding at the towel trolley.

In a microsecond, she had grabbed his pistol hand and simultaneously swung a kick right at his face, her heavy boot landing with a thud like a boxing glove on a heavy bag. The weapon scattered across the steel floor, and he reeled backwards under the force of her kick.

"You bitch, you'll die for that." Blood was pouring from his smashed nose. He pulled a short knife from his belt, then grabbed the end of the chain she was standing on and yanked. She fell backwards. He laughed and wrapped the chain around his arm, leaving a meter out, which he swung in a lazy, dangerous circle, advancing on the girl.

Alistair jumped out of his hiding place and grabbed the chain arm from behind, and punched a rapid fire of uppercuts to the man's kidneys.

The brute staggered forward under the blows, gasping. Then, seeing his Glock on the ground next to the open doorway, he bent down to grab it. As he did, a piercing whistle from a tug rang out, and the deep throb of its engine bellowed as it pressed into the side of the ship.

As the man grabbed the gun, the tug popped the ship from its stationary position. The ship lurched, and the man disappeared out the door, the heavy chain still wrapped around his arm and spooling out after him.

Alistair and the girl ran to the door as the end of the chain clattered out and saw only a whirlpool of water churning from the tug and prop. The man must have sunk like a lawnmower.

"Perfect," the girl said in Russian accented English.

She was grinning at him as if she had just poured him a cup of tea. Her smile made her look like a princess in boots.

"Um, thank you. I'll just wait for the tug to move around to the stern, and then I'll swim back," Alistair said rather awkwardly.

She nodded, still grinning.

The tug looked like a toy against the wall of the ship, pirouetting and powering its way to the stern.

"Bye then."

He dived into a long shallow dive and struck out to the opposite shore with a powerful crawl, hoping to hell no ships were coming in the opposite direction. He rolled onto his back once he was well clear. The ship was well under way and the door he had jumped from was dark and closed.

9

Back at Base

Alistair climbed up the bank of the Canal and walked the 500 meters back to the pub, its warm lights beckoning him in the darkness. Paloma, Dr. KV and Misha were waiting for him, relief etched on their faces. He tugged off his pack containing the waterproof pouch and gave it to Misha. Dr. Kitts-Vincent handed him a glass of Laphroaig malt whisky, which he downed with relish, the smoky flavor transporting him to Scotland for a brief moment.

"We have just four hours before the ship finishes its transit of the canal and passes through Miraflores locks. Then it will begin the sea journey to San Francisco," announced Misha, looking around. "We can't open this here in public," she said, patting the bag with the doll inside. "We cannot monitor Athena's cameras. Do you have somewhere secure we could go? Preferably, with lab equipment so we can analyze the contents of this baby."

Alistair, Paloma and Dr. KV looked at each other, nodding in response.

"We have the perfect place. It's called THE MAGIC SHOP. Give me five minutes to change. Dr. KV, maybe you can grab some food supplies to keep us going," Alistair said, as he ran upstairs to change.

On the drive Alistair explained everything that had happened on the cruise ship, slightly editing his encounter with Sandy. Then they took turns telling Misha the story of the discovery of THE MAGIC SHOP.

"This is perfect. Like I am back with the KGB, but is warmer than Moscow."

The Landy's headlights formed a narrow tunnel and dark silhouettes brushed the doors as they drove along Pipeline Road to their destination. No one spoke as Alistair led the team through the forest to the bunker, pulled Gibson's file, and punched the numbers to the secret door. Misha took in the sight of the vehicle warehouse with a nod of approval. Paloma steered everyone into the 'OFFICE' and once the door had closed behind them, she carefully extracted the contents from a serious-looking suitcase onto the largest metal table and snapped open several laptops. They flickered on, two of them revealing live images from 'Athena' in room 737. Alistair searched the screens, hoping to see a glimpse of Sandy.

Misha extracted the doll from Alistair's bag, turned it over, and examined it carefully. It had survived a pretty rough journey across the Canal. "Well, I can't see any obvious way to open it, can you?" Misha asked, passing the doll to Paloma.

Paloma pulled at its head to see if she could get it off.

"Wait, wait, we have an X-ray machine," Dr. KV said, smiling as he grabbed the doll and marched off to the medical clinic. The team followed.

Dr. KV seemed to know how to operate the complex machine and soon they were looking at an ancient TV set with an X-ray image of what looked like a dozen slices of manioc inside the doll. They could also make out a hidden zipper that looked like it had been sewn over. Misha meticulously unpicked the stitches, pulled down the zipper and took out a vacuum-wrapped plastic bag. Dr. KV handed her a scalpel, and she cut a tiny hole in the bag to let the air in, then slit it open.

Pulling out the rough discs, she held one up. It looked like fossilized vegetable slice. It smelt of wood smoke. It smelt of Africa.

"It's rhino horn. I recognize it from when I volunteered for an anti-poaching charity in Kenya," Paloma said, putting her hand over her mouth. "Rhino horn is worth about three times as much as gold per kilo." She placed the contents of the packet on a set of scales. The number read '1.6 kg.' "Right. Here we have $160,000 worth of Rhino horn. If each couple has at least four dolls, that's around $640,000 per couple."

"Misha, how many couples have dolls in their rooms?" Dr. KV asked.

"We counted 312, but we may have missed some."

"So just roughly that cruise ship is carrying... $200 million dollars' worth of Rhino horn. Or put another way," added Paloma sadly, "each doll represents one dead Rhino. 1,248 in total.. Seeing one dead rhino out in the bush with its horn hacked off was deeply shocking. This is almost too much to think about. This feels like an apocalypse."

They stood silently, staring at the slices of horn on the table.

10

P of A

The OFFICE in THE MAGIC SHOP was now an Ops Center, with rows of monitors playing live feeds from the cruise ship. Another displayed a map of the world, a blinking dot indicating the current position of the 'Unicorn Quest' and a line tracing the dolls' journey from Mombasa, Kenya. But all eyes were on the red banner scrolling across the live BBC news feed. 'Breaking News, US Ambassador to Panama shot dead by sniper while attending outdoor music festival.'

Paloma's eyes flashed. "We have to get Grandpa and Grandma off that ship now. The Admiral phoned the Ambassador. And now the Ambassador is dead."

Misha spoke up, "We have four assets and two risks."

"Asset One: There are a pair of CIA operatives in The Admiral's suite right now; they are both armed."

"Asset two: My granddaughter Tatiana. Alistair, you met her already. She opened door on lower deck for you. She got on board at the same time as the CIA men. Dr. KV had to pull some strings. It took some work, a girl trained by a former KGB officer joining forces with the CIA."

Alistair's eyes grew wide. Now he understood.

"Number three: We have what I believe to be secure communication with both Tatiana and The Admiral."

"Four: We can watch everything." She lifted her tiny glass of vodka towards the screens.

"Number One risk: The Admiral and his wife or the CIA guys and Tatiana could easily become compromised.

Number Two risk: They are stuck on the ship until it docks again."

The blinking dot was now heading toward the narrow Culebra cut which lead to Pedro Miguel locks.

"Right," said Dr. KV, "Let's make a 'P of A.'"

Misha tilted her head quizzically.

"Plan of Action."

"Paloma and I have a plan," announced Alistair. "We need to show you something," nodding for them to follow. "We spent most of last week exploring the all the goodies in the bunkers. Dr. KV, you'll recall, we never explored the entry route."

Together they walked across the vehicle warehouse. He punched in the code for the door marked IN. Immediately to their right stood another door, labeled HUG.

Alistair, having memorized all the codes now, pressed 4 black buttons and led the way into a massive hanger. As the door slid open, the smell of avgas wafted over them.

In the center was a fully armed UH_1D_Huey Gunship.

"We already fired her up, she's ready to go. The roof opens up," said Paloma matter-of-factly.

Dr. KV had a look of incredulity on his ebony face. "Wait a minute Paloma, you haven't got your heli license yet and you are proposing flying this 70-year-old machine from the forest, land on the deck of a moving ship—possibly under fire—to rescue two people in their seventies who need to sit down after a short game of tennis?"

"Do you have a better 'P of A'?" asked Alistair.

There was a pregnant silence.

"Then the Alistair and Paloma, 'P of A' it is!" added Paloma with a grin.

Dr. KV looked anxious.

"Once the ship clears the Pedro Miguel locks, it will no longer be surrounded by jungle and it will be getting close to a populated area. Then there will be no way we can use weapons to defend ourselves. Right now, it's only a six-minute flight."

Paloma pulled a bright yellow lever, motors connected with grinding chains, and the domed roof split open. The morning sun and the bright clatter of jungle sounds streamed into the hangar. They both jumped into the Huey's seats, Paloma on the right as the pilot with Alistair beside her. They strapped in and started preflight checks.

"Misha, tell Tatiana to meet us at the helipad on the stern of the ship as soon as they hear us. Grandpa will remember the sound of a Huey. We'll take all five of them: Grandma, Grandpa, the two CIAs and Tatiana."

"You two be bloody careful and come back whole. I promised your dad I would keep you safe."

"We will, Dr. KV. What could possibly go wrong with Paloma in control? Dad would have loved this."

With that, the massive rotor blades began to turn.

11

The Rescue

The Admiral and his wife, Georgina Rowena, sat uncomfortably on the dining chairs in their suite, their hands zipped tied behind their backs. On the floor—hands, feet and mouths wrapped in duct tape—lay the two CIA operatives, both bleeding from the nose and the deep cuts in their faces.

The man in the Hemingway suit stood alongside a guard. Both pointed Heckler & Koch machine pistols at the trussed figures.

Talking and pacing was a bull of a man in a white shirt, sleeves rolled up. His face bore the marks of a life of battle under the sun—skin like an old saddle, one eye covered with black patch. He wore a shoulder holster with an old Nazi Walther P38 pistol in it. His accent was American, mixed with an Afrikaans lilt.

His Name was Piete Van Olenburgh.

"Well, Admiral, it's so good of you to join us. Your presence on the ship has given us an excellent level of additional insurance. If anyone objects to our little expedition, I merely need to suggest that one of America's best loved war heroes might meet with a nasty accident. Not that we expect any trouble. I have hosted half the US Senate on my wonderful safari ranch for decades. Ah, they are always so desperate to bag something more interesting than a zebra." He leaned close to The Admiral. "And the fact that I have it all on film will perhaps persuade them to look the other way when we bring in our little collection you so artfully discovered."

He smiled, running his finger down the nose of The Admiral's wife.

"You leave her alone, you son of a bitch. Do what you like to me. But she had no idea what was going on until you gangsters barged in." The Admiral struggled to free himself from his chair and failed, glaring at Van Olenburgh with pure hate.

Van Olenburgh laughed. "You have no idea what you have got yourself into." He paused. "Imagine an Admiral getting himself out of his depth." He smiled at his own joke. "You don't even know what's in those dolls, do you?

"I know it's worth killing for."

A walkie talkie squelched, and his second in command, the man in the Hemmingway suit spoke. "Sir, the sergeant says we've got an inbound helicopter requesting permission to land." He handed the walkie talkie to Van Olenburgh.

"Sergeant, position the snipers so they have a clear shot of the helipad on the stern. Let them land and then fire on my command. Over." He turned and said, "Number Two, and you," he said, pointing to one of the guards. "Stay here. If they so much as fart, shoot them in the kneecaps."

"Roger that," they replied in unison, shouldering their weapons and pointing the muzzles at the legs of the elderly couple.

Van Olenburgh swept from the room, talking rapidly on his radio as he went.

When the door closed, the guard said, "Go on, you old fogey... fart. I need the entertainment."

There was a knock on the door. "Room service, Admiral. I have brought your morning rum ration," a sweet female voice announced.

"Tell her to come in. She can provide us with the entertainment," Number Two hissed.

The Admiral hesitated. Hemingway suit lowered his weapon and aimed it at Georgina Rowena's foot. "Say it or I'll start with her feet and work upwards."

"Come."

The door opened, and a petite girl in a steward's uniform entered. She was pushing a little trolley covered in a white linen cloth.

As soon as she walked in, the guard leapt behind her and shut the door.

"Hello, sweetie pie, wanna have a little fun?" Number Two said, his smile sickly sweet.

She smiled back. "Sure boys. Can I offer you a drink?" Waving her hand over the trolley and taking off her hat, she spun it onto the table as if someone had unexpectedly invited her to a party. The guards' eyes instinctively followed the spinning hat.

Without seeming to move, her hand reappeared with a silenced pistol. Two low mechanical plunks rang out, and both men crumpled to the floor, neat black holes between their eyes.

"Perfect," she said.

She flicked out a knife and cut The Admiral and his wife free. They stood and rubbed their wrists, too shocked to talk.

"I did actually bring you a rum, Admiral. It's on the trolley," she said calmly.

The Admiral poured two shot glasses and handed one to his wife. Georgina Rowena and The Admiral, hands steady, looked each other in the eye and sank the rum in a single swallow.

Tatiana was speaking into her sleeve as she cut the two CIA men free. "Whisky? This is Vodka. Rum and Bourbon are free and ready to move."

Back in the Huey, Alistair answered, "Roger that, Vodka. I understand they are going to let us land, then attempt to take us out with snipers."

From her ship's communications monitoring, Misha had intercepted the plan and passed the information to the team in the helicopter. "We'll come in low from the bow; then pop up at deck height on the starboard side and take out the snipers. Be ready to move but stay under cover. I'll be firing the door gun and it will be messy up there. Over."

It had started to rain heavily, muffling the sound of the helicopter and blurring visibility. Van Olenburgh stood on the flying bridge port side, scanning for the incoming helicopter. His three snipers were lying under lifeboats 100m from the helipad on the stern, their weapons ready on their bipods, rounds in breeches. They were using heavy Barrett M82 sniper rifles with a kill range of over 1800m. They would drive huge holes through the helicopter and anybody in it at this range.

The upper deck was awash with rainwater and scattered with outdoor furniture, which the guests had rapidly abandoned when the rain came.

Paloma was approaching the ship a few feet off the rain dashed Canal. The ship had entered the infamous Culebra Cut, the narrowest part of the waterway where steep rocky banks towered over the ship. It was here that so many men lost their lives as the cliffs collapsed again and again during construction.

Alistair moved from the copilot's seat to the gunner's position in the left door. He cocked the swivel mounted M60 machine gun, put his hands on the handles and thumbs on the trigger.

"This is Bloody Mary to Vodka. We are going in." The *chop chop* of the twin blades reverberated off the rocky walls of the cut.

"Roger that. We are moving." Tatiana opened the cabin door, checked the corridor and said, "All clear, let's move." She led the way with one CIA covering her grandmother and one bringing up the rear with The Admiral. The CIA agents had taken the HK MP5s from the dead guards.

They moved forward cautiously, shifting from one section of hallway to the next. It was breakfast time—they met no one.

54

They approached the last corner leading to the deck. Tatiana peered around the wall and at that moment a deafening explosion, bits of wall, a light fixture and the remains of a potted plant ricocheted all around them.

Tatiana urgently commanded everyone back with her hand.

Half a dozen armed thugs had seen her and they had instructions to kill on sight.

Paloma guided the helicopter level with the water, the vast wall of the ship on her left, the rock wall on her right: there was no room for error.

"Ready," she said into her mike.

"Ready."

She pulled the heli straight up and they cleared the deck. The noise bounced off everything, making it impossible to tell where it was coming from. The three snipers, suddenly realizing what was happening, tried to roll out from under the lifeboats, pulling their ungainly weapons with them.

The M60 burst into action, turning the snipers and most of the furniture into tangled splinters. The snipers' lifeless bodies jerked under the heavy rounds as brass shell cases rained down on the water below. Alistair kept firing.

"All clear."

Paloma swept the heli back down below the stern of the ship, ready to snap up and make a landing on the pad.

Inside, Tatiana used the diversion of the helicopter and M60 to look around the corner. Half the guards had disappeared to obey a command to take down the heli. Before the remaining three could bring their weapons up again, Tatiana dropped them with neat slots from her silenced pistol.

"Let's go."

At the same moment, the Huey popped up behind the stern of the ship, Alistair firing short bursts at the guards on the deck. Several holes ripped through the plexiglass in return.

Unnoticed, a gunman appeared behind Tatiana, Georgina Rowena and one of the CIA men. He opened fire, hitting The Admiral in the leg and wounding the CIA agent who returned fire on fully automatic.

The ship was now in chaos. Screams rang out, and panic set in as the roar of automatic gunfire filled the corridors.

The CIA agent bore The Admiral down the corridor, his leg bleeding heavily.

Up on deck, Paloma set the Huey down on the helipad. Tatiana and the other CIA operative guided Georgina Rowena towards it as Alistair covered them with the M60. The three of them climbed on board.

"Where's the Admiral?"

Tatiana looked around. He had been with them only moments before.

"Man the guns. Grandma, buckle in." Alistair grabbed a short shotgun from the gun rack at the back of the aircraft.

"Paloma, do we have comms?" he said, checking his radio and headphones were attached to his tack helmet.

"Roger that, loud and clear."

More armed men and women in black combat gear appeared on the deck and opened fire at the helicopter.

Rounds started pinging through the fuselage.

Tatiana got herself behind the M60 and Alistair shouted through the noise, "I am going back for Grandpa. Drop Grandma and the Langley man at the World War Two anti-aircraft battery just above the cut and then wait for my signal there. It's only three minutes away, don't bring Grandma back to the battle. We can collect her when we have the others—it's too hot for you to wait here."

He dropped out of the side of the helicopter and rolled away to the metal steps that would take him down to the next level.

Paloma lifted the heli off the pad like a champagne cork—Tatiana covering the deck with neat bursts of fire from the door, the black-clad figures dispersing—then dropped it down below the stern of the ship and raced down the canal, at last popping up and over the steep sides of the cut. It was still raining heavily, and they disappeared from sight .

Seconds later they spotted the old military bunkers that squatted on the top of the carved cliffs of Culebra Cut. Paloma landed near the concrete circle that was once an antiaircraft battery, and Tatiana jumped out as soon as the skids touched the swirling grass. She helped Georgina Rowena and the CIA man over to a doorless bunker out of the driving rain. Then Tatiana returned to the machine, and she and Paloma waited for Alistair's call.

12

Saving The Admiral

Stealthily, Alistair worked his way back to level seven, down the corridor where they had last seen The Admiral. Twice, he had to stuff himself into cleaning cupboards as groups of armed men ran past. There was a lot of confusion. He grabbed a radio off one man Tatiana had killed earlier and he could hear Van Olenburgh howling blue murder because they had let the prisoners escape. They were clearly unaware that The Admiral was still on the ship—but it wouldn't be long before someone reported seeing only one old person climb aboard the helicopter. The Admiral was a distinctive figure, even out of uniform.

Alistair reached his grandparents' suite. But the door was open, and clearly no one was there.

He was edging his way back along the corridor when he heard booted steps coming from both directions. Trapped, he was just considering returning to The Admiral's room and climbing to another level from his balcony when a voice made him look up.

"Psst, towel boy, I need some fresh towels."

"Sandy, what the hell...?"

"Get your ass back in this room, quick."

She pulled him in and quietly shut the door just as the footsteps reached them. The Admiral and CIA man were lying on the floor. Luckily, the carpet design was a deep red. Sandy had dragged both the bleeding men from the corridor. Alistair dropped to the ground, begging his beloved grandfather to be alive.

Alistair checked both men. The CIA agent was dead. His grandfather was pale, unconscious, but still alive. His training and instinct kicked in—emotion took a step farther back into his mind.

He ripped a trauma kit from one of his pockets and passed a pair of shears to Sandy. "Cut his trouser legs away, all the way around."

He sprinkled QuickClot onto the bleeding wound.

"God, Sandy, you are incredible. How the hell did you manage to drag these two in here?"

She was covered in blood from the two injured men.

"Don't forget I'm from Texas. As kids we're trained to wrestle calves, rodeo style."

Smiling grimly, Alistair bound the leg with a bandage.

"Bloody Mary, this is Whisky. Do you read me?" Alistair said into his radio, confusing Sandy for a second. "I have Rum 1, he's injured but will make it. Bourbon 2 is finished. I'll tell you when we are ready to roll. Over. Standing by."

They looked up at one another.

"I think I prefer this outfit to the last one," Sandy said, appraising Alistair's full combat uniform for the first time. "But I'd love to see the whole collection before deciding."

"Hey, where are your parents?" Alistair asked. "And where are the dolls?"

"As soon as the shooting started," she said, "everyone was moved to the lower floor ballroom with their dolls but I doubt it was for tango lessons. I hid under the bed, fairly classic escape story I am afraid. Your escapes seem a lot more imaginative. Was that your helicopter shooting up all the garden furniture? Nice touch. Somehow I've always hated garden furniture." Sandy was under the influence of adrenaline. "Take me with you," she blurted. "We could live in a little cottage on the edge of Dartmoor and breed ponies. I have an English granny who lives there. She could put us up until we find the perfect place."

Alistair looked Sandy in the eyes and said, "How old are you?"

"What the hell do you mean by that, does it matter, is there an age limit to breeding ponies on Dartmoor? I'm seventeen." She lifted her chin. "Seventeen and three-quarters, almost exactly," she added.

"How come you are at University?" asked Alistair.

She sighed, "I think you're changing the subject from our pony breeding again." She looked serious. "OK, OK I'm smart, super smart. Really, truly. I started University at 16... could have been earlier if it hadn't been for my 'behavior problems'. Not sure where I got my brains from because my parents are like a couple of Dray horses."

"Ahem. Do you mind if I interrupt you two little birds?" The Admiral asked, raising his eyebrows.

"Grandpa! Are you OK?" Alistair knelt and hugged his grandfather's broad shoulders, something The Admiral was not used to. His face softened, and a tear rolled down his cheek.

He cleared his throat. "Yes, yes, I'll survive. I've had worse."

"OK, let's move before we are too close to Panama City to be rescued by Paloma," said Alistair.

"Who's Paloma?" Sandy sensed a rival.

"My baby sister, who is also a wicked pilot."

Looking relieved, Sandy repeated, "Take me with you."

The Admiral and Alistair looked at each other.

The Admiral spoke. "You are clearly a remarkable person who has probably saved my life and his, but we cannot take you with us. Apart from the fact that you are still under the authority of your parents and you need to finish university, you would most definitely trigger a massive hunt. They will say you were kidnapped and—I daresay—you would actually be very useful to us as an insider."

She looked disappointed, but resigned.

"As soon as we leave, get out of here. Don't shut the door, as if we came in here without your help. And then, you must pretend to 'get lost' looking for your parents."

"Thanks, Sandy." He kissed her cheek in front of her ear, smelling her skin and storing it in his memory. She stuck her tongue out at him, but the look on her face was one of possession.

"Bloody Mary, we are moving to the aft deck. Come and get us."

As fast as they could move with The Admiral slumped on his grandson, they worked their way back to the underside of the helipad. They left the body of the CIA agent in the room.

They hoped Olenburgh wouldn't spot the helicopter on radar as soon as it was airborne. Alistair knew the riskiest part of the rescue was coming up. As the helicopter came to pick them up, the machine would have to touch down, therefore motionless and completely exposed. This gave him an idea.

"Vodka, get the longest rope you can find. Attach a harness to the end and drop it under the machine. As soon as we are in it, Bloody Mary has to go like a bat out of hell."

The 'Unicorn Quest' was powering its way towards the locks. The distinctive *whomp, whomp, whomp* of the twin Huey blades was drawing closer.

"I love that sound," said The Admiral, his eyes sparkling at the distant shape approaching.

The deck, recently deserted, suddenly erupted in a hive of activity at the unexpected return of the helicopter. Feet clattered down ladders, weapons cocked. Suddenly the heli screamed down the length of the ship, small canisters dropping from her as she sped along.

Thick red, orange and green smoke plumed and billowed across the decks. "Smoke grenades... bloody genius!" shouted Alistair.

The ship barreled forward, and the stern was blanketed in colored smoke.

A harness emerged into view, followed by a thick black rope. Alistair guided The Admiral into the harness and then clipped his own combat rig onto it.

"We're on. Go. Go. Go. Go!" he shouted into his mike.

As they heard the Huey ramp up the speed, three armed men came running onto the helipad. Alistair fired the shotgun from his hip, just as they brought their weapons up. The force of the buckshot pushed one of them right off the pad. The second dropped, clutching his arm, blood streaming from his face.

The recoil force of the shot sent the harness and its human cargo into a spin. The last man aimed and hit Alistair in the chest, knocking the wind out of him as the slugs struck his Kevlar jacket.

Alistair and The Admiral whirled fast across the pad and rose as the helicopter pulled them away. Alistair thrust his leg legs out horizontally—becoming a high speed, spinning pair of combat boots—and smashed into the third gunman's jaw, flipping him neatly off the stern and into the churning water. The helicopter lifted itself and its cargo up into the air and away from the chaos it had created. The two men were winched on board as soon as they were out of sight of the ship.

13

Home Sweet Home

Georgina Rowena, her face grey with worry, climbed out of the old bunker and started half dragging the Langley man as the returning helicopter landed. Alistair and Tatiana jumped out to help. Once aboard the aircraft, Georgina Rowena climbed across legs to reach her wounded husband. He put his arms around her and shouted in her ear as the helicopter lifted off again, "Sorry dear, I got hit again." It had been nearly fifty years since she had last heard this.

The weather slammed against the Plexiglass, which was so full of holes everyone got soaked by warm tropical rain.

Paloma skimmed low over the jungle canopy until she reached the opening dome of their hidden hanger. She dropped the Huey down through the hole in the roof which started closing the moment the skids touched ground again.

It felt safe.

Lights came on and Dr. Kitts-Vincent and Misha ran out, pushing two stretchers.

As they strapped The Admiral and Mike the CIA man onto the stretcher, Dr. KV introduced everyone.

Traveling through the labyrinth of tunnels to the clinic, the vastness and condition of the place stunned Georgina Rowena into silence.

But despite his wound, The Admiral couldn't help asking questions.

"This place has the air of a US military base and I had top clearance, but I have certainly never heard even a rumor of this even existing. Who on earth did it belong to?"

"Grandpa, we are still trying to work it out, but we will give you the full tour once you are back on your feet. Hey, did you like my flying?"

"You were like an angel on a mission, my excellent granddaughter."

Later, after they finished treating the patients, the group found their way to the mess, where a lovely surprise greeted them. Laid out across the bar was a beautiful collection of cakes and pastries, along with several pots of tea and Marmite sandwiches. Dr. KV smiled at the team's surprised faces. In all the excitement, appetites had been forgotten, but seeing the food awakened their hunger.

Through the murmurs of appreciation, Dr. KV introduced a new team member.

"Ladies and gentlemen, I would like to introduce Chef McDonnell. He works for me at the pub but things are quiet there and I thought we could do with a treat. "

McDonnell was a veritable battleship of a man, as wide as he was tall. He had such a thick Glaswegian accent that even after several years of knowing him, Alistair still struggled to understand what he said, which was probably a good thing, because whatever came out of his mouth was so foul he could make a sewer blush. As soon as they tasted the cakes, everyone discovered he could really cook, and he cooked with a delicate, light touch.

Later in the day, Alistair went to see how his grandfather was getting on. He found him fast asleep, comfortably tucked into the medical center bed. The CIA agent, Mike, had been shot many times and was still unconscious. After removing the bullets, the team had decided to let him be while his body mended.

Two sentinels, Misha and McDonnell, sat at a low table close by the beds, drinking malt whisky and playing poker.

Misha spoke softly, "Where on earth did you find this foul-mouthed, impossibly behaved Scot?"

The huge Scot bellowed, "Ack wee lassie, you're only miserable because I'm stripping your wallet before yer very eyes."

Alistair left them to it, satisfied his grandfather was OK. There were enough rooms for everybody and he was happy to crash into a cot. Before going to sleep, he checked the ship tracker on his phone and saw that the 'Unicorn Quest' was already halfway up the west coast of Costa Rica.

Next morning everybody met in the mess; McDonnell had prepared a lovely breakfast buffet with fresh croissants and he was making eggs Benedict to order, a favorite of Alistair's. The Admiral was in a wheelchair tucking into his breakfast, looking none the worse for having been shot the previous day. Georgina Rowena was having her usual breakfast, prepared by McDonnell under her strict instructions: Bloody Mary in a cocktail shaker with a crushed scotch bonnet chili pepper. McDonnell was having one too. He met Alistair's raised eyebrows.

"Aye laddie, I need t'add a wee bit of lead to m'pencil this morning—that Misha could drink a Glaswegian dockworker under the firkin table."

Dr. KV called everyone to order "Right, let's do a debrief."

14

Debrief

D r. KV, ever the army officer, moved to the front and cleared his throat. "Right, everyone. First, I want to run over everything that happened yesterday so we all have the full picture. Alistair you start." Alistair went through the details of the rescues, and the rest added their parts of the story.

The Admiral finished by adding, "I haven't had that much fun in decades," which won him a reproachful look from Georgina and a laugh from Alistair.

"Thanks Grandpa, we'll see what we can organize for tomorrow. OK, here's what we know about the background. Chip in if we missed something. We put this together in short time."

There was a projector set up. Tatiana and Paloma were manning laptops. They carried on with the presentation while they ate the rest of their breakfast.

Tatiana dimmed the lights and Paloma clicked to a stock photo of a black rhinoceros with a man standing beside it clicked onto the screen, illustrating the scale of the massive five-foot horn.

"The estimated value of the horns on the Unicorn Quest is around $200 million dollars. We are pretty sure this is African Black Rhino horn, but we will confirm today. Black Rhinos are critically endangered: it is estimated there are only 5, 600 left in the wild. Therefore, we could say that this ship is carrying the equivalent of one quarter of the world's remaining Black Rhino horns," Paloma explained, shaking her head.

Alistair took over.

"The 'Unicorn Quest' is due to dock in San Francisco in seven days.

Misha, please can you tell us more about Van Olenburgh? We know he is running the operation on the ships. But he may be the person in charge of the entire organization."

The screen filled with the image of a younger version of the man who had terrorized Admiral and Georgina Rowena on the ship. The photograph showed a man without an eyepatch. He was tall, solid like a rugby player and good looking, with blonde hair and blue eyes that pierced through the screen. He was wearing short shorts, a safari shirt, and was holding an expensive looking rifle.

"Misha, I'm pretty sure that's him, but he's much older now and he's missing an eye," The Admiral said.

"Thanks, Admiral. This is the most recent photo we have, and it is at least fifteen years old. Piete Van Olenburgh: Born Rhodesia (Now Zimbabwe) 1966. His father was Rhodesian special forces, Selous Scouts. KIA 1976. His mother continued to run their 120 square kilometer big game hunting and cattle ranch. As you can probably guess, the family held firm beliefs on the superiority of the white race."

A Google Earth image of Zimbabwean landscape came up.

"They were forced to sell the ranch by Mugabe's government in 2000." A picture of a tough looking tanned woman in a summer dress carrying a Sten gun appeared. "His mother was executed by 'war veterans' of Mugabe's regime when she refused to leave the ranch. The family had colossal sums of money tucked away in Swiss accounts. They owned diamond mines. And with the profits, our friend Olenburgh went shopping for land in Africa—vast amounts of land. He also bought real estate in California. He then stocked the African ranches he purchased with big game under the auspices of conservation. Van Olenburgh created a super high-end safari company—starting at $9,000 a day per person—which seems to do more than average tourism: there is hunting too. The safari company is called 'Pamwe Chete,' which means 'Together Only,' in Shona. There is very little information about 'Pamwe Chete' available but from what we can work out, it is much favored by the most influential people in the world. I will keep digging but I have already found several US Senators, British Ministers and a few super rich folks amongst their patrons. That's it. Then he seems to disappear from everything in 2015," Misha finished.

"'Pamwe Chete' is also the motto of the Selous Scouts," added Alistair.

"OK, thanks Alistair. Good to know. 'Unicorn Quest' is part of the Unicorn cruise liner fleet which appears to be affiliated with the Pamwe Chete safari company," said Misha. "The same company owns land and a five-star spa retreat on the coast of California. It is a bit confusing, so let me summarize and make some assumptions:

Piete Van Olenburgh owns large tracts of land in Africa which he stocks with endangered big game in the name of conservation. But it is actually the opposite—those animals are walking targets. The ultra-wealthy and ultra-influential pay to go on hunting safaris. They become exclusive members of his 'Last Club,' specializing in hunting the last of the species.

He then monetizes the valuable bits of the endangered species by smuggling them out. So far we have seen rhinoceros horns hidden in dolls. Paloma, it looks like you stumbled on part of the process in Lokichogio, Kenya?"

Paloma nodded.

"Using his Unicorn Cruise ship company, he invites retirees with perhaps his politics to join his cruise club, known as 'Unicorn League'.

Members get super rates and all sorts of extras in exchange for the minor effort of taking dolls across the world, originating in Mombasa. The ultimate destination: California. Some clients belong to both clubs: 'The 'Last Club' and 'Unicorn League'. Platinum members, I suppose.

And this is where we run out of information. We do not know what he is going to do with so much rhino horn in California. The market for rhino horn is in Asia, no?"

Tatiana interrupted, "Guys, you need to look at the news." Someone turned on the ancient television and it hissed into life. It was tuned to CNN.

The image materializing on the screen was that of the 'Unicorn Quest' and it looked like something out of a war film. Furniture was exploding everywhere and there were vague images of people being hit by the heavy rounds of the M60. The footage cut to bloody figures lying crumpled on the deck, dressed in colorful Hawaiian shirts and dresses."

"Hey—what the—?" said Paloma. "They dressed those people up! Everyone we hit was in full combat gear and shooting at us!"

The banner running across the bottom of the screen read 'Deadly terrorist attack on Unicorn Quest Cruise Ship as she transits the Panama Canal. Unverified number of passengers killed. Among the dead, one CIA agent. War Hero Admiral William Hagler and wife kidnapped. This is breaking news... stay tuned for updates from our reporters rushing to the scene.' There was a stock image of The Admiral and Georgina Rowena together at a charity ball.

"Well, I can put a stop to that right now. I'll just do a news conference," said the Admiral. "Those bastards."

Dr. KV spoke up. "Admiral, in my opinion, as soon as you stick your head over the metaphorical parapet, they will blow it right off. I can guarantee they have left a hit squad in place. When they kill you and Georgina, they will simply blame your deaths on the 'kidnappers'. As Misha has pointed out, they have friends buried deeply in the US

69

Government and probably many governments across the world. So you do not know who you can trust. I recommend you stay here until we have found out more. It seems to me they do not know where you are." Dr. KV concluded, "I think the only people you can absolutely trust are the ones in this room right now."

The Admiral turned to Alistair and Paloma. "You are right, I hadn't thought of it in such broad terms, but I hate to see you branded as international terrorists on worldwide news."

"So, we need a plan of action," Alistair said decisively. He was not ordinarily this assertive, but the clock was ticking and his thoughts kept returning to Sandy, trapped on the ship.

"Ok, now we have hard evidence. There is a ship en route to San Francisco. Half its passengers will disembark carrying hundreds and thousands of dollars' worth of smuggled rhino horn. Plus, amongst the passengers are about forty men and woman who are wanted by INTERPOL. Why don't we just inform the authorities, and they can raid the ship as it docks?" Paloma looked around at everyone.

"Paloma, you are right. That is exactly what should happen. But these people are not playing by the rules as we saw when we informed the Ambassador. The chances are that they will have organized 'friends' in high places to make sure those rhino horns get off the ship without a hitch. I expect they will also have US customs officials on their payroll. These people have vast amounts of money and almost everyone has their price. To raise an alarm won't stop the rhino poaching. It would merely serve to make them alter the shipping method and we will lose track of it. To stop them, we have to play them at their own game—the one without rules." Paloma was nodding as Dr. KV spoke. She knew it was true.

"Ok Alistair, so what is your plan?" Paloma asked her brother, palms up.

"We need to go to California and find out what goes on when those dolls reach their destination. We have to find out what they are doing with the horns and importantly find evidence of who is involved. We need to build a complete story including photographs, documents pertaining to financial structures, smuggling routes and even film of the actual people killing rhinos if we can find it. I believe the evidence is in Van Olenburgh's lab. Once we have enough indisputable information, we can release it to the world press. No amount of high-level connections would be able to stop it then.

But before that can happen we need to answer a question my father was always drilling into me: how are going to fund this?"

He looked around at the crowd.

Misha stood up.

"Alistair, you British grow up reading those Robin Hood stories, no?"

He nodded and smiled, knowing where this was going.

"So, my band of Merry Men—and women—" she swept her hand across the assembled team.

"Aye, I know what's comin', you've even got a Friar Tuck." McDonnell put his hands on his belly and mimicked an exaggerated Friar's walk.

"Exactly. But this is the twenty-first century and our bows and arrows are automatic weapons and our Sherwood forest hide-out is the jungle of Panama and," she winked, "the internet."

"Yes, my grandmother and I have been 'reassigning assets' from the lowest forms of life for several years now. Not for our personal gain but to finance worthy causes—and this is one such cause," Tatiana interjected.

Misha continued, "In fact we have just broken into the accounts of a known ivory buyer in Hong Kong and I think her funds will be ideal for this job."

There was applause around the room.

"Brilliant, Misha and Tatiana, then let's plan our mission. Tatiana,

Paloma, we are going 'surfing' in California."

Alistair laid out his plan and listened to input and suggestions from the rest of the team. In two hours they had it worked out.

"Excellent. So, let's select a vehicle from our 'stable.'" They strode out to the main warehouse, where the remarkable vehicles were lined up, all painted in military colors.

15

Inspector Clouseau

Alistair walked amongst the rows of vehicles. He passed an armored car and lifted a tarp to reveal a desert-ready Land Rover known as a Pink Panther it was without a roof and bristling in guns. He then surveyed a compact tracked car; an amphibious truck and stopped,- he put his hand on a 1968 Chevy Impala Station wagon painted in the ubiquitous flat army green.

"No, really, Alistair?" cried Paloma. "We have a choice of all these cool vehicles and you choose the 60s soccer mum's car? I mean—what about this puppy?" She jumped up on the running board of a 4x4 ambulance with a boxy back. "We could live out of this thing—go anywhere in it. We could take on anything."

"Well, this Impala will need some modifications, I agree. But we want to look like we are just a bunch of surf dudes hanging out on the beach. Also, it is low profile so we can easily camouflage it in the desert. It has masses of space for all our gear and it does actually have a 4.2-liter V8 engine. And Paloma, you are absolutely right—this car is unremarkable. If we cruise California in an M725 ambulance, however we modify it, everyone will remember it. Plus, that truck, nice as it is, has a maximum speed of 60 mph and it is really, really uncomfortable. I am sure Dr. KV and The Admiral remember painful journeys in them?"

Both men nodded grimly.

"The Impala is specifically designed for long, comfortable journeys on American roads. And don't forget, in the 60s a lot of roads were unpaved, so cars were actually designed to drive in the conditions we'll be facing in the desert."

Paloma held up both hands in surrender but added, "OK fair enough, mum's car it is. But even though you and I are pretty decent mechanics, I'm not sure we have enough time to make sure she runs perfectly or do all the modifications we need. We still have to get it and us to California, pronto."

"Exactly. Charlie Patel will be waiting for us at G57 Pub in." Alistair looked at his watch. "30 minutes."

"Who's Charlie? I've never heard of him?"

"Actually, Charlie is now, technically speaking, a 'her'. She is the person that helps me prepare my vehicles for my annual expedition with my mate Leboo. Charlie works for her dad at Patel Motors in the city. She seems to be able to build or repair anything that moves. You'll love her."

Half an hour later, they were waiting under the Myrtle tree at G57.

They watched as a beautiful, army green classic from the 1940s glided into the tree lined parking space on fat tires. Black and white triangles were painted on the bulbous wheel arches.

Paloma whistled, "A Humber Staff car from World War Two!"

'Very good Paloma, you remember your Dinkys, but wait until you meet the driver."

The front right door swung back and out stepped a statuesque woman dressed in what looked like a British ATS uniform, the kind of uniform Alistair and Paloma recognized from family photographs from World War II.

Alistair stood up and greeted her. "Charlie, you look brilliant.

Splendid uniform. You don't know why I asked you here, but that is exactly what you should be wearing. This is my slightly wild baby sister Paloma."

"Hi Paloma, pleasure to meet you at last. I have heard so many stories about you."

Paloma gave Alistair a look, trying to work out exactly what he had told Charlie. "Hi Charlie, love the Humber. I've always admired those. We have pictures of our great grandad being driven around in one of those by an ATS driver. Can I look inside?"

"We are a bit short of time, Paloma. Why don't you ride with Charlie in the Humber and I'll follow in the Landy? That way you can give Charlie the rundown on what's happened. You can tell her everything."

Paloma trotted happily over to the Humber and opened the door. As she did so, she closed her eyes and breathed in deeply. The car smelled like a real car—old leather, oil, fuel, cigarette smoke—mixed together with a hint of Charlie's perfume.

When they reached THE MAGIC SHOP and showed Charlie the collection of vehicles, she was in raptures and immediately began referring to them as her 'little orphans.'

They finished at the Impala.

"This is a lovely, lovely car with a marvelous engine. After we have finished servicing it and tuning it, I recommend we lift it a bit to give her more clearance and improve the suspension. Then you can round corners at speed and not feel like you're aboard her majesty's yacht." She swept her hand across her brow. "Let's add a differential lock in case you get stuck in sand. What else do you need?"

Alistair listed, "A hidden safe, hidden weapons case, extended fuel tank, serious communications, tracking and GPS systems, camo net that is easy to deploy. What else?" He looked around at the team.

"I guess we need to carry basic camping equipment, food etc. but that can be put into boxes in the back," added Tatiana.

"I have a lovely new toy for you." Misha appeared and placed a large Pelican case onto a table and flipped it open. "This, ladies and gentlemen, is the latest in drone technology. A tethered drone. Attach it to this box, with this wire." She snapped open another Pelican, revealing a bank of screens, keypad, joystick and several switches. "This little bird will be your guardian, your protector, and your eyes. It can hover at 200 meters and see over 10 kilometers for 24-hours." She spun it around. "It is fitted with infrared cameras, motion detectors, 50 x zoom lens and a little sting that I added: a single, guided, micro missile that has a range of 500 meters. Just in case it meets with any airborne foes. Plus, it acts as an aerial to communicate with us. So everything you see—we can also see back here."

"Wow, that is incredible. Perhaps I shouldn't ask where you got it," Alistair said, smiling.

"I think in England you say 'it fell off the back of a lorry'."

"OK, so we need to disguise these two Pelicans so they don't look like high-tech military hardware casings. After all, we are playing the role of surfers in search of the Big One."

"Good point. So, we need to strap three surfboards to the roof rack. Nothing says surfers more clearly than surfboards on the roof, right dudes?" Paloma finished her sentence with a good California drawl.

Charlie smacked her hands together and said to Paloma, "Right, Chica. Get your overalls on, we've got some man work to do." They both grinned.

"Wait. We can't leave the car army green. It still looks military," Paloma said.

"Misha, can you pull up a view of the terrain around Van Olenburgh's land?" Alistair asked. Her iPad screen showed Google Earth. A red dot marked a place 300 kilometers from San Francisco. The pixels focused into a dry desert scene running alongside an impenetrable coast line of rocky cliffs. They could see why he'd chosen it. The roads were unpaved.

Buildings were sparse. The only green area was labeled 'spa', hugging the edge of a cliff. Misha said, "We have been looking at this," her cursor circling a boxy shape. "We think it is a lab of sorts. We still don't know the importance of this building."

"Boy, that is going to be a tough place to hide," said Paloma.

"If the SAS can hide in the middle of an open desert surrounded by Nazis, so can we." Alistair's reference to Nazis was not lost on his audience. "On that note, I suggest we paint the car pink."

"Pink? Pink! Alistair?!" Paloma was hopping from one foot to the other, opening and closing her mouth like a bullfrog. "Pink? Coming from the boy who forced me to respray my mountain bike from pink to matte black—otherwise I couldn't ride with the 'Muddy Street Gang'? PINK coming from the boy who told me when I was six-years-old that I had reached my 'lifetime quota of pink' and I couldn't go shooting with him unless I purged my wardrobe of pink?!"

Alistair, to his credit, was looking very embarrassed. Paloma went on, relentlessly, "Not only are we driving a soccer mum's car, but now it's going to be pink. Pink?!"

Alistair cleared his throat. "Thank you Paloma, I apologize. That was all a bit mean, I admit. It was the fuchsia pink I was objecting to. It really didn't suit you. If you recall, in the 60s, the SAS conducted extensive research on the best camouflage color for the desert. And they came up with this dusty pink color. As a result, they painted a bunch of Land Rovers pink. The SAS referred to them as 'The Pink Panthers'. Like the one we have one over there," gesturing to the car with the tarp half covering it. "I think you'll agree it is incurably cool and it must have worked because they were still using them right up to the 80s."

"OK, OK then we have to call the Impala 'Inspector Clouseau'. It's part of the Pink Panther team," Paloma relented.

"Really? Couldn't think of anything shorter?"

16

California

Alistair, Paloma and Tatiana landed in San Francisco International Airport, passed through immigration and collected their bags. They made their way toward a card that read 'Whisky, Vodka, Bloody Mary'. Behind it was a man in a well-cut black suit with a look of relief on his face. He was obviously getting a little tired of the 'I'll have a double of everything,' comments from the general public.

"Good Afternoon. Mrs. Shepherd sent me. My name is Carl. Please come with me." He had a warm smile and his accent was sing-song Scandinavian. He was very blonde and, by the way he walked, obviously fit. Carl picked up two bags, and they followed him out to a new long wheelbase Range Rover that sat on the curb, daring anyone to come near its dignified presence. "Mrs. Shepherd is waiting for you at the house."

Mrs. Deirdre Shepherd was an old friend of the Stuart family. She had joined them for a number of happy Christmases in Scotland.

Deirdre had led a colorful life so far. Born into wealth, she married a fearless international journalist, Pete Shepherd, whom she had met while attempting to cross Northern Kenya alone on a camel. They were both fanatical advocates of wildlife, and much of her wealth went to support anti-poaching charities. She once bought a helicopter for an eco-guard unit in Gabon. Pete had been killed by poachers several years ago. He had been researching the poaching story from their side but it proved too much for the people who paid them a pittance to do the dirty work, the kingpins.

Carl drove them in silence for an hour and paused at an understated gate with a simple sign that read 'Tangulbei Ranch'. The gate glided open to reveal a winding drive. Desert Willows threw squiggly shadows across the Range Rover as they drove deep into the estate. Soon Deirdre's sprawling home came into view, perched next to the crashing ocean. Alistair checked his bearings. They were now about an hour's drive from Van Olenburgh's land.

The Chevy Impala had already been delivered to Deirdre's stables inside a horse lorry. Misha had sent it by DHL to San Francisco airport. Panama had the great advantage of being at the center of the world's transportation systems.

They would leave under the cover of darkness that night to stake out Van Olenburgh's estate. Deirdre's house would provide a useful bolt hole if they had to make a run for it. Tangulbei had an airstrip for the lovely old De Havilland Twin Otter that she had brought over from Kenya after Pete had been killed. It had been their 'safari' plane.

Paloma and Alistair introduced Tatiana when they arrived. They had told her all about Deirdre and Pete on the drive down.

"I am glad you have met Carl; he's a retired professional Swedish rally driver and my general fixer of everything. He and his wife live in the gatehouse cottage. I trust them deeply." Deirdre smiled at Carl.

Carl looked honored. He bowed his head, smiling. "Your toy arrived. I fired it up. Nice engine and nice color."

Eager to be reunited with their most important piece of equipment, they followed Carl to the stables. The Chevy Impala did look very laid back—big tires, dusty pink coat of paint, surfboards strapped to the roof rack, 'Inspector Clouseau' inscribed in 60s bubble style on the rear.

In the cool of the stables, surrounded by the balmy smell of horses, leather and hay, they unpacked and checked every piece of equipment. Tatiana marked everything off on her cell phone.

All was in order. Once they had packed the equipment back in the car, they locked the stables and walked back to the main house.

They spent the rest of the evening with Deirdre on her veranda. The sun appeared to hiss when it set onto the Pacific horizon. The sound of the sea and the glasses of champagne made the three young people feel like they wanted to stay there forever, just like that.

Tatiana surprised them by telling her story. Although she had never met her father she knew he was an officer in the KGB based at the embassy in Nairobi and had acquired a reputation for consuming vast quantities of vodka. Her mother, Natasha, was a scientist who studied the rhinos of East Africa. When she had become pregnant with Tatiana, the father left. Most of Natasha's work was in the field, and Tatiana and her mother had spent much of their time living in safari tents close to her study sites.

When Tatiana was six, poachers had come to their tent and killed her mother. The rhinos she was studying had been fitted with radio collars, so the poachers had used the equipment to track and shoot all the rhinos on her database. They cut off their horns with chainsaws.

Tatiana was found wondering in the bush three days later by Maasai. Her grandmother Misha had looked after her ever since.

Tatiana's story impressed Deirdre. She understood her past had set her future—not through pity or sorrow—but through determination.

Deirdre didn't have any children of her own and didn't approve of sentimentality. Neither did she approve of mollycoddling child, which was why Alistair and Paloma were favorites. They had spent most of their waking hours, and many of their sleeping ones, outside exploring the jungles, forests and mountains of wherever they were, repairing themselves as they went. Both of them learned to drive the Willys Jeep their father had given them as soon as their feet reached the peddles and their eyes reached above the dashboard. Paloma had rebuilt the engine at aged eleven. Deirdre always gave them free rein when they came to stay, smiling when they came back to the house. Muddy and bloody, but happy and exhausted.

As the sky became studded with a million stars, they told her the complete story about the dolls, jolting them all back to the importance of the present mission. Before their eyes, Deirdre turned from a buoyant, carefree host into a steely woman. Determination and anger blazed in her eyes.

She looked at Alistair and Paloma and Tatiana and understood the courage they would have to summon to cope with what was coming next.

17

Let's Go Surfing

At midnight, dressed in dark clothes and light combat boots, Paloma, Alistair and Tatiana eased the Chevy on to the quiet highway outside the gates of Deirdre's ranch. On the backseat sat a basket with a thermos of coffee, fresh fruit, and croissants that had been pressed into their arms by an emotional Deirdre as they said their farewells.

They could hear the waves above the hum of the V8 as they gathered speed, the smell of hot asphalt filling the car along with the damp, salty air.

By studying satellite images, Misha had found an old track that would lead them into the back of Van Olenburgh's ranch. Although it looked unused, the image was a year old, so they couldn't be sure. They had an hour's drive ahead of them before they would meet it. Meanwhile, Paloma was checking the position of the Unicorn Quest as it approached the port of San Francisco. They estimated they had between four and five hours before the dolls would arrive at the ranch—if the dolls were coming to the ranch. There was no certainty, but they wanted to be ready in case. Snippets of conservation Misha had picked up from the cameras aboard the cruise ship seemed to indicate that everyone was heading to Van Olenburgh's Ranch to enjoy two days at the spa. 'Athena', the doll that they had planted in Sandy's parents' cabin, would give them both a video feed and live location of the movements of the smuggling operation. The risk was that Van Olenburgh's men would collect the dolls from customs, open them up, and remove the Rhino horn slices there and then, immediately discovering the camera and tracking device. This would put Sandy and her parents in a very dangerous situation.

"Our track is coming up on the left. Three hundred meters, two hundred, one hundred and—pull off." Tatiana was navigating using a 1:25 scale satellite image she had on her iPad, tethered to GPS by Bluetooth.

Alistair drove off the asphalt into the scrubland, clouds of dust filling the car as they came to a halt. He turned off the lights, grabbed a torch and some wire cutters.

A pair of headlights appeared on the horizon. The team quickly pretended they were having a break from a long drive. The girls started doing stretches, using the car like a ballet rail. Alistair peed against a nearby fence. He whistled the tune of 'I'm not doing anything, officer,' as he peed. Paloma told him to shut up.

The approaching car swept past in a rush of noise but didn't seem to notice them.

"See, the pink works," Alistair said.

"Come on, let's find this track." Paloma did not like that they were parked on the side of the road. They would be easy to spot.

"Hey, this looks like it." Tatiana knelt down to inspect a part of the fence that had been patched haphazardly. Beyond the fence, two shallow ditches appeared to extend into the distance—old wheel tracks—though it looked like nobody had driven that way for years.

They cut the fence and drove the car through, going 100 meters before stopping. Then Paloma and Alistair ran back, mended the fence, cut some scrub bushes and swept over the ground to obscure their tire tracks. At least nobody from the road could see they had been there.

Tatiana navigated. Alistair had on night goggles so he could steer without headlights. The tires made a nice singing sound as they drove along the soft sand. Stubby grasses on the center ridge of the track swept the bottom of the Chevy, pinging the chassis. Sometimes they had to push through mounds of sand; they were glad Charlie had suggested lifting the suspension.

They drove on in silence, each of them thinking about what they were trying to do and, most importantly, how not to get caught. They already knew the men and women they were dealing with wouldn't hesitate to kill them if they were seen. Equally, their capture would blow the entire operation and potentially expose everyone associated. The problem was that there were many unknowns, so they would have to make it up as they went along.

First, they had to locate 'Athena' and switch her back to the original doll before Van Olenburgh's team cut the dolls open. They hoped that because there were so many dolls to deal with—over 1,000,—Van Olenburgh's plan would be to gut them all in 'The Laboratory' and take out the rhino horn there.

Second, they had to find out what on earth they were doing with so much rhino horn in California instead of just sending it to Asia where it was already worth three times more than gold?

Tatiana watched the live feed from 'Athena' on her screen. They could see from the GPS it was just going through customs in what looked like a duffle bag. She could hear the customs officers talking.

Using satellite images, Tatiana navigated them to the place that they had chosen as their observation post or OP. They left the track and headed towards a dry river bed surrounded by oblong boulders the size of overturned telephone boxes. In the gravel and sand, their tires left no marks.

Even though they could see the night sky lit up like a shopping mall in the distance, there were no lights nearby. They guessed that the lights must be coming from what they called 'The Laboratory', a good 2 kilometers away.

They tucked the Chevy between two boulders and strung the camo net just above head height over the top of the vehicle. From ten feet away, it was invisible.

Alistair rigged up the tethered drone and sent it up into the sky. He had been worried that it would make too much noise and give them away, but the drone itself was quiet and the noise of the nearby surf crashing against the rocks cancelled it out. Putting out two canvas camp beds, they took turns sleeping and watching the feed from the cameras of the drone for the remaining hours of the night. The soft, green glow of the infrared camera and the sound of the sea made sleeping easy.

18

Reconnaissance

Sunlight traced the distant hills. Alistair, Paloma and Tatiana could hear the soft coos of doves as they sat in the emerging warmth. Alistair opened up Deirdre's picnic basket and handed out goodies. While they ate breakfast, they studied the live feed from the drone. In the bright sunlight the image was remarkably clear and they could zoom right up to the doors of The Laboratory and zero in on some patrolling guards.

The Lab itself comprised six Quonset huts, their long cylindrical forms set out in a parallel formation, with a straight corridor connecting them all, intersecting each hut on the northern end. The huts looked unremarkable, painted in a kind of dirty gray, which they decided was surely deliberate, camouflaged by the rocky desert expanse all around. There was a loading bay on the end of the rightmost southern hut in their view. Other than that, what they had dubbed 'The Lab' had no windows. A concrete track the width of a golf cart encircled the compound. A field of well-tended gravel filled the space between the track and a chain linked fence, coils of vicious razor wire spiraling along the top. A short distance from that was another fence of the same description. As they watched, a man with a sidearm and a German

Shepherd at heel patrolled along a well-worn path between the two fences.

Tatiana recorded the time in her notepad while Alistair sketched The Lab's path and fence from a bird's-eye view in his, labelling them and estimating distances.

Tatiana checked the location of the doll 'Athena' and sure enough, she was moving toward Olenburgh's ranch. Although Tatiana calculated they had about half an hour before 'Athena' and all the other dolls arrived at the ranch, they could not be sure of the sequence of events once they got there, or even if they would arrive at The Lab, but they decided it was a good bet.

They estimated there were six guards in rotation around the compound at any one time, two with dogs.

"I can see a CCTV camera on every other building all the way around; no way security won't see us coming," Paloma said, peering at the screen.

They connected with the ops center in THE MAGIC SHOP. Alistair spoke. "Misha, do you think you could hack into those CCTV cameras, record the images, and then play it back in a loop when we go in?"

"Great minds think alike, I am already making the job."

Tapping his drawing, he said, "OK, let's work out how to conquer each element: fence, guards, dogs, noisy gravel, guards, cameras and what looks like highly secure doors. We have got to enter in a way that never reveals we were here."

Getting into The Lab compound would not be easy. Once they had got into the building, they couldn't tell what they would encounter on the inside.

"We can cut fences just under ground level. We can lift it and roll under. They set the fence in gravel so we can push it back over the cut when we leave." Tatiana held up a pair of black World War Two British army wire cutters in a canvas pouch. "I'm assuming that because there are dogs the fence is not electrified."

"Yeah, about the dogs?" Paloma asked. "They'll smell us a mile away," she finished, looking at Alistair and holding her nose.

In response to this remark, Tatiana put her hand in the side pocket of her backpack and held up a plastic bag containing something slightly damp, brown and heavy. "Yes, I have something here that will drive the dogs away and not only that, it will make them crazy."

"Dog shit!" exclaimed Paloma "How does that work?"

"Close. It's not dog shit. It's jaguar shit. In Africa I learned dogs are terrified of leopards. Large, predatory cat species prey on the dogs and the dogs know it instinctually. Jaguars, leopards, same shit, different spots. I keep a supply from Summit Zoo and before we left Panama, I packed some. It comes in handy more often than you'd think. If a dog gets so much as a slight whiff of this jaguar shit, he will not come close. Even the best-trained German Shepherd in the world won't come near us. The guards will be stuck holding them back from running in the opposite direction."

"Very good. I love it. OK, how do we cross 20 meters of really crunchy, noisy gravel?" Alistair asked. "The only thing I could come up with is to get something that makes a louder noise than us. But I am not sure what. The road is too far away."

Paloma's face lit up. "Hey, do you think Deirdre still has that amazing yacht she hosts parties on? How about she throws a raucous party, fireworks, music, the Full Monty, and it happens to pause on this lovely bit of coast, just as we are breaking in?"

"Brilliant, Paloma. Hopefully, the show will captivate the guards. Meanwhile, we cut across the gravel around the back. And if we really get into trouble, we can always make a run for it and swim out to the yacht."

"And leave our lovely Inspector Clouseau? I am growing rather fond of him," Paloma teased.

Undeterred, Alistair added, "We'll wait until nightfall to pull this off. Let's call Deirdre, she'll be delighted to do an impromptu party but she'll need some time to get it together."

As they spoke, giant clouds of dust barreled across the landscape. As the clouds drew nearer, they could make out three large coaches turning off the main road and heading towards the factory.

Tatiana checked the moving dot on her iPad. "Confirmed. 'Athena' caught the bus to The Lab.'"

Alistair thought of Sandy. He hoped she might be on one of those buses, but he also hoped she was miles away.

The coaches swiveled into The Lab gates, hissing air as their brakes went on. The doors whisked open and couples dressed in colorful shirts and shorts filed out. Each person was carrying one or two dolls.

"Are you getting this, Misha? See if you guys can count the dolls."

"Yes, we are and we are watching the feed from 'Athena's' camera."

They switched to 'camera view' on the iPad so they too could receive the feed from 'Athena's' artificial eye and saw part of Mrs. Kelly's arm and a very heavy Mr. Kelly with two more dolls. There was no sign of Sandy. Alistair let out a breath of relief that the other two missed. The Kellys were walking through the doors of the lab.

Like an old thief, Tatiana was talking them through the locks as they passed through each door. "Yale double NS dead bolt—easy. Bike chain and padlock—interesting."

Soon, 'Athena' and the Kellys reached a room with rows and rows of tables. They heard Mr. Kelly breathing heavily from the short walk. The scene jerked along tables set with four stands, each one labeled in alphabetical order. When they reached the K's, Mrs. Kelly's wide bosom came briefly into view. She positioned 'Athena' in her stand and then awarded them with a perfect view of the entire room. The rest of the couples were finishing arranging their dolls and walking out chatting happily, glad to be rid of the ugly things and looking forward to their dividends.

As soon as the last person left, they heard the door shut, lock, and the lights went out. 'Athena's' camera automatically switched to night vision and the ghoulish sight of thousands of silent dolls—all sat upright, staring into space—filled their screen.

19

Lab Watch

The couples filed back onto the coaches and headed towards the spa to their facials, pedicures, and piña coladas.

Alistair, Paloma and Tatiana realized that by nightfall they would need to have completed their plan and be ready to move. They had eight hours.

The drone captured the scene of six golf carts arriving to The Lab, bearing men and women dressed in white technicians' coats and carrying small briefcases. They pulled up to the first Quonset hut and then marched through the front doors.

Alistair connected back to the Ops room. "Hey Misha, any chance of more cameras inside the buildings?"

Misha, who had already exceeded everyone's expectations with her computer skills, instantly linked them to cameras inside the buildings where they saw the techs walking down the corridors of the huts. "I'm using the drone to intercept the feed. This is good stuff. I am loving this drone."

Tatiana said something to her grandmother in Russian. Although Alistair and Paloma didn't understand, her voice was full of warmth, affection, and admiration. Tatiana's face softened as she spoke, and they saw a new side of her.

Each time the techs walked to the limit of a camera, a new view from the next camera filled the screen. Eventually, the people in white coats reached the sixth and last building. Each technician reported to a lab bench with an identical set up: scales, glistening test tubes, burners and an expensive-looking stool where they each put on surgical masks, goggles and gloves. Then they concentrated on their tasks, filling, measuring and mixing. After an hour, one technician collected all the test tubes. She walked over to a large stainless-steel contraption that looked like something off a Star Wars set and poured the contents of each test tube into a funnel.

"OK, so here's what we have at The Lab: Building 1—offices and admin. Building 2—dolls. Buildings 3, 4, 5 and 6—laboratory equipment." As Alistair spoke, more techs arrived and soon all the laboratories were full.

Once they had settled in, one person from each laboratory went to Building 2 and collected dolls, working systematically in alphabetical order. Four 'Atkins' dolls were first. Four dolls to four labs.

Alistair said what they were all thinking. "Let's hope the Kellys' dolls won't be processed today. If they work in shifts through the night, we're back to square one with the plan."

Misha's voice crackled over their coms. Her tone was urgent. "Incoming Helicopter. Pull the drone down. They might see it—or run into it."

Tatiana grabbed the drone controls and hit the red 'home' button. The quadcopter began a rapid descent. Alistair reeled in the cable. As it got closer, it sounded like a swarm of bees. Paloma ran outside and caught it by its legs before it landed and created a mini dust storm. She ducked under the camo net just as the helicopter, a fast AS350, roared over their hiding place, throwing an ominous shadow over the boulders.

The helicopter descended towards The Lab compound and they could

hear the rotors' *chop, chop, chop* as it flared back to land. After a minute
it was airborne again, heading over to where they knew the spa was.

Paloma hastened back outside with the drone and Tatiana toggled the
controls, sending it skyward again. Without the drone they couldn't
see the CCTV, video feeds or communicate. Without it, they were lost.

Once the drone reached 200 meters, everything came back on line.

From the CCTV, they watched Van Olenburgh and two men dusting
off their clothes as they walked towards the main door.

As they entered, a black Mercedes AMG pulled up and waited by the
gate.

"Misha, who are those two men with Van Olenburgh?"

"Just running it and... the tall guy in the blue suit is the Sheriff and
the other one with the beer belly is the attorney general."

"Yeah, looks like he's got some good 'protection.'"

They watched as the three men inspected the dolls and toured the
labs. Two armed guards kept close to them the entire time. After ten
minutes, they marched out, ducked into the waiting car, and drove off
in a cloud of dust.

Alistair, Paloma, and Tatiana went over their plan. The goal was
to gather as much data as they could—but they had to do it without
getting caught. If Van Olenburgh and his gang suspected that anyone
outside his trusted circle had knowledge of the rhino horns, they would
probably shut down their operation temporarily and move it elsewhere.

They had to find out what they were doing with the horns and,
importantly, find evidence of who was involved. They were going to
build an unequivocal truth about Van Olenburgh's crimes—and release
this information to the world press.

The descending afternoon sun was easing off the heat.

Alistair, Paloma and Tatiana would raid the labs at 3 am, the deadest
part of the night. It was the part of the night that a guard, getting
complacent, might drift off or search their phone for that new F150

pickup truck they had their eye on. Once they had conquered the fences, the gravel, the guards, the locks and got inside, they had decided that Tatiana, who had been well trained by Misha, would go to the offices and try to hack into the computers. Alistair and Paloma would go through the labs, get samples, and replace 'Athena' with the real one, carefully sewn back up. They had given themselves 20 minutes based on the routine of the guards.

They would carry silenced pistols and dart guns—both of which they would only use as a last resort.

Then they would simply drive Inspector Clouseau out the same way they had come in and back to Deirdre's ranch.

At least that was the plan.

As darkness fell across the scorching desert and the night filled with unfamiliar sounds, the trio watched the lab techs begin to leave. They had stopped for the night at the 'Higgins' doll. 'Athena' was still sitting upright broadcasting an unobstructed view of the room.

20

The Raid

Once it was dark, Alistair, Paloma and Tatiana sat down together and shared a meal of bread, olives, prosciutto and parmesan cheese that Alistair carved off with his Kukri, the Gurkha's knife. His father had left him this knife—it had a simple black ebony handle and an edge like a samurai sword.

"Alistair, isn't that a little excessive for cutting cheese?" Paloma was drinking a little bottle of Bordeaux Sauternes Château Suduiraut 2011 Premier Cru. "Lovely wine, they were serving it on the plane, so I got myself a small supply." She showed them her bag stuffed full of little bottles. "You never know when you might need a drink," offering them around. The other two declined.

Settling down to rest for part of the night, they took it in turns, keeping watch over their screens and sleeping, or trying to sleep. Alistair and Paloma couldn't sleep. Their nerves were like violin strings. Tatiana dropped off instantly. Alistair always admired people who could do that. He couldn't even sleep on long plane journeys.

Giving up on sleep, Alistair and Paloma sat up, trying to work out what Van Olenburgh was doing with the rhino horns.

"I think he's grinding them up and mixing them with candy or something, so they're easy to transport to Asia."

"But Paloma, he could do that in Kenya. I think he must be selling to someone in the US. But for what?"

Paloma said, matter-of-factly, "You are aware that pretty much everyone knows that rhino horn doesn't give men a good stiffy? Anyway, now you can just use those cheap blue pills." She looked pleased with herself. Her brother was pretty easy to embarrass when it came to discussing sex. As she expected, he changed the topic.

"But there are 3,000 years of Chinese medicine, prescribing it for various cures. Maybe it's something as obvious as that?" Alistair said.

"OK, you might be on to something. Maybe that's what the spa is for? We can't find out a thing about the spa and you certainly can't just call up and ask for a massage."

"Yeah, but if they are dealing in rhino horn cures, they're not going to pick up the phone for any old chica who tries to book a massage. You need to be really rich, well-connected, and a little bit naïve to get an appointment."

"Like Deirdre Shepherd."

"Yes, like Deirdre Shepherd. She would love to play spy. Perhaps she could have an excuse to 'pop in' after she sails past in her yacht tonight and see the spa?"

"That. Is. Brilliant. Let's ask her when we get back."

"If we get back. I'm getting nervous. Well, actually, I am already nervous," Alistair said with a weak smile.

Waiting was both interminable and too fast. At 2 am they packed up all their gear except the drone, checked their communications, and talked to the Ops center in Panama. Misha had been busy; she had found out the names and details of every guard on duty tonight. They were all either a wanted war criminal, an ex-mercenary, or had a history so nasty the world would be a better place without them. Van Olenburgh had chosen well. For their unswerving loyalty, they got fat wallets and protection from the law. Misha had even found out the names of the two German Shepherd guard dogs on duty that night: Jeeves and Nightfang.

Paloma, who was the friend of every living creature on earth, however vicious, had convinced more than one snarling guard dog to be her friend. She always carried a bag of bacon for this very purpose, but a name would certainly help her gain their trust.

On cue, at 2.55am, thumping music came roaring from the sea—Jimi Hendrix's 'Purple Haze'. A wild scene, pulsing in lights, appeared around the headland on a dead calm sea—Deirdre's 1920s, 40-meter yacht. These lights were not just emanating from the vessel, but from a dozen mini drones zooming in a swarm and changing colors in the starry night. At the stern, a series of high-powered jets fired a six-meter water screen into the sky. On it was projected an image of a girl in a bikini dancing to the music, her body moving in a mesmerizing 1960s pulse. The actual girl was a tiny figure on a stage at the bow of the ship, lit up with strobe lights.

The total effect was utterly mesmerizing.

"Woooow, Deirdre is an animal! To heck with this—let's go join the party!" Paloma joked. Deirdre's party was having the right effect on the guards. As they watched the camera feed, one guard after another abandoned their post and walked towards the sea, almost as if they were being remotely controlled from the yacht.

"OK, let's move." Alistair took his eyes off the scene and pulled down his night goggles, scanning the area behind the labs. Their entry point. They crouch-ran down the dry riverbed towards the rear of the buildings. No one was around.

Misha came in over their earpieces. "OK, I'm looping cameras with old footage. I might try to add the sound track back in as a noise for authenticity. Let's hope she sticks to the 60s and nobody remembers the actual tracks."

Misha had become someone they would trust their lives with. She had the incredible intelligence to see all the chess pieces on the board at once and always seemed to think of solutions before they even realized there was a problem.

They had reached the 'loud crunchy gravel' as Paloma had labeled it, but Deirdre's party music—'Good Vibrations' by the Beach boys at this very moment—was so loud that they could have fired an M60 machine gun and nobody would have heard.

Tatiana rolled on her side by the chain-link fence, dug down into the gravel a few centimeters with her hands, and started clipping the wire with her cutters. She hesitated, pulled a plastic bag from her pocket and drew out a handful of the jaguar dung. Alistair and Paloma winced at the smell.

"Whoa, no wonder dogs run a mile. God, that's truly nasty," Alistair whispered.

Tatiana shrugged her shoulders and rolled under the fence. On the other side, she scattered the dung and rubbed her hands. The other two followed. Paloma smoothed the gravel back over the fence where they'd come through and Tatiana cut through the next one. They crawled underneath and lay flat, waiting. Although they were in a dark spot between lights, their next move would take them into the sharp floodlight that poured out from the buildings.

"All clear." They could see the guards along the coastline, absorbed in Deirdre's show. She now had two girls projected on the water screen at the stern of the boat, dancing with each other to the Rolling Stones' 'You Can't Always Get What You Want.'

Rather than worry that some senior officer would snap the errant guards back onto duty, they sprinted across the floodlit scene, feeling like they were escaping from prison—instead of potentially running towards one.

Once they reached the doors, Tatiana pulled out a black suede leather roll that looked like it belonged to a Victorian surgeon. She rolled it open on the ground and selected a tool that must have come from a jeweler. "You, my little darling, will be perfect," she said. Then, humming to the music which was now 'I Feel Good' by James Brown, she set to work on the lock.

Alistair wished he had 10% percent of Tatiana's cool under fire—his heart was going so fast he felt it might pop out of his chest. He had to keep wiping his hands on his combat trousers, he was sweating so much. They were so exposed right now if one guard even looked in their direction, they would completely trapped—and dead.

"... like sugar and spice," James Brown crooned. The door clicked open.

They slipped in and snapped the door behind them. The change in temperature was so dramatic it was like they'd put their heads in the fridge after a hot run. The room was also dark and quiet.

They each turned on head torches—now they could get to work. They looked at their watches. Alistair calmed down with effort and concentrated.

"OK. It's 3:07, agreed?"

They checked their watches and nodded.

"Meet here at 3:27. Let's go."

Tatiana headed to the office. Inside her mini-Pelican case backpack, she had stashed a collection of digital wizardry that could help her mine her way into pretty much any computing system on earth.

Paloma and Alistair found the corridor to the labs. Alistair disappeared into the room full of dolls to switch Athena back to the original, and Paloma dashed on to the last laboratory.

They both had a little Pelican case filled with foam cutouts, each with sealed test tubes for collecting samples. They needed to take enough samples to analyze the results, but not so many that someone would notice them. Each sample required careful photographing to show which doll it had come from, and then the tubes needed labelling. Misha had provided them with a set of bar code stickers that would make it work.

They had to move efficiently and with precision. They took the pictures using the tiny Sony RXO II cameras with incredible Zeiss lenses that worked in low light. These cameras were also filming everything—streaming straight back to the Ops center.

"Five minutes baking time left folks...five minutes." They heard Misha doing a bad British accent on their earphones.

Alistair heard Paloma muttering something about 'not exactly a bloody cakewalk.'

At 3.26 am, they all met again by the door.

"Wait, wait—clear. Go. Go!" Misha was monitoring the guards.

They slipped out of the door, relocked it, and sprinted back to the fence where they had cut their holes. The heat was still in the air, and the sound of Deirdre's party seemed to have reached a crescendo. The speakers were playing Martha Reeves & The Vandellas' 'Nowhere To Run'.

"Honestly, just what we need," Paloma said, referencing the choice of music.

They rolled under the first fence and had just finished tucking the cut section under the gravel when they heard a dog barking. It wasn't the kind of barking you might hear when you live in the city, where dogs just seem to bark for the hell of it. This was the deep, aggressive bark of a German Shepherd doing what he was trained to do—hunt intruders.

The dog was getting closer, coming towards them fast. Tatiana pulled out her silenced pistol, and Paloma gasped, pulling out her dart pistol and waving the other two under the fence.

The massive dog was running towards Paloma at a flat sprint, so fast that when he stretched his legs out his entire body was a horizontal line. His handler had obviously released him. Paloma lay flat on the ground, dart pistol pointed at what she hoped was the speeding dog's chest height.

As the dog caught sight of Paloma on the ground, he seemed to break his stride. Then he slowed to a trot and advanced with caution.

Tatiana said through clenched teeth. "Shoot him. He's trained not to attack but to keep you cornered until his handler arrives."

But Paloma said, "Hello beautiful boy. Let's go for a little walkie."

The dog cocked his giant head, and his attitude changed. She held out her hand, palm down, and he sniffed it. Between her fingers was a bit of bacon.

She talked to him softly, and his tail swept side to side a little.

Then she said, "Come on then, I've got a much better life for you than with these nasty men."

She crawled under the fence, then held it up for him and he crawled under on his belly. He waited while she buried the cut section.

There was no sign of his handler. All the guards seemed to be still entranced by the yacht, where the show was getting increasingly raunchy. The boat was much closer to land, and the girls were beckoning the guards to swim to them like Sirens from Greek mythology. Several of the guards had taken off their boots and were wading into the sea. One was already completely naked and was marching into the water, his clothes, boots, and weapon strewn on the beach behind him.

Paloma looked at the dog's tag and said in his ear, "Hello Jeeves. Welcome to the team." Together, they ran back to the hidden car.

When they got there, Alistair had already retrieved the drone.

Tatiana was shaking her head, "You British and your love of dogs!"

"Well, he's not scared of your Jaguar shit, and he likes me. So I think we have one very smart dog here." Paloma said, stroking his ears. He looked up at her face.

They all hopped in the Chevy. Paloma was in the back bench seat with Jeeves' enormous head resting on her lap.

They reached the asphalt without a hitch and called in. "All clear, no problems... and we gained a team member."

Deirdre's party came to an abrupt end, leaving the guards on the beach in a seething fury. One of them, with fists like joints of meat and a scar that went straight through his lips and down his chin, started shouting,

"Jeeves! Jeeves? You stupid bloody dog—Jeeeeeves! Bugger. Where the hell did he go?"

21

Playing Without Rules

When Alistair, Paloma and Tatiana reached Deirdre's estate, her party was still going on, having shifted from the yacht to the main house. Carl welcomed them at the gate and ushered them towards the stables, where they slipped the Chevy through the main door and into a large stable. He showed them into the empty grooms' rooms around the back, where they showered and crashed.

Late the next morning, the three went over to the main house. A remarkably fresh-looking Deirdre was drinking coffee on the verandah.

She looked up and said, "Morning campers, you missed one hell of a party. And, hello, who is this?"

Jeeves was trotting on Paloma's left side, as if he had always been there. Paloma wore short riding boots, sand-colored jodhpurs, and a white shirt. Around her neck was a silk scarf with flecks of green, the same color as her eyes. The outfit and German Shepherd accessory made her look like she had just walked off a Ralph Lauren photoshoot.

"Deirdre, meet Jeeves, a new member of our team," Paloma said, lifting her finger and looking at Jeeves. He sat down neatly, his huge tail sweeping the cool marble floor backwards and forwards.

They told her the whole story while staff plied them with rich coffee, fresh fruit, toast and, of course, Marmite.

Paloma said, "Those raunchy Sirens were certainly effective."

Deirdre threw back her head and laughed wickedly. "I thought they might do the job."

Alistair said, "So, let's go through what we now know, or think we know. We think Van Oldenburgh's operation poaches rhinos. We now know the smuggled horn comes from the black rhino—which is critically endangered. They then place the sliced rhino horn into the dolls in Lokichogio. We know they probably move it from there to Mombasa, Kenya. From Mombasa the horn moves in Unicorn Cruise ships carried by retirees.

Finally, the horn stash reaches the lab in California where it is ground up and mixed with six other ingredients and as soon as we get our samples tested, we will learn what those are. Tatiana not only managed to copy all the hard drives from the office but also planted a bug so we can now see everything they do on their computers.

Which leaves us missing two bits of evidence. One is the actual hunting of the rhino and how it happens. We hope to find something about that on the hard drives.

Secondly—and this is where you may need to play a part Deirdre—what the hell does the Aura Spa have to do with this?"

They explained how she might 'drop in' and try to work out, or at least record what was happening at the spa. They were not at all sure it was connected.

Deirdre clapped her hands together. "First, I love spas. In my opinion, it's one of the most pleasant ways to spend a day, or two. I own several.

Second—and Alistair and Paloma already know this—since Pete, my husband, was killed by poachers, I have become more and more passionate about stopping this catastrophic annihilation of wildlife for the purpose of some ridiculous human obsession. Pete was not only a brilliant journalist, but he was also an incredible investor. He turned my not insubstantial wealth into an incredible fortune.

I intend, in his honor and for the good of our dear planet, to demolish by whatever means every single illegal wildlife operation out there.

So yes, I am part of your team. I want to play a part as you suggested, Alistair, not just in this operation but in every operation when you need me or my resources, or both.

I have been thinking about this every day since Pete was killed, and I want to share it with you. But I want to see if you agree with my vision:

All over the world there are governments, agencies, charities and foundations working hard to stop poaching and wildlife trafficking, and my hat is off to them. These are all good people trying to win a serious game. The problem is, they are playing by the rules of the game while their opponents are ignoring all the rules and winning every time. The natural world is simply running out of time.

What we need is a group of people willing to play dirty. A group with the right skills, the right resources, the right motivation to stop this annihilation of the natural world.

The world needs a team who can fight these criminals outside the rules of the game. A group who is going to make the poachers extinct before they make more species extinct."

"The Poachers of the Poachers," Alistair interjected with conviction.

"That group is us," Paloma said.

"Yes, and our client is the natural world." Deirdre continued, "But, we have to operate completely autonomously and anonymously. We do not exist. In fact, we ourselves are 'extinct'." Deirdre drew quotation marks in the air. "There are four targets for eliminating these illegal wildlife trafficking organizations:

We break into their financial systems, drain all of their funds and repurpose them to operations that are working to protect the very wildlife they are trafficking.

We destroy every piece of infrastructure they use to facilitate the trafficking process: from cars, to offices, ships, planes, guns, everything... smash them up.

We make sure that anybody involved at the top level is prevented from ever operating again, either through conviction and prison sentence or something truly permanent.

And finally, we expose the complete operation and everyone associated with it, using thorough research and hard evidence which is then released to the world press. What do you think?" She looked at their faces.

Alistair said, "I think you just put into words exactly what we were thinking and doing. We are 'poachers of poachers'. What do you think should be the next step?"

Deirdre looked at the three of them.

"It is already in motion. The next step will happen soon."

22

Deirdre's Spa Treatment

"The other piece of the puzzle we are missing is Van Olenburgh's motivation. Usually, when people find extreme ways to generate vast sums of money, especially when they already have a lot, they have a specific need for those funds." Deirdre was thinking out loud. "What is that evil creature up to?"

Deirdre couldn't get an appointment at Aura Spa for several days. She said it felt like they were giving her a background check and a sly bank inspection.

In that time, Misha had flown in carrying a large bag of gadgetry. She was there to kit out Deirdre's small 'and tasteful', as Deirdre put it, Robinson 55 helicopter. They had the plan worked out. Deirdre would arrive at her spa appointment in the Robinson. Not only would they equip it to take high-quality pictures of the spa but it would act as a kind of repeater to harvest data. Misha would also wire Deirdre to record everything.

Misha and Deirdre hit it off immediately.

As Misha showed her the wire, Deirdre said, "Don't forget it's a spa appointment; part of the process is to get down to one's smalls."

"Well, we Russians don't believe in smalls, owing to our climate, so for spas we use what you call the 'birthday suits'. And Deirdre, excuse me, you have several useful creases to hide listening devices."

Deirdre exploded with laughter.

This was far too much for Alistair, who slipped out and found Paloma preparing for a ride on one of Deirdre's immaculate horses.

Spending the rest of the day riding, enjoying Diedre's excellent hospitality, and sharing it with their teammates, Alistair and Paloma felt like teenagers again. But they missed the most important person—their father.

The Robinson helicopter, landing on the lawn outside the french windows, interrupted next morning's breakfast. Deirdre wafted through the breakfast room, dressed in baggy silk trousers and a fancy dressing gown, flapping dramatically in the downdraft of the rotor blades. Deirdre knew how to make the best of the artificial wind and struck a pose before hopping in, putting on the Peltor headphones and giving a royal wave as the machine rose above the house.

The team sat down in front of a bank of screens to watch the show: Dierdre's landscaped estate from above, followed by scrub and barren land and a rocky, tempestuous looking coastline.

After twenty minutes of this mesmerizing scenery, the helicopter's camera captured the spa, a flat-roofed, concrete structure that appeared to be clinging to the cliff above the foaming waves. There was a big 'H' 100 meters away from the building and the Robinson settled on it gracefully.

A golf cart with a clean-looking blonde girl dressed in white approached. As Carl shut down the engine, the blades slowed to a halt.

"Mrs. Shepherd, my name is Ileana. Welcome to Aura Spa," the girl said with a sophisticated Argentinian accent.

"Good morning, Ileana. Thank you. This is Carl. Please make sure he is comfortable while I have my treatment."

They nodded to each other.

For the next three hours, Deirdre enjoyed a delicious sequence of skillfully applied treatments and then a lovely, light lunch, which was served to her on a private veranda overlooking the sea. The decor was subtle and contemporary, with just a suggestion of something exotic.

When she finished lunch and a twenty-minute nap, Ileana came in.

"Mrs. Shepherd, Aura spa has, over the last few years, been developing a remarkable new product based on 3,000 years of Chinese medicinal wisdom. We are able to offer this to a few of our most distinguished clients. Our owner decided that as you are almost a neighbor who we hope will become a member and frequent visitor, we would like to give you a chance to try it."

"How exciting. Do continue."

"May I show you a presentation we prepared?"

Deirdre smiled and nodded her consent.

Ileana flicked and swiped her iPhone. Curtains drew across the windows in a neat swish, the lights dimmed and a large screen television slid up from inside the table.

Ileana nodded and left the room.

Deirdre started talking aloud, as if talking to herself. She expected they were watching her.

"How exciting. I love a good presentation."

The rhythmic sound of African drums filled the room, and a narrator with an Afrikaans accent began speaking. He told the story of a miracle Chinese medicine made from rare ingredients from around the globe. A medicine that made the old young again, infusing them with new vitality and energy. The word 'elixir' was even used. Deirdre crushed a smile.

The speaker's tone turned confidential. There was a problem—one of the essential ingredients comes from a rare animal that is being hunted and is now close to extinction.

The film showed a massive rhino charging like a steam train through the African bush. It was easy to see the allure of drawing power and energy from the beast.

But they had found a truly remarkable answer to the problem. The narrator continued, and the scene shifted to a rhino's peaceful form, lying in a massively scaled human operating theatre, surrounded by men and women wearing gowns and masks. An innovative solution, he explained. A win-win. By surgically removing the rhino horn, and replacing the real horn with something of equal strength but no value, the rhino could continue to live. To thrive. Footage of a 'replacement' horn complete with gps tracker being installed on the rhino issued onto the screen.

Then, the scene switched to a wide-angle view of a rhino with its replacement horn smashing a tree trunk to pieces in an idyllic savannah.

The narrator continued to explain how, by performing this harmless and humble procedure, no one wanted to shoot the rhinos anymore because their new horns were worthless. The prosthetic horns were instantly discernible by their conspicuous white color and poachers would leave them alone.

But, his voice now collegial. The activities necessary to capture and perform surgery on the rhinos were complex and expensive. And so, the answer was - and here the narrator's tone turned noble—to provide privileged clients the opportunity to benefit from the potent and extraordinary youth elixir made from the real rhino horn and, in turn, these select clients would have the honor of saving the rhinos.

The voice then extended an invitation to purchase one dose of the elixir and, if desired, to come to the spa's laboratory for an exclusive look at how the rhino horn is processed.

As the presentation finished, Ileana swept back into the room and the lights gradually came back on.

"I love it! You must of course know of my dearly departed husband and his mission?"

"We do, and we know from your party last week that you have a young heart and no doubt our rhino elixir would appeal to you."

Deirdre smiled angelically.

"Shall we go and look at the laboratory? It is only a few minutes' drive from here," Ileana suggested.

"Certainly."

Two hours later Deirdre was back at the estate, debriefing Alistair, Paloma and Tatiana. Misha was processing the 'elixir', the ochre-colored pill, the size of a sovereign, that Deirdre had bought for $50,000.

At 4:00 p.m., on schedule, Carl glided into the room and gently released the cork on a bottle of champagne.

Deirdre sighed, satisfied. "So much more civilized than tea."

Alistair, back to business, said, "Well, they have certainly got their rhino horn system worked out .They are taking a highly illegal material and turning it into a 'clean' conservation strategy and they are selling it at ten times the street value. $50,000? Wow."

"Yeah, and all they need to do is dart a few rhinos, paint their horns white, and show pictures to their clients as due diligence. Meanwhile, they just continue to kill rhinos and cut their horns off with chainsaws. If they were actually operating on rhinos, it would need to involve the authorities in Africa. Everyone we have spoken to has never heard of this." Paloma added.

"Because the spa is so secretive, no one can know how many rhino pills they are selling. Tatiana, how is the data farming coming on?" Alistair asked.

"So, we know that almost every first world county has a spa like this and they all sell the rhino pills to so-called 'select' clients. In the last six months they sold just over 17,000 pills at their spas. That's $850 million." Tatiana replied, looking at her screen.

Misha darted into the room. Her wise face showed she was full of news from her work in the portable lab. Mike poured her a glass of champagne. "So, each pill contains 25 grams of black rhino horn. Meaning each horn makes 60 pills, precisely."

Paloma did a quick mental calculation. "That's $3 million per horn. So, if on this shipment they have, as you say, around 1,250 horns, that means the income is $3,750 million."

Alistair said, "But that means they have to sell 75,000 pills. There are certainly not enough wildlife loving Deirdres to make that number. Certainly not just spa clients,"

Deirdre sat forward. "No, but probably enough well-heeled middle-aged people seeking eternal youth? I wonder how they sell them?"

Satisfied with a mission accomplished, the team headed back to San Francisco airport in Inspector Clouseau. They would drop the car off at the FedEx Depot so it could be flown back to Panama in cargo.

PBR

23

PBR

A listair was happy to be driving his old Landy down the muddy Pipeline Road again.

They were all looking forward to getting back to the sanctity of THE MAGIC SHOP's solid walls. Alistair had realized that humans had evolved in caves, and somehow THE MAGIC SHOP evoked some kind of sense of safety that was deeply rooted in their DNA.

They left the main track and followed the almost invisible route to the hidden entry door.

"Open Sesame!" Grinning, Paloma spread her arms, and the door disappeared with a hiss, revealing a long, arched tunnel made of corrugated metal. Dr KV would have seen them coming from the hidden CCTV camera and activated the door for them.

Loops of industrial looking cables ran along the sides and top of the tunnel. Dusty lights in glass and wire cages studded the roof.

The door hissed shut behind them, sealing out the sounds of the forest.

Since Alistair, Paloma and Tatiana had been gone, the rather institutional Magic Shop had been seriously upgraded. Dr. KV took them on a tour.

The bedrooms had been redecorated into very pleasing rooms, but they still maintained their 1970s style. The mess had been left as it was except that someone had added some photos of their own adventures, including one of the team when they landed the Huey after the rescue of The Admiral and his wife. It looked strangely like it had always been there. The old TV was still there, but the screen was now an LED high-definition flat screen.

The Ops room now looked like something between NASA headquarters and a military forward operating base.

The rest of the team were sitting on tall architectural drawing chairs around what looked like a large plotting table and swiveled around to welcome Alistair, Tatiana, Paloma and Misha back.

Jeeves dutifully trotted around and introduced himself to everyone. Dr. KV had installed empty wooden ammo crates in most of the rooms, which he piled with old army blankets. Jeeves stepped into the one in the Ops room, made three circuits and lay down with a sigh.

On one wall was a large digital world map dotted with pins and lines. Dr. KV zoomed into their own location and showed individual trees in sharp definition. "See, we don't exist." There was no sign of the bunker. Their entry and exit roads were just lush green forest.

Dr. KV moved their attention to what he called the 'cast of characters screen' showing mug shots of every single person involved and lines indicating their connection to others. They were color-coded: red for working for Van Olenburgh and green for a friend. Even Jeeves had his picture up there; Paloma was pleased to note they had updated his color to green. Misha explained that the people who had been eliminated had a line through them.

They were surprised but happy to see The Admiral there, seated in front of the map.

Alistair was ready to get to work. "So where are the funds going? What did you guys find?"

114

Walking over to the map, Dr. KV touched the screen, zooming in on Algeria, Libya and Egypt. Large chunks of these countries were colored red.

"Olenburgh has been acquiring land, massive amounts of it. So much, in fact, that you could almost say he has created a country. You can see most of the land he has is contiguous." Dr KV pointed to what looked like a red river across north Africa. "In a way, he is recreating an Axis power occupation. This may look like desert to you but there may be valuable minerals here that are worth exploiting."

Paloma stood up. "I think we are speculating. There are too many unknowns. We should have a look. Misha, have you noticed an area in the vicinity with a high volume of air travel in and out?"

"Yes, actually, that was my next point. We are seeing intense focus on an airfield in North Africa. There is constant air traffic heading to a single point in the middle of the desert. It's like watching a beehive. Everything is flying in from all over. Question is—what for?"

Dr. KV patted his pocket with a look of a man who just remembered something. "Oh yes, we got a strange message. It was left at the G57 Pub."

He handed a brown manila envelope to Alistair, the kind that has two little round discs and a bit of string to tie it together. The string was sealed with an embossed wax two-headed eagle.

On the front, in elegant handwriting in rich ink, was the word 'Whisky'.

"I guess that's for me," Alistair said, pulling out his knife and neatly slitting open the envelope.

A small card fell out. Alistair caught it below his knee. Embossed on thick, luxurious linen card was the name '9th EARL OF GODOLPHIN'. Alistair turned the card over. On the back was a handwritten message: 'I am a friend. Meet me 10.10.10 9.595867 -79.667083

"OK, that sounds potentially very dangerous—but exceptionally intriguing. Where is that?" Alistair moved the curser on the huge digital map. He punched the coordinates from the card into the keyboard and, hitting enter, the map zoomed to a little island in the Caribbean coast of Panama, just North East of a town called Portobello. Portobello was once a port where the Spanish hoarded the gold they'd stolen from the Americas before sending a Galleon-load home to Spain. Captain Morgan and the English pirates cleaned it out on three occasions. Now it was a rain soaked and faded village with a population of stranded yachties, wanderers and poets.

'Isla Baile del Mono.' The map curser settled on a strip of yellow beach on the small island otherwise covered in vegetation.

Paloma picked up the envelop and turned it over. "Wait, there's something else in here." Peering inside the envelop she pulled out a tiny USB.

Misha held out her hand "I think I should test that before we plug it into our system."

She plugged it into a small computer that was disconnected from everything else.

"It's clean. It's a GPS track to the island."

"10.10.10 I guess that's 10 am, 10th October. That's in two days. We'll need a boat," Alistair said.

"We have a boat - in fact, we have an amazing boat - come with me I will show you our baby," Charlie said. She was turned out in perfectly pressed World War Two overalls, tightly belted at the waist. She led everyone out of the Ops room, through the main vehicle room, and along the 'OUT' corridor.

"I was repairing all the holes you lot put in the poor Huey and needed some parts. I figured these boys would have spares somewhere, and I found this door marked 'PBR.'" Charlie opened the door and beamed like she had just pulled a perfect souffle out of the oven. She led them down a narrowly lit passage. Steel cages covered every light fixture.

Thick cables ran down the sides of the walls in loops. They passed a Bakelite telephone hanging on the wall with the words 'Emergency Only' written in red stencil underneath.

At the end of the tunnel was another door with the spin handles, the same as watertight ones found on ships. Charlie spun the handles, pulled a lever, and stepped through the steel door.

They all followed her, wide-eyed.

A domed roof dominated the concrete bunker. In the center, a wide ramp led to a massive steel door.

But the biggest surprise was perched on a wheeled cradle and attached to a monster winch. Alistair's mouth dropped open in amazement.

In flat green was one of the Vietnam War's famous PBRs: 'Patrol Boat River.' The boat was a 32-foot fighting machine. Mounted in an armored swivel housing at the bow were twin M50 Caliber machine guns, and on the rear, twin M60 machine guns, plus an assortment of other interesting weapons. Two jets made it highly maneuverable at high speed.

Paloma walked over to the fiberglass hull and patted it like a horse. "Incredible. Does she have a name?"

"Nope, right now she is PBR 116. Shall we try her out? I've serviced her as best I can without actually putting her in the water. Jump on, we are doing a wet launch." Charlie pulled another lever and the immense doors slid along the rails to the roof like a car garage.

Outside, the jungle cascaded down either side of the launch channel, which curved away to the left.

"Wait. Paloma, we've kayaked down here exploring when we were teenagers, remember?" Alistair smiled at the memory.

"Yeah, I remember. It never stopped raining, and you kept on saying 'just one more corner' and we ended having to sleep in the forest because it got dark."

"Well, see, I was right. One more corner and we could have found this!

But this means these channels lead to that bridge under the railway. We always wondered why it was there."

"It connects this channel and leads to the Canal," Paloma finished for him.

"Which means we can get to sea and to our meeting with the strange Earl. Dr. KV, do you still have a mate who runs the tugs? Remember how he let us go through the locks with the tugs when we had that speedboat we built?"

"Yes, in fact, he has gone up in rank, Juan Sandoval. I'll ask him. Now listen. You must dismount all the weapons and stow them if you go through the locks. Nobody will be happy seeing a heavily armed boat driving up to the Panama Canal locks. They are still recovering from our last little escapade."

"But we'll keep them on for the test run, right?" Alistair pointed out hopefully.

They were climbing up the rear ladder onto the boat. It was in perfect condition, and the weapons were oiled and armed.

"Hey, remember in 'Apocalypse Now' when they pick up that PBR with a Huey and drop it in the river mouth? I've always wanted to do that. We could pick it up and drop it on the other side of Gatun Dam in the Chagres River. It would be so cool, save going through the locks, much faster—and much more fun."

"Sorry Paloma, I am still doing my checks after patching all the holes you put in the Huey. Picking up an PBR is not exactly the first test flight I had imagined," Charlie explained.

"Plus, I need you to drive the boat," Alistair added.

"I will be driving the boat for this mission." This was a command from The Admiral. Everyone turned, faced him and saluted, grinning.

Dr. Kitts Vincent stepped off the boat. "I'll hold the fort." He walked over to a lever marked 'Rapid Deployment' and pulled it down with a sharp tug. The boat seemed to groan and then screamed down the ramp on its trolley.

Paloma waved one hand in the air like a cowgirl. "Yeee Haw!"

The boat hit the water like a lifeboat going out on rescue—everyone got soaked. Charlie hadn't stopped grinning and—as she fired up the twin jet engines—she was more smile than face.

The fiberglass hull powered up the waterway, jungle slipping by them at high speed like some kind of green curtain being ripped open. Within minutes, they came to the railway bridge that led to the canal. Charlie flipped the thrusters, and the boat came to an immediate rocking halt.

"We'll call her 'Marmalade'," Paloma announced.

Alistair shook his head and rolled his eyes. He knew better than to ask why Paloma had decided to name a heavily armed fighting boat after a breakfast preserve.

"Perfect." Charlie lit a cigarette and half shut her eyes as the warm sun filtered through the canopy of trees above them, making patterns on the surrounding water. "And let's call her dock 'Paddington Station.'"

They all laughed, and Charlie buried the hammers as they blasted under the bridge to the open water of Lake Gatun.

Paloma sat in the cockpit at the bow with her tongue out like a dog with its head out a car window. Jeeves, sitting next to her, was doing the same thing.

Charlie took a picture.

They spent the next two hours testing the boat, taking it in turns driving, learning the sounds of the engine and enjoying the pleasure of riding a fast-moving boat through the myriad of jungle cloaked islands that dotted the canal. Charlie spent the whole time tweaking the engines, listening to them like a piano tuner.

Pulling back into their hidden dock, the roar of the engine rang in their ears and stayed with them long after they had shut it down.

24

9th Earl of Godolphin

Early next morning, Paloma and The Admiral sat in the PBR's cabin. He looked like a schoolboy on his first outing to the beach. "Damn, I haven't driven one of these things since 1968. I feel like I just stepped back in time. I feel good..." he drummed on the dash.

They were all wearing a mishmash of Vietnam era uniforms, including the tiger stripes favored by special forces. Charlie had found a room containing enough different uniforms to make a documentary on the subject. One compromise was that all of them were wearing the latest Sonetics hearing protectors with mics and headphones incorporated so they could communicate over the noise of the boat.

Georgina Rowena had tried to prevent The Admiral from going on the expedition, but there was no way he was going to miss this.

He was telling Paloma some marvelous stories from his time in these boats. It was rare for him to talk about his war experiences, and she listened carefully, wishing she could record everything he said.

Tatiana and Alistair were organizing equipment in the small cabin. Charlie was checking the gauges on the engines. She was also wearing a 1960s outfit, but hers was the black 'pajamas' of the Vietcong. She had even braided her hair before going to the dock that morning. "I like to be the odd one out."

Alistair stuck his head through the small door. "OK, ready to launch!"

Misha pulled the launch lever, and the boat rolled down the ramp and through the open door. It was 6am, and the sun was just rising, sending long shafts of light through the mist over the water.

The name 'Marmalade' had been neatly painted in black on the stern.

The Admiral drove the boat through the jungle with the expertise of an Olympic tobogganer; he seemed to know exactly when to pull the power back the moment before anyone else might have driven them unceremoniously into the jungle.

It seriously impressed Charlie. "So that's why they made you an Admiral!"

As soon as they reached the Gatun locks, the tug 'Chagres' was powering up to go through the open gates of the first chamber. They maneuvered alongside the tug and the crew expertly lashed together the two boats.

The Admiral received a salute from the tug captain. Paloma asked if he was loving being in charge of a boat again. "The last one was a bit bigger," he said, his eyes twinkling in remembrance of his US Navy aircraft carrier.

The nearly 700-ton lock doors shut neatly behind their sterns.

The lock's century-old engineering functioned perfectly and within minutes the water began to drain and the 'Marmalade' and the 'Chagres' began their descents to meet the Caribbean Sea. Once they dropped into the concrete chamber and out of the fresh breezes, the air was hot, wet and still. The 'Chagres' crew had put rubber protectors around the hull of the tug. Once the water level equalized with the lock below, the doors at the bow end pushed open and they crept forward to the next chamber.

Twenty minutes later, they were out in the blue waters of the

Caribbean. It would take them an hour and a half to get to Isla Baile del Mono. The PBR was not designed for open seas and the Admiral was grateful for the rainy season's relatively calm waters. And he guided the 'Marmalade' to ancient Portobello in good time.

The crew pointed at the ancient Spanish forts' funnel-shaped openings, which had been designed for cannons, almost at water level. As they passed by, Alistair noted that those cannons could have annihilated any ship approaching. In fact, many cannons were still pointing menacingly out to sea. Paloma reminded them all that Captain Morgan had avoided the cannon fire by landing his men a few miles west and then attacking overland.

Once beyond the town of Portobello, the younger crew remounted their own weapons on the boat while The Admiral scoured the waters with his binoculars. They had no way of knowing if this was going to be a trap but at least they would be well armed and had a fast escape.

They were feeling the adrenaline running as they locked the heavy machine guns into their mounts and loaded the ammo belts into the breaches.

Alistair was pulling on a black rash guard and strapping on a jungle knife. He would jump off the stern of the boat as they went around the back of the island. While he swam ashore and worked his way through the jungle to the beach, The Admiral would drive the PBR towards the beach with Paloma and Tatiana on the guns, with Charlie ready with a grenade launcher.

The Admiral swept the boat in an elegant arc around the back of the island, barely easing off the 38 knots of top speed. Alistair rolled off the stern at Tatiana's signal. He had less than 20 meters to swim. On his back was a small Arctrex waterproof bag and tucked inside was a stubby UZI submachine gun—a wicked little weapon made by the Israelis.

As his feet hit the sand, he could hear the PBRs' twin engines throbbing until the boat disappeared.

He checked his wrist compass and headed for the trees that were dipping their leaves in the crystal waters.

The jungle was his natural environment, having grown up in a house surrounded by forest. Most kids have streets and playgrounds. Alistair and Paloma had the rainforest. He could name every bird, hundreds of insects, and he knew what plants he could eat, and what plants would rip his skin or stick needles so deep into his flesh that they wouldn't come out for months.

As children, he and Paloma would take it in turns to camouflage and hide in a small patch of forest until the other one found them. It required moving and concealing in a spot while the other, with their back turned, would listen and wait.

Alistair could move through the jungle more quietly than a blue morpho butterfly flying. He left no trace of his passage.

Within a few minutes, he saw a flash of ochre sand. And, 100 meters away, in the shade of an Indian Almond tree, was a man. He was, somewhat bizarrely, sitting at a small wooden desk. The man wore a white shirt with the sleeves rolled up neatly, braces looped over his shoulders, a deep crimson tie, and dark pin-striped trousers—his whole look had an air of Saville Row. Except that the trousers were rolled up nearly to his knees. He had very pink feet and his rather round head was bald. Through small circular glasses, he peered at a gilt-edged leather-bound book.

He reminded Alistair of Winston Churchill.

The man was dabbing his forehead with a handkerchief. Alistair smiled to himself. A cool breeze wafted up from the water. For him, this place was air-conditioned.

On the beach was a black RIB speedboat with a 200 HP engine and center consul. It looked military. No one else was around. This must be The Earl.

As he was taking this scene in, the PBR rounded the corner and came into view. The Admiral was at the helm carefully following the GPS track they had been sent with Charlie beside him. In the bow, Paloma was tucked in behind her twin M50s. Jeeves was beside her with his tongue flapping in the wind. In the stern, Tatiana was swiveling the big M60 towards the beach.

The Ear' looked down his nose over his glasses with an expression of distaste, as if he had been sitting at a traffic light and some yobs had pulled up beside him blaring music.

Alistair used the distraction to drop into the empty chair. He had the Uzi in his lap, hand around the grip and finger lightly on the trigger.

"Good Morning Alistair," the man said in a plummy voice, without taking his eyes off the boat in the bay.

"Good Morning, Sir."

The Earl's pale blue eyes met Alistair's. They were kind, and he was smiling.

Alistair eased his grip on the Uzi.

"I apologize for the subterfuge, but it looks like you were prepared for anything." He nodded his head towards the heavily armed boat in the bay. "My name is Peregrine De Montfort, 9th Earl of Godolphin. I am the director of WT 8 Anti-Wildlife-Trafficking at INTERPOL. It is a pleasure to meet you. As far as we are all concerned, this meeting is not taking place. Here is my ID."

Alistair looked at the ID and took a photo, which he sent to Misha. Fifteen seconds later she sent a thumbs up emoji to everyone.

Alistair put the Uzi on the table. The boat dropped its anchor, and the girls got out of their positions behind the weapons.

"Most people both inside and outside the organization do not know what I or my team at WT 8 do. We are a small team and I trust everyone. My assistant, for example, is also my niece. My wife, sadly no longer with us, the Countess Jasmine, came from an old and well-connected Panamanian family. She inherited this island, which is where we also have an office. The Admiral followed the exact course I sent. If he had deviated from it, the boat would have smashed into hidden rocks. No one, except a few trusted and well looked after fishermen, knows how to get in here."

The Earl fished a bottle of Domaine Jean Paul & Benot Droin, Chablis, Burgundy, 2010 from a canvas covered tube beside his chair. Ice clinked as he lifted the bottle and placed two simple wine glasses on the table. After pouring each of them a glass of the cool pale liquid, he continued.

"Our job description is straightforward. We gather information on wildlife trafficking. The way we do it is complex. We have a world-wide network of highly paid informers from almost every aspect of the trade; from lowly hunters with decrepit shotguns to the most powerful Ivory Mogul in China. We assess the data and assemble the most complete and up to the minute picture of wildlife trafficking activities across the globe. If another agency within INTERPOL needs information, we connect the dots and pass it along. Does this make sense?" The Earl sipped from his glass.

"Yes Sir, this is jolly interesting but I am not sure where we fit into your picture?"

25

The Extinct Company

The 9th Earl of Godolphin continued explaining to Alistair as they sat on the beach of Isla Baile del Mono.

"So, I have two problems. Number One: Lately, when my team passes information along to authorities, even within INTERPOL itself, it spells a death warrant for anyone providing that information. The trafficking organizations are now so powerful and so well connected that they themselves trace all of our sources quickly. This means that although we have a wealth of good evidence that should put people in prison, it is now actually working against us, destroying our most valuable assets—our sources. These relationships often take years to cultivate." They both took a healthy drink of wine.

"Number Two: Wildlife extinction is happening so fast, estimated at between 10,000-100,000 species a year, that the tools we normally use against people like poachers are simply too slow, too complicated and it feels like we always show up to a gunfight with a penknife. For example, at this rate we have ten years of wild rhinos left."

Alistair was nodding—he knew what was coming.

"So, Alistair Gordon Stuart, you and your team can do what the rest of the official," and he emphasized the word, "world cannot. That is to say—wipe out wildlife traffickers using the same ruthless means that they use."

"You want us to poach the poachers until they become extinct?"

The Earl smiled at the last word.

"Exactly, that is very well put indeed."

"But I am not talking to you in my official or unofficial status with INTERPOL. This is not an official partnership. You and your team would receive no official recognition, and if you get into trouble, we cannot bail you out. INTERPOL can, though, provide information, and we can reassign valuable resources for you to use. What do you think?"

"I don't need to think about it. We are already there, so to speak, and if you can help us, then yes. We've realized we are up against something far bigger than we ever imagined." Alistair drained his glass.

"Excellent." The Earl put his hand across the table and they shook.

"Is there some kind of other group involved?" Alistair had a sense The Earl still had more to reveal.

"What I am about to tell you is about a secret organization that has been kept that way for several centuries. Men and women have died keeping the secret. Once I tell, you will be bound on pain of death to keep the secret."

Without hesitating, Alistair responded, "I understand. I give you my word and my trust."

"The organization has existed since 1627.

It was founded at the first recorded extinction of a species by man.

Its mission is to stop that extinction of species by whatever means necessary. It is known as 'The Extinct Company.'"

"That is incredible. How much can you tell me, how do we join?"

"First, you have already joined. You and your team were nominated, and you have been accepted."

Alistair leaned back in his chair, mouth slightly open. He put his hand on his chest, "Thank you Sir, we are honored."

"We have limited time, and I will present you with more details soon. For now, you need to understand that there are two wings of the organization. One is purely financial—their mission is to support through anonymous funding and gifts. So, for example, if there is a rare, endemic frog in Mongolia and the government wants to destroy its habitat to push an oil pipeline through, you will find a series of anonymous donations going to the NGO fighting to save it.

The second wing has not been in operation since the end of the Vietnam War.

It used to do what you are now doing.

The poachers of poachers. A Commando unit. A highly trained, diverse unit committed to the extinction of poachers.

It was Deirdre Shepherd who nominated you. The California mission was your selection process. You exceeded expectations.

Welcome to The Extinct Company.

Questions?"

"Gosh, yes, one immediately, probably a hundred later. Why did the Commandos stop operations in the 70s?"

"Three reasons. One: the Inner Guild of the Extinct Company wanted more peaceful solutions—they believed they could make things happen without resorting to violence. It was a response to decades of war around the world, the conflict in Vietnam was the final straw.

Two: several members of the Commando unit were killed during their last operation because of a leak in the organization—they decided the means could no longer justify the end.

Three: of the remaining survivors, we could only trust one man. Someone you are aware of—Sergeant Gibson.

He eliminated those we could not trust and then shut down the headquarters. Otherwise known as THE MAGIC SHOP. I believe you know it?"

Alistair was stunned. Both men sat in silence and watched the peaceful scene unfolding on the clear, tropical waters in front of them.

Meanwhile, the girls had changed into bikinis and were diving off the boat while Jeeves was happily paddling around in the cool water. The PA system was original, so as The Beach Boys emerged from the speakers in a tinny form it somehow seemed perfect. The Admiral was drumming his hands on the dashboard and smoking a cigar; he had really gone back in time. The heat, the jungle surrounding them, the loaded weapons on the PBR. Tears were streaming down his face as the faces of a hundred missing friends passed before him.

The Earl poured them another glass. "So, tell me about Van Olenburgh, what you know and what you don't know, and I'll try to fill in the blanks. We've been watching him for the last five years."

Alistair drew himself up and reported, relaying all the details of the dolls, the fact-finding missions to the laboratory and the spa.

"So, yes, this aligns." The Earl looked at Alistair intently. "Van Olenburgh has a series of Aura Spas based in every developed country, just like the one Deirdre visited, except the only laboratory appears to be in California. What we have gathered is the spas are a front for their principal business, which is selling their 'rhino horn elixir of youth' pills online. His network of salespeople performs a virtual version of what Mr. Tupper's did back in the 40s. It's a club and the more you sell, the better the benefits. Every buyer is invited to the 'club,' the network of Aura Spas. Though in reality very few visit the spas, they are deliberately remote and not everyone has a helicopter.

What you may not be aware of yet, Alistair, is that Olenburgh has created a colossal online community. And it operates like a cult. Extra status for the more often you buy these pills and at $50,000 a pop that requires a major investment. There are carefully curated 'influencers' who push the virtues of the pills and the significant difference they are making to saving the rhinos. This is invitation only, making it even more desirable."

"The propaganda is brilliant and perverse," Alistair said.

"Yes, it's clever," The Earl continued. "People become obsessed with this community. They mortgage their houses, leave their families, everything. Van Olenburgh sells at least 500 pills a day worldwide. That's $25 million a day."

"But what about technology, security?"

"All transactions are done on encrypted iPad, part of members' benefits. And, Alistair, I know what you next question is…" He leaned forward. "We both know he is buying vast chunks of land with that money but what is he doing with that land? We, at INTERPOL, have tried to find out, attempted to fly drones over it. We have tried to send teams in but they always get stopped by layers and layers of bureaucracy."

"Which is where we come in," interrupted Alistair.

"Exactly, my good fellow. We need you and your team—for a mission that doesn't exist." The Earl drained his glass. "A trip to the deserts of North Africa." He handed across a sophisticated-looking phone. "Use this to communicate with me. It can only call one number—mine. The calls and data are encrypted."

Alistair took the phone and, standing up, he put out his hand out and they shook once more.

"Do you mind if we spend a few hours on your beach? It's been a rather crazy few weeks and this is a perfect patch of peace."

"Please do and please use it whenever you need some R and R. My security crew knows all of you."

Alistair had seen no security crew. He turned and walked down to the edge of the water and waved for The Admiral and the girls to come up to the beach.

When he turned back again, The Earl had gone. On the table was a sand-colored Pelican cooler. Alistair opened it. Inside were three large, very ancient-looking keys. The bows of each were distinctive, in the shape of curved horns. The three keys were lying on the top of two chilled bottles of 2002 Taittinger Grand Cru.

26

The Chest

For several days Tatiana, Paloma, Alistair, Misha and Dr. KV had been searching THE MAGIC SHOP to find something to use their three keys to open. Speculation had gone on day and night.

Each evening, the five of them gathered in the mess to solve the mystery.

"I think they are keys to a chest that holds an amazing weapon," Alistair declared, and had spent two slightly distracted days searching every nook and cranny of the DOGS OF WAR armory and firing range. He kept on discovering new weapons, which he would bring to the MESS.

"This, ladies and gentlemen, is a Heavy Dragoon Carbine Pattern 1770, from the Battle of Waterloo if you didn't know."

"Alistair, does that gun require three large keys?"

"No, Paloma it does not, but it is very exciting to be holding something that was actually used in The Battle. It must be worth a fortune."

Dr. KV stepped in. "Thank you Alistair, it is a beautiful, but according to what The Earl told you we need to go back another 150 years to 1627 right? It must be something that holds great secrets, and that is why it is so valuable."

Paloma's eyes lit up. "Wait, we are searching the wrong way. We are looking for something that the keys fit; but the way THE MAGIC SHOP works is everything is given its own special room or locker. I think we are looking for a safe or something; whatever those keys open will be inside there."

"By jove, Paloma, you are right." Dr. KV pulled sergeant Gibson's notebook out of his pocket and started scanning the pages. "Come on Gibson, give us a hand here," he said to the notebook.

"Alistair, why don't you just give The Earl a ring and ask him where it is; didn't he give you a special phone?" Tatiana asked.

"Yes, I considered that, but I think if he knew where it was, he would have just told me at the beach. Maybe Gibson didn't want to tell anyone. Remember, this place was locked up by him over forty years ago and he couldn't trust anybody. He was right because Gibson was killed soon after locking it up. Any luck, Dr. KV?" Alistair looked at the professor, who seemed to be inspecting one page.

"Maybe, maybe. How does this sound? It is next to a drawing of a Tarantula Hawk wasp if that has any significance: TEC_MAA 631627?"

"TEC, The Extinct Company? Not sure what MAA stands for but I'll bet that's it. Not sure what 6 or 3 stand for but 1627 is the year it was founded? So I think Paloma is right, it must be a safe. Let's search?" Alistair was already looking behind the bar.

Misha was holding one key and looking up at a military shield on the wall. The shield had a punished appearance. It looked like it had been in battle. Most of the paint had been scratched off. It had deep valleys cut into it where a sword or axe had been used against it.

Everyone stopped what they were doing when they noticed the look of triumph on her face. Lining the key up to her eye like a gunsight, she looked through it at the shield.

Without talking, she handed the key to Alistair, who mimicked her. When he brought the key up to the shield, it completed the symbol of horns with an arrow through a skull.

Stepping forward, he ran his hands around the edge of the shield, which was at the same level as his chest. There was a neat click, and the shield swung open, hinged on the left.

"A safe!" Paloma shouted, delighted. In the center of a very sturdy steel door was a keypad numbered one to zero through nine. On one side was a handle.

Dr. KV repeated the numbers and Paloma punched them in "6-3-1-6-2-7" and pulled the handle, opening the door.

Barely fitting inside the safe sat an ancient-looking chest. At first nobody in the room moved towards it, feeling like they were raiding a tomb.

Finally, Alistair grabbed the one of iron handles at the end and pulled it out. Paloma grabbed the other end, and they heaved it across to a coffee table.

"Damn, that thing must be full of gold or something," Paloma said, putting her end down with relief. They all gathered around and stared at it. The excitement filled the room.

Thick, battered wrought iron encased each edge and corner. Heavy rivets studded the entire box. Solid rings with rods running through them adorned both the front and back. Dark green painted wood filled the remaining spaces between the metal. It looked like it could tell stories, nearly four hundred years of them. It even smelled of the past—iron, musty sandalwood, smoke from a thousand hearths. One side looked like it had been attacked with an axe. The paint was chipped, and the iron was dented.

Dr Kitts-Vincent pulled one of the large keys from his pocket.

Alistair and Paloma had one each.

They looked at each other.

"Ready? On three." Dr. KV counted "One. Two. Three."

Simultaneously, they inserted their keys, Dr. KV's at the top and

Alistair's and Paloma's at each end.   Turning the keys together, satisfying metallic clicks came from inside the chest. They withdrew the keys at the same time. Everyone was utterly silent.

Dr. KV pulled the iron rods from the sides of the chest and put them carefully down on the table. Putting his hands on each side of the lid, he lifted it up. It swung open on well-oiled hinges and folded backwards. He put on white cotton gloves and reached inside.

Paloma spread a soft cloth on the table and Dr. KV pulled out a long, red leather box that looked and smelled like it had been sitting in a whisky cellar for years. Their nostrils filled with the aroma of peat and mold. He laid it on the cloth. Engraved in gold on the lid of the box was the same symbol as the keys.

Dr. KV put his hands back inside the chest and, with utmost care, lifted out a large leather satchel with something heavy inside. Clearly, one side of the satchel was polished smooth, as if it had been carried for a very long time. On the other side, the leather was thick and uneven, covered in contours and stains. The satchel had a sturdy strap with a buckle. The edges were crudely sewn together with leather cord.

There was a flap of leather covering the opening, which was roughly tied closed.

Dr. KV laid the battered bag on the cloth and undid the strap.

27

1627 Men at Arms

D r. KV drew out a large leather-bound book from the bag and laid it reverently on the soft cloth. The book was a deep and worn red. Parts of the cover were thin and almost pink, others stained dark crimson. Thick ribs reinforced the spine. The edges of the pages must have once been gilded gold but were now thumbed and worn, so only hints of its original glory showed.

On the cover was a date and writing, also once embossed in gold but now mostly just an impression, with gold remaining only in the deepest crevices of each figure.

Inscribed was the following:

'1627'

'The Honourable Extinct Company,'

'Men at Arms,'

'Nobis Non Est,'

The assembled team were awed and silent. They realized they had become part of a very long line of history.

"Love the motto 'Nobis Non Est.' If my Latin is correct it means 'We Don't Exist'."

"Correct, Alistair."

Dr. KV turned over the cover of the book, revealing the first pages. Richly illuminated on the back of the cover was the same symbol as the keys to the chest—two long curling horns on the skull of a bovine-like animal, an arrow piercing one eye and reappearing out of the top of the skull. The symbol was encased in a heraldic shield, making it military in appearance.

On the facing page, with the first letter illuminated, were the following words:

'In the year of our Lord 1627, we men and women of sound mind and true heart do hereby declare the formation of the Honourable Extinct Company. We dutifully commit our souls, our swords and our monies to the defense of those creatures of God who shall be struck down into extinction by the hand of man.

We commit ourselves to defend those creatures to the death and to destroy all those who seek to take from this earth those creatures who hath been put here by God.

We shall not rest until our work is done.

We shall not be beholden to any other man, state, king or law whom shall bar our path.

6 day March 1627

Castle Moy, Lochbuie.

Signed.

8th Earl MacLean of Lochbuie

Sir Francis Godolphin

Sir William Stuart of Wynards

Lord Ramsey of Barns

Lady Ann Cunningham, Marchioness of Hamilton

Lord Murray of Lochmaben

Lady Elizabeth Dowell

Arther Wellington Carver

James Tregarthen'

"Gosh. So, it looks like the Godolphins have been involved since the start. Well, well, here is Sir William Stuart of Wynards. That must be your great, great, great Grandfather." Dr. KV was trying to count back how many greats it would have been.

"Wow, so our family must have been members of The Extinct Company from the start. Gosh, do you think dad was?"

"Alistair, we've been to Moy Castle. Remember, there is that amazing beach, Laggan Sands, on the South-East coast of the Island of Mull? The castle is a ruin, but the beach is a massive expanse of white sand that runs into the clear water of Lochbuie that runs out to sea. We used to go there with dad on day trips from Wynards Estate."

"Yeah, I remember. Ben More rises in the distance and the highland cows wander the beach. It feels like it has been like that for hundreds of years."

"Can you imagine those guys meeting in that castle? Must have been cold in March. What made them do it Dr. KV? It seems like a pretty heavy commitment—their swords, their lives, their money."

"Let us see." turning the page revealed perfectly scribed and tightly written text.

"They had printing presses then, but this is handwritten so it probably means this is the only copy, right?"

The writing was tough to read, even for a native English speaker and the font was small.

Dr. KV put on his reading glasses and gave a synopsis as he read each piece.

"The Articles of the Honourable Extinct Company."

"This is basically the code of conduct." He scanned the document. "Each of you will need to read these and memorize them. I think the most important message here is that we are sworn to utter secrecy, to death."

"It also talks about the two wings of The Company—the financial side and what they call 'Men at Arms' which is us. We are deliberately completely separate and only the head of the entire organization knows who is in both wings."

"Can we change it to Men *and* Women at Arms? It looks like women have been part of it from the start." Paloma looked at the doctor.

"Actually, this document is pretty democratic, you'll see that down here," he pointed to article number 6 that stated that; "If all agree articles can be changed, both words and means must have full consent of all members of the wing and the head of the Honourable Extinct Company."

"So here in article 72, 1942 they changed the words from 'Men at Arms' to 'Commandos' which I believe means that it includes everyone. And don't forget two of the founding members were women.

And actually in 1963 the name of the entire organization changed from The Honourable Extinct Company to The Extinct Company—which given some of our recent activity is perhaps appropriate!"

"Is the Head The Earl of Godolphin?" Alistair asked.

"I assume so, but I'm not sure."

"When you read this, wear the white gloves when you do so. The pages are over 400 years old. We will keep it in the safe, only the five of us can know the combination."

"So, let's see." Dr. KV turned the page. At the top was written:

'The History Of The Honourable Extinct Company.' The pages were filled with different handwriting, dates, sketches and, as he turned the pages to more modern times, photographs.

"So, this looks like almost a diary of every action taken by The Extinct Company, carefully filled in by individual members." They all drew in closer.

"Wow, I would be a bit nervous about making a spelling mistake on 600-year-old paper. It's not like you can use white out! Listen to this about Lady Ann Cunningham, Marchioness of Hamilton: 'She goeth in armour and with a pistoll by her side readie charged, and wishes him there, saying shee would burie the bullets in his bowells.' Wow, I can't wait to read it all," Paloma added.

Dr. KV returned to the first page and read.

"The Honourable Extinct Company was formed by nine men and women, good and true. Four were men of Arms, four were men of monies and one was a man of both and he was elected leader:

In The Early days of the year 1627 the last breeding pair of Aurochs were hunted down, killed and roasted on a spit by Prince Charles Stuart known as King Charles I of England.

This hunt made the noble beasts no more on earth. They were extinct."

"Dr. KV, what is an Auroch?"

"Paloma, you have actually seen prehistoric paintings of them in the caves of Lascaux in France. They are huge Bovine creatures that stood at least six feet tall at the shoulders, with long curved horns. During Roman times, they were almost completely hunted out of Britain.

They were greatly prized as hunting trophies by nobleman in the 1500 to 1600s and they are the first known extinction caused by man."

"The words continue: We have sworn to protect beasts from extinction through the frivolous folly of man. We are sworn to punish those who lead to the extinction of animals. The horns of the Auroch and arrow will be our symbol and the reminder of our task."

Dr. KV turned the book cover back over and showed them the symbol on the cover.

"They executed King Charles I in 1649. I wonder if the Extinct Company had anything to do with it." Alistair looked at the rest of the team.

"It seems we are honored to be in such exalted company."

"I have another question, Dr. KV."

"Yes. Tatiana?"

"What is in the beautiful red box?"

'Oh gosh, I completely forgot about that. Let us see."

The box, a deep crimson leather, was held shut with two straps and buckles. Dr. KV freed them and lifted the lid.

The inside was lined in black silk and slotted into perfect cutouts were five knives in black leather sheaths. He pulled one out and drew it out of its sheath. It was a very simple shape with a dagger point. Its handle was made of black wood.

"That is a Sgian-dubh or black dagger used by Scots in the 17th and 18th Century. The name implies a covert weapon." Alistair picked one from the box and drew it from its sheath.

"It's exquisite... and very sharp." He said, looking at a tiny drop of blood on his thumb.

They each took one from the box.

"Look at the end of the handle. There is a small metal emblem. It's the Auroch horn symbol in reverse. I guess this is like a seal to make in wax? That is quite a membership card." Paloma admired the knife.

"We all need to read The Extinct Company book and learn its history. I have a feeling it is full of hard-won lessons for us."

Over the next few days, they took it in turns reading parts of the book. Some parts were read aloud to all of the team by Dr. Kitts-Vincent. They were ancient stories of battle, of the evil of humankind, but also of hope. It was just what the team needed ahead of their mission to Africa.

28

Preparing for the Desert

The Earl had promised them a Military Airbus A400M Atlas, the plane with which armies had replaced the old and much-loved Hercules C130. The Atlas would take them from Fort Sherman, the abandoned US base on the other side of the canal, all the way to a desert airstrip in North Africa. The plane could take six fully laden Land Rovers, but they needed a light load to increase the range of the plane. As it was, they would stop to refuel at St. Kitts, and then on the island of Madeira. The last island refueling would be Malta.

They had identified Youks Les Bains in Algeria as their landing site. An airfield used by US fighters and Bombers during the Second World War. Youks Les Bains was truly in the middle of the desert and it didn't look like it had been used since the war. It was perfect for their operation. The Atlas was designed to handle the rough, short airstrip they'd find there.

Charlie had been working on the Pink Panther from their 'collection' in THE MAGIC SHOP. This was a 109 series two Land Rover, painted dusty pink. It looked like it had already been in a few fights—faded and sporting several patches. Some original green paint was showing through. Charlie confirmed it had served with honors in Aden, with the

SAS regiment. The Land Rover was fully kitted out for desert battle. It had no doors or roof. On its solid roll cage were mounted twin GPMGs in a swivel housing. The rear gunner, by standing behind the driver and passenger, could fire in any direction. The passenger side was equipped with a single GPMG.

But Charlie had 'upgraded' the power system. She was a great fan of the formula one racing champion Lewis Hamilton. She had got ahold of one of his Extreme E electrically powered off-road racing prototypes and was under the chassis wiring it up.

"It is sooo wicked, over 500Bhp. Each wheel has its own motor."

She shot out from under the Panther on a car creeper. "So, I sort of borrowed the technology and put it in the Pink Panther. That means you don't need to carry fuel, just these super high performance solar panels that will fast charge the Lit-ion batteries. All the Bedouins have solar panels outside their tents, so it won't look odd. Plus, you'll be charging every time you move. Remember those old ram pumps? Same principle, the movement creates power which creates movement. The big difference is this baby makes no noise, perfect for creeping about the desert at night."

"So, what's her range without sun?" Alistair questioned.

Charlie wiped her hands on a cloth, avoiding soiling her overalls. "I estimate you'll easily be able to do 700 kilometers at night and when the sun is out, you won't need to stop."

Every surface was loaded with equipment: sand ladders, tools, desert camouflage netting, Jerry cans for water, ammo boxes. The complete collection looked evocative of the images from the original SAS in their Jeeps. The car appeared to demand to go to battle.

Charlie also showed them a traditional Bedouin tent with two central poles that slotted into tubes fore and aft on the Land Rover. The tent would cover the entire vehicle, giving them deep shade and an excellent disguise. Much of the desert they would operate in was flat and open.

So, however well they camouflaged the Panther, it would still look like a lump sticking out of the sand. Bedouin tents, although not common, were unremarkable. She had even found them Arab robes. "You'll have to get your own goats once you're there," she teased.

"Charlie, you are a genius. Brilliant. Fantastic."

"Yup, this is part of our mission, right? Environmentally friendly while blowing the baddies to bits," Paloma added.

Tatiana raised a finger. "Sorry to be practical, but what about mechanical failures?"

"No, important question. I replaced every original part I could, given the time. Your call to The Earl delivered us two complete sets of parts for everything. So, you have a set of spares for the most likely stuff to break, like drive train and shocks. I want to go through the car in detail with all three of you in about two hours. That way, if something happens to one of you, there are still two that know how to fix stuff. And, the advantage of having four electric motors is that even if you are down to one, you can still drive. Just don't get stuck in the sand with only one motor running."

That evening, they were ready. Alistair, Paloma and Tatiana had reviewed and loaded the vehicle and drove the Pink Panther down a service road to a small beach. Their rendezvous was a neat-looking aluminum landing craft. Waiting, its bow ramp was down on the sand. They could see ships gliding almost silently past them, only their navigation lights showing. As each ship went past, they heard the wash roll up the banks in the dark. Paloma backed the silent vehicle down into the craft so that she could drive out forwards on the exit.

The crew knew Alistair and Paloma from when they were kids. The small community of Gamboa was also home to the Canal's dredging division. There were certain characters that seemed to always be hanging around.

"Hola, Alistair, Paloma! You owe me a beer—o tres!" Shouted

Carlouchi, the captain.

The banter went on as they shackled the Panther down and covered it with a blue tarp. They didn't need some observant Canal Pilot reporting a heavily armed car in a landing craft going by.

As soon as there was a gap between ships, they crossed over and headed North outside the main channel. They pulled up at an old concrete ramp next to the remains of a building, a relic of the canal defenses from World War Two.

Alistair and Paloma had explored most of the old buildings buried in the jungle along the Canal. There was such a wealth of hidden goodies, everyone had left their mark: Spanish conquests in the 1600s, the French, World War One, World War Two, the Vietnam war.

They unshackled the Land Rover and, thanking the canal guys on the way, drove up the track towards Fort Sherman. Fort Sherman was a ghost town of old military buildings and hangers. Parts of the original docks had been 'upgraded' for yachts to park in a marina, but the whole place had an air of abandonment. They splashed through big potholes in the road.

As instructed, they headed to the airfield, stopping in the shadows between rusty hangers that still bore the marks of the last inhabitants 'JOTC,' 'The Green Hell.'

"2000 hours. Perfect timing."

In the distance, they could hear the growing, high-pitched whine of the Atlas' four turboprops.

Almost immediately, the dark, fat plane appeared, and the whine became a powerful roar that shook the night air. It tucked itself neatly down onto the runway and taxied towards them, and the eight fat tires in the middle of the aircraft squeaked in complaint. As it turned on the tarmac in front of them, the tail ramp dropped. The red lights illuminated dark figures dressed in black uniforms on the inside.

One figure trotted down the ramp as it touched the ground and indicated with a sweep of both arms that they should drive up the ramp into the glowing belly of the beast. The engines had hardly slowed, and the whole area was throbbing with their power.

They quickly put on their headsets, and Paloma drove the Panther into the plane. As they clanked up the steel ramps, the team of black clad crew moved into position like members of the Russian ballet. They clamped a winch onto the front of the Land Rover and pulled it into blocks. The crew swarmed the wheels and cinched the clamps down. When they finished, they stood back in a neat line and saluted in perfect symmetry. The person who appeared to be in charge, although as they all looked alike it was hard to tell—masked headsets, black uniform and goggles—indicated the three should follow her. The ramp shut and they could feel the aircraft move. She ushered them through a small door and into a room on the port side of the aircraft. Inside were four comfortable chairs with five-point harnesses. They sat down and buckled in. The rest of the crew filed past through another door. As they walked, Paloma recognized the delicate scent of perfume, even through layers of tactical clothing and by the way they walked—she could tell these were not men.

"Yes! All the crew are women!" Paloma was thrilled.

Alistair, Paloma, and Tatiana took off their headsets. The cabin was blissfully peaceful after the noise in the cargo bay. They felt the plane surge forward and take off. Unlike a passenger jet, the Atlas seemed to pop straight off the runway, leaving their stomachs on the tarmac.

"I want one." Paloma shook her head in delight as soon as they leveled out.

"Yes, dear..." Alistair closed his eyes. It was past midnight, and he was exhausted.

29

The Axis of Evil

Alistair woke Paloma and Tatiana as the plane circled the airfield at St. Kitts. The island was deep, lush green, and poking out of a sea so clear and blue it looked like a cartoon. The Atlas performed its short landing, and the engines roared in reverse to pull the plane to a stop. As the props wound down, a stubby grey tractor came bumping out to meet them and pulled the plane into what looked like a disused RAF hanger. As they came to a halt, a British Racing Green Range Rover with dark tinted windows pulled in at high speed, causing a cloud of dust to rise. A person dressed in a black flight suit came through the door of their cabin. She removed her helmet and goggles and introduced herself as Captain Taboga King.

"You can call me Taboga. I am your pilot for the expedition." She had a rich, lilting accent from the Caribbean, cheekbones of a supermodel and the body of a gymnast.

They all jumped up and shook her hand.

"I love your plane—what a wonderful machine." Paloma said.

"We are very proud to have the privilege of flying her, thank you." Taboga lowered the stairs of a side door.

The door of the Range Rover opened as Alistair, Paloma, and Tatiana descended the steps of the Atlas. The Earl emerged, looking resplendent in a three-piece cream linen suit and light brown suede shoes. "Good morning everyone, lovely to see you all, I hope your flight was comfortable?"

"Good morning, Sir. This is a surprise."

"Yes, I have some important updates. You three jump in and we will have breakfast while Taboga and her team refuel."

"Two hours max," said Taboga. "And, Alistair, please bring me some of those lovely croissants Peregrine always gets, would you?" She said over her shoulder, standing in the doorway of the Atlas.

Alistair blushed at the unexpected attention.

"Alistair, it sounds like you have met Taboga before," The Earl said as they climbed into the cool, dark interior of the Range Rover. It smelled like new leather.

"No, girls just like to give him jobs to do." Paloma announced, sensing Alistair's discomfort and exploiting it in the way only a sister could. Their capacity to tease each other was endless, affectionate, and kept them both with their feet firmly on the ground.

The 9th Earl of Godolphin roared with laughter as he started the engine.

They eased along the winding, dusty roads and slowly climbed a ridge. At the top was a small, slightly ramshackled, tropical house encircled by a deep veranda. They pulled up in front and standing on the landing was a small, very weathered man. He had a gold earring in one ear and a starched white apron around his waist.

"Good morning, my lord. Your usual table?" he said with a French accent, gesturing to a table on the corner of the veranda. The view was breathtaking, the sea below flashing light from the sun. From here they could see the track they had just followed all the way down the green neck of the island, sparks of white sand to each side. No-one could come up here unseen.

"Good, morning Jacques. Perfect, thank you."

Jacques reappeared almost immediately with a pot of coffee, butter, and small baskets of heavenly smelling croissants. He withdrew with a slight nod of his head.

Alistair pulled a small jar of Marmite from his pocket.

"Alistair, you are disgusting."

"Actually, Paloma, I think Alistair has an excellent idea. May I try?"

"Please do. I never leave home without it. I think the combination is perfection. In fact, I believe it really is the only time the English and French have ever worked well together."

The Earl put the butter and Marmite on his croissant and took a bite.

"You are right, quite perfect."

Tatiana picked up the jar and warily edged her nose in its general direction, like one would do with a bottle of milk from the fridge of suspect vintage. She jerked her head sideways, closing her eyes.

"See? See?" Paloma chimed in, opening her eyes as wide as they would go, holding her palms upward.

The croissants were soft, buttery, and hot. Just the smell of them took them all to Paris for a moment, despite the interference of Alistair's marmite.

They sipped their coffee from delicate white cups, and The Earl began. "Your mission has been upgraded. Several things have come to light in the last few hours. The information you gave me, Alistair, allowed us to make much more direct investigations." He assumed the tone of a commander now.

"Firstly, there seems to be a global event planned two weeks from now. It's called 'March for Nation First' and it is being organized by extreme right-wing cells, in every major capital. I would call it a fascist event. The rhetoric is pretty vile. Although from the outside it appears to be organically organized, we have traced a central source for all the internet traffic."

The Earl opened an iPad and tapped on a map area that looked like an empty desert. "Someone is feeding the fire, pouring material into the internet from this location." Alistair, Paloma, and Tatiana leaned in. "It's pushed through VPNs and all sorts of wizardry. Tatiana, your grandmother is quite capable—she beats our best IT people." The Earl pointed at the screen as the pixels began to clarify. "This vile rhetoric originates here. That's about 350 kilometers from where you are landing, across the desert. It is one of Rommel's old bases. Sidi Haneish."

The Earl looked up at them for questions.

"Whoah, really? That's where David Stirling and his boys in the newly formed SAS did their most famous raid, knocking out dozens of Nazi planes." Alistair was beaming. He knew his military history. In a split second, his smile faded. "Wait, the SAS did it with eighteen heavily armed Jeeps, if I am not mistaken?"

"You are correct, Alistair, and that is the bee hive I was referring to earlier. There seem to be dozens of planes that have landed there and not left. We have looked at the satellite images and," The Earl pulled the view in closer and pointed "here is what looks like a mini city—or maybe a movie set—only 150 kilometers from your landing site." They were now looking at a very pixelated image of what appeared to be a city street. "Strangely, the streets look European." He waited for them to take it in. "Well, good news is you don't have to attack the base or the 'city'. Just get close enough to send your drone over, sit, watch and report back. Our satellite data is not good enough—there have been constant dust storms, so we really don't know what Van Olenburgh is up to. "

The Earl poured another cup of coffee. "Second, the Aura Spas we talked about, we have concluded that they form a sort of extreme Nationalism recruiting agency. The spa clientele are being fed a fairly constant stream of powerful fascist propaganda through their iPads.

150

Deirdre's iPad has been invaluable."

The Earl continued, "On top of all that, we are seeing a huge uptick in 'Big Game' hunting bookings to a ranch in Tanzania called 'Risasi Nzuri'. It seems like many of the most influential men and women in the Western world are going on hunting safaris starting in the next ten days. My team is working on getting an invitation to Risasi Nzuri for me. Generally speaking, if I wave enough money, sorry to be so vulgar, and make the right noises, I can get invitations to things. It is one of the few times having a title has its advantages."

"We know the people on the guest list are renowned for their right-wing and nationalistic views. This also rings alarm bells because our unofficial data shows that no more than 40% of the world's rhinos have been killed by what we would call low-income poachers. These poachers are paid by a syndicate. So, it seems the rest - 60% - have been killed by high wealth clients paying for the privilege to take out endangered species.

"We know this from forensic evidence and also by following private, social media accounts of known 'hunters' who post images of themselves with their quarry. When we find a Rhino that has been killed by a single .375 round manufactured by one of the exclusive British gunsmiths, we are pretty sure that it is not the same character that takes out other rhinos we find killed with 27 AK47 Chinese-made rounds. To put it simply, this is the group going off on safari in the next two weeks. The intelligence you can bring in from your desert mission will help us establish how the right-wing propaganda. Sidi Haneish and the hunting safaris are connected. You need to keep your ears and eyes open to anything that might join the dots."

Jacques reappeared with a basket covered in a checkered cloth. When he saw the Marmite, he gave it a look as if a fly had landed on the starched damask tablecloth. He put his hands behind his back in an effort not to pick up the offending jar and throw it in the forest.

Paloma looked at him and said, "Exactly," reading the man's thoughts, while Alistair grabbed his precious pot and returned it to his pocket.

There was no bill. They thanked Jacques, Alistair clutching the warm basket for Taboga, and walked back to the Rangy and climbed aboard.

When they were halfway down the hill, they saw a plume of dust traveling towards them at high speed. They heard a sound like a rally car, a deep roar coming from its exhaust and the high-pitched whine of a turbocharger. It closed the gap between them in seconds.

"Everyone down!" The Earl shouted.

An AMC Mercedes G Wagon, menacing in black paint and tinted windows, exploded into view.

The Earl wrenched the Range Rover up the bank, but there were too many trees to get around the Mercedes, which had crunched to a halt in the road.

"Paloma and Tatiana—quick—shotguns and buckshot in the boot."

Just as he said this, four men dressed in black combat gear sprung out of the Mercedes, holding AK 47s. Opening fire, the armored glass around the driver's seat became an ice pond after a pebble shower.

"You two—get ready to open fire through the rear window. I am going to ram their car off the road."

With that, The Earl turned the Range Rover perpendicular to the Merc and raced down the steep embankment. One man realized what was happening and ran towards the Merc. He was just sliding in the car's doorway as the Range Rover hit it, severing the man's legs just below the knees. Even with all the noise, they could hear him scream.

The three remaining men were changing their magazines, having emptied everything into The Earl's armored Range Rover.

The Earl kept pushing the Mercedes, flicking into low range until the Merc popped up the side bank, tottered a second, and then rolled down the embankment towards the sea. Paloma and Tatiana, in the back, pressed the button, flipping open the rear glass and opening fire with their shotguns. With an unspoken understanding that the men were wearing bulletproof vests, they aimed at their heads, taking one man from each side with one barrel and then blasting the remaining man with the combination of both their other barrels. His head and body flung backwards with the blast.

The Mercedes caught fire with a boom somewhere down by the sea.

"Everybody alright?" The Earl asked in a businesslike tone.

Everyone was.

"Nice pair of Purdy's, my Lord," Paloma said, admiring the weapons for the first time.

"Thanks. They were my grandfather's. They've seen some action in their time. Let's see who these clowns were and then get out of here, fast."

They climbed down from the battle-scarred Range Rover and inspected the figures on the ground, making sure they were dead and checking their pockets for clues.

Tatiana found a cell phone and immediately hooked it up to a tiny, waterproof laptop. "This will suck all the data from the phone and if anyone calls it, it will start a trace before we pick it up."

"They weren't exactly pros, all getting out the car like that," Alistair said, turning one body over. He pulled out a wallet with a driving license. He gave it to Tatiana, who scanned it and sent it to Misha.

"I suspect they thought I was alone and unarmed. Just an old man by the sea. My fault. I can't resist Jacques' croissants and the view, so I have been coming up here every morning at the same time for the last week to get some work done. Because the windows are tinted, they couldn't see you chaps in the car. Not the best way to find out, but I am now certain I am being followed and I have someone in my office giving out my location, either deliberately or by accident. Let's get back to the airfield."

They jumped back in and The Earl made a call using the speaker.

"Sebastian, good morning, we've run into a spot of bother, and I need to leave in a bit of a hurry. Please get the plane ready and park it in the old hanger next to the Atlas. I'll fill you in with the details when I get there."

"Certainly Sir, I was already by the plane doing some checks."

"Excellent, thank you."

"Standing by."

Twenty minutes later, they pulled into the hanger. Next to the blunt shape of the Atlas was a sleek Citation jet.

Taboga passed her eyes over the shape of the Range Rover, peppered with hundreds of bullet holes and said to Alistair as he got out, "Wow, good job, I didn't ask you to get me some fresh lobster too!"

He smiled and handed her the basket of croissants, which were still slightly warm.

"You should see the guys that tried to take them off me."

Sebastian, The Earl's pilot, was looking at the Range Rover, shaking his head. The headlights and the front of the car were smashed. Every window had hundreds of white galaxies where the rounds had sunk into the armored glass.

"What shall we do with the Rangy, sir?" Its normal parking spot at the club was out of the question.

"Throw a tarp over it for now. Taboga, do you think you could take it to Panama on your way home?" The Earl wasn't really asking questions, they were instructions politely delivered. "Perhaps you could take it to Charlie in Gamboa? She'll enjoy thinking of a new role for it on the team."

"Alistair, Paloma, and Tatiana, best of luck on your mission. I will see you soon. I trust you will tell me if you need anything urgently. Taboga and her team will wait in Gibraltar in case you need a resupply. They can air drop emergency equipment if you are desperate or, if you can get to a decent airstrip, she can land and do a casualty evacuation."

"Let's go."

The Citation jet gently taxied out of the hanger first and then blasted down the runway, followed in short order by the potent Atlas. Its exit could be heard across the island.

30

North Africa Landing

The rest of the journey was not exactly fun, but the team spent it usefully studying the route, the hiding places, the landscape and the conditions they would need to tackle between their landing place in Youks-Les-Bains, the abandoned US air force base from the Second World War, the strange 'city' that had popped up and Van Olenburgh's presumed new base 350 kilometers away in Rommel's old Luftwaffe base in Sidi Haneish.

Flying over the desert at night was eerie. The normal twinkling, friendly lights from human habitation were absent, a silent reminder that they were about to enter a vast void, populated by a few, possibly very hostile, people.

"Going dark in five," Taboga announced over the intercom. They all reached down into their packs and pulled out their generation X27 goggles. These models gave them full-color night-vision instead of the usual green monotone.

"I am going to buzz the airstrip once to make sure it's clear." The Atlas descended quickly and leveled out. "Please look out the side windows to spot any potential threats."

"All clear starboard," Alistair said into his mike.

The Atlas was equipped with forward looking infrared enhanced vision system (EVS) which allowed the pilot to see the airstrip even in complete darkness.

Taboga banked the Atlas neatly, and after a final approach, they felt a low thud and swells of dust obscured the windows. Taboga turned the plane around so it was facing back down the runway, ready for a quick exit, and the ramp light flashed from red to green.

The crew swarmed the Land Rover, undoing all the straps and removing the wheel locks. Alistair, Paloma and Tatiana secured themselves into their seats using the five-point rally harnesses Charlie had added.

Their plan was to rotate jobs so that everyone would do everything. These were the rules of David Stirling's newly formed SAS back in 1942, and they applied here. Alistair was starting as driver, Paloma navigator, and Tatiana would be lookout/rear gunner. Every two hours they would stop, have a quick brew of tea and switch around. Driving in the dark using night vision goggles was tough enough—driving across raw desert with countless escarpments, rocks and in some places soft sand was very dangerous and required high concentration.

Alistair pulled out of the rear of the throbbing plane and down the ramp.

"Welcome back to Africa," Paloma said over their headsets.

The pitch of the four turboprops increased, and the Atlas roared down the runway like a mad dragon.

Paloma leaned over towards Alistair in the driver's seat and indicated with her hand. "OK, I need you to drive on this bearing as close as you can for 5000 meters, then I'll give you your next bearing."

Clipped to the dashboard was a rubberized iPad that was hooked up by Bluetooth to a highly accurate GPS. It showed their present position and their route as a dotted line. Alistair turned the Land Rover to the correct bearing and read the degrees on the ship's compass mounted on the dash. Any movement of metal in the car, including the jerry cans, and the compass could play up. The sound of the Atlas disappeared, and they got that thrill of feeling completely alone. They could smell the clean sand beneath them. The air was chilly, almost freezing.

Alistair was wearing a vintage World War Two sand colored duffle coat with wooden toggles over a high-performance military jacket. The duffle coat was popular with British Special Forces and immortalized in the famous photo of David Stirling standing in front of a line of rugged warriors in their heavily armored jeeps.

"OK, let's go, Paddington." Paloma had started calling Alistair 'Paddington Bear' as soon as he had put the duffle coat on.

Alistair gave Paloma's synthetic puffer jacket a snobbish once over. "Just you wait while your fancy, modern materials get shredded by the desert."

Tatiana, in the back, was dressed in a threadbare Russian Navy sweater, a French Foreign Legion kepi on her head and a cream-colored silk scarf around her neck. "You two do not know what cold means." She was marking their route on a paper map.

Paloma turned to look at what Tatiana was doing. "Tatiana, you're usually the high-tech girl."

"You never know when all your electronics and satellites might fail. The desert does funny stuff to the equipment."

They pulled away. Everybody was smiling because they were expecting the sound of an engine and all they got were the stones crunching under the tires. The electric motors of the car were completely silent.

Alistair was a skilled desert driver. As an eighteen-year-old, he and a friend had taken a battered Range Rover across the Sahara from Algiers to Niger and then across to Mali. They had broken down and got stuck many times and lived off dwindling supplies of tinned salmon and rice. But they had not got lost once during the adventure and had even driven all the way back after crossing to Gibraltar, through Spain, and had taken the ferry to Portsmouth and on to his grandparents' estate in Scotland.

He drove at a steady speed, sticking to the bearing. They had set the tire pressure low to give them maximum flotation on the sand. Here the desert was flat and the very fine sand was studded with little pebbles. The combination of dew and cold night air would support the weight of the Landy as long as Alistair didn't turn, brake, or accelerate hard. The trick was to spot super-soft patches before you hit them and either drive around them or hit them at a high enough speed to take you across them. It was like running on thin ice. One wrong move would have them digging below the axle to extract themselves, causing them major exertion and thus forcing them to drink more water from their limited supply.

Alistair had learnt this the hard way. As he was the only one with this kind of desert experience. He soliloquized Paloma and Tatiana through the process for twenty minutes, until Paloma told him his mansplaining was well received and no longer required.

After two hours they reached a rocky outcrop with a wide vista and a good exit route. Alistair pulled the Landy close to the rocks facing forward and rolled it to a stop. They all piled out and swept the area, checking to see if there were any other residents nearby.

They took off their goggles and rubbed their eyes in the darkness. As they acclimatized, the sky opened up. With a flat horizon and no artificial lights for more than 200 kilometers, the stars put on a glittering show. In the utter silence of the desert, it felt like they were floating in space.

Alistair pulled out a Trangia, the Swedish army cooker he always carried on expeditions, and put some water on to boil for tea. The other two scanned the horizon. It was truly peaceful. They sat on the cool sand with their backs against the wheels glad of the rest.

Alistair handed them each a tin mug of steaming lapsang souchong and honey. It tasted of sweet smoke. They put their hands around the warm mugs. Without a windscreen, they were chilled to their bones in the cold desert air. They felt like an aircrew in an open biplane.

Tatiana pulled out a small metal flask covered in Cyrillic writing and a red hammer and sickle. "A little vodka to keep you warm on the inside?"

They each took a swig and felt the liquid burn warmth down their throats.

After fifteen minutes, they were moving again—Tatiana driving, Alistair navigating, and Paloma in the rear. They had covered 170 kilometers, good going considering the surface they were crossing. They still had 180 kilometers to go.

Driving conditions got more difficult. Several times they reached escarpments that looked drivable on their maps but proved to be too steep and too rocky to risk. Each time, they had to set out on foot to find a point where they could descend. In one place it was so steep and the material so loose that they decided to lower the car down backwards using the winch with a wheel wedged between two rocks as an anchor.

Paloma, who was afraid of almost nothing, hated taking the car down rocky cliffs. She had once witnessed a friend, showing off, drive his Land Cruiser up a sharp escarpment until, wheels spinning, it had tipped over backwards. She could still hear the crunching and smashing as the car disintegrated on the way down, crushing her friend in the process. So they avoided steep rocky cliffs whenever they could.

The further they went conditions got worse so progress was slow, and they got stuck in soft sand several times.

Finally, the dark night was punctuated by a thin, warm line of light. Dawn was breaking.

They knew they were getting very close to the border of Van Olenburgh's vast tract of land. Their final target Sidi Heneish was still a very long way away but the so called 'city' was getting closer.

For a rest, they found a perfect crack between two boulders, big enough to get the Landy in with good escape routes, a long vista and a place for the lookout to hide. They quickly covered the car in camo netting. Paloma went on lookout duty, Tatiana checked the car for damage while Alistair prepared a meal of British army rations. Alistair and Paloma grew up eating them on expeditions with their father, who had been in the British Special Forces. So the food had many happy memories. Alistair handed Tatiana her portion and carried Paloma's up to her lookout post and sat down beside her, facing the rising sun. "Sausages, baked beans and oat cakes, all washed down with lashings of lapsang souchong tea. What more could a man ask for?"

"Well, this woman would like a nice hot shower, crisp sheets and a dark room... mmm thanks, that actually smells divine."

"Any movement?"

She pointed. "Yes, three goats around 700 meters that way."

Alistair lifted his 10x42 Zeiss range-finding binoculars and scanned for the goats. "Where there are goats, there's a goatherd. And where there's a goatherd, not far away is a village. Or it's a Bedouin, so we'd better be careful." He held the binoculars on a fixed point. "Yup, there he is. Boy, he looks rough. Have a look."

"Damn, does that mean I can't string up my orange aerial hammock and do my morning yoga?"

"Yeah, if you remember, I said you should get the camo one."

"There's something fundamentally wrong with a camo yoga hammock. I think it might be time for you to grow out of your camo phase and move into pastels, Alistair. Dusty pink suits you."

Chuckling and walking back to the Land Rover, he said over his shoulder, "We'll send the drone up and then you can come down. Keep an eye on the goatherd and call us if he gets too close. Enjoy your beans."

He told Tatiana about the goatherd as she was finishing her breakfast.

"That tasted pretty good. We Russians are told so many ghastly stories about the British Army I am surprised to find out they don't breakfast on small children." She looked into Alistair's eyes without smiling, and it took him a second to realize she was pulling his leg.

"Let us send up the drone and have a look around. Has Paloma given the drone a name yet?" Tatiana said.

"No, she hasn't. Let me ask her when she comes down."

Alistair cleaned away the breakfast things, while Tatiana set up the drone. Zipping up into the sky, it sounded like a swarm of bees.

The two huddled around the screen as the thermal camera picked up the goats and goatherd.

"Hey what's that? Can you zoom in?"

The camera zoomed into what looked like a small village. As they got closer, they realized it was a shambolic settlement made up of scraps: plastic, cars, and junk. Some shelters were fashioned from old coats.

"That's strange. This camp wasn't on the last satellite image and it's only eight weeks old. Hey, isn't that close to the border of one of Van Olenburgh's properties?"

Tatiana tapped the keyboard, and a series of overlapping polygon lines appeared over the satellite image, showing the areas where the drone was filming.

The tethered drone was also their communication system. Now the drone was up, Tatiana contacted the Ops center in Gamboa. "Vodka One, this is Vodka Two. Do you read me?"

"Loud and clear, and the video is coming in."

"See that settlement? Those people weren't there eight weeks ago, that's—" Tatiana measured using the computer, "300 meters from Van Olenburgh's border."

Paloma appeared from her lookout post and started cleaning her plate with sand and then with a cup of water that the other two had already used.

"I think we should go and look at that settlement. Tatiana, how is your Arabic?"

"Good, I am fluent," Tatiana replied in perfect Arabic.

"Mine is passable. Paloma sounds Dutch for some reason."

Paloma threw the tea towel at Alistair. "Tatiana, I have a question."

"Yes?"

"What can't you do?"

Tatiana looked into Paloma's face and smiled a melancholy smile. "I cannot fall in love... I have tried. I have read all the books. Misha has found all perfect Russian boys, but nothing happens. I am, how do you say it, frozen, cold... not moving?"

"Unmoved?"

"Exactly, these boys are not moving me here." She thumped her heart.

"Paloma has the opposite problem." Alistair chipped in. Paloma took a swipe at him, but he ducked and she hit thin air.

Tatiana ended talking about herself abruptly. "I think we go back to our original problem. How do we get in there without the entire camp just swarming over us and asking us questions? People don't just 'pop in', as you Brits say, here in the middle of the desert."

"The only thing I can think of is we go in at dusk and if we need to get out fast, we can disappear into the night with our goggles on. Paloma can wait with the Landy ready to take off."

They spent the rest of the day taking turns getting some sleep and searching the iPad screen for other surprises around Van Olenburgh's property.

The drone was picking up a range of 10 kilometers. From these images, Tatiana had identified at least three very similar-looking refugee camps.

The team's assessment from just watching with their drone was that these people in the settlements were desperately poor. They watched girls walk off with empty plastic containers and return heavily laden hours later. It was a universal sign that water was a long way away and located somewhere they couldn't settle.

At three in the afternoon, they spotted a cloud of dust in the feed from the drone. It was heading along a track on the limit of Van Olenburgh's property line. As it got closer, they recognized it as a twin cab 76 series Toyota Land Cruiser. It was painted matte sand and looked kitted out for anything. On the roll bar in the rear was 30 Caliber machine gun, and behind it balanced a man. It was less than 2 kilometers away.

Tatiana zoomed the video feed as close as it would go and set the camera to track the vehicle. "Look at the logo. NF. 'Nation First.'"

"Olenburgh's lot. Wow, we are 150 kilometers from his main base. I guess this is the border patrol?"

Until now the Pink Panther had felt over-armed, too military with all their heavy weapons. Now, suddenly, Alistair thought of the rest of David Sterling's team of misfits and their eighteen Willys Jeeps armed to the teeth. "If that is what Van Olenburgh is using to patrol a distant border, can you imagine what he has at Sidi Haneish?"

The Land Cruiser disappeared in a cloud of dust in the distance. Tatiana set up a call between the Ops room. Everyone had seen the images.

The Dr. KV spoke. "OK, let's do a quick recap and make a P of A. It looks like Van Olenburgh has created a 'state' under the title 'Nation First'. That vehicle is patrolling the border. It is clear he has displaced the indigenous population from the property he controls. These people are now living in ramshackle camps along the edges of the property. Clearly he has a well-armed and well-equipped gang under command here."

Dr. KV paused. "Misha please share the new satellite images." The screen flickered. "At last, we have clear images from Sidi Haneish and inside Van Olenburgh's property. Look carefully. There are towns under construction and some are very urban looking. But, and this is important, one place is only a film set—the buildings are only facades. This fake city is only about ten kilometers from your present position and on route to Sidi Haneish. We do not know what it is for, but it must be important. It looks busy."

Dr. KV was a retired British Army Officer and accustomed to holding briefings. He continued. "Rhino horn is funding this new 'Nation First' state. Olenburgh's high-end hunting safaris are supplying the horn and his high-end rhino horn supplements are supplying the cash. Nation First owns massive tracts of land across Africa. It is peddling extreme right-wing politics through the internet. There is a huge right-wing march happening across the first world in 12 days' time. Finally, and this is vital, although we have a lot of evidence, we don't have enough to make the world react. Any comments?"

Misha spoke. "Yes, I do. We have been analyzing the data from California that we collected from the offices. We found videos. The videos show people on safari with the Van Olenburgh safari company. These include many powerful people."

"Safari hunting is not illegal, Misha." Alistair said.

"Let me explain better. The videos include shooting and killing endangered species, rhinos included. They are very short videos, like something you might find on Twitter. But they are very clear." Misha snapped the screen to a video showing a nervous-looking man wearing what was clearly brand new 'safari' gear. He was carrying a heavy rifle with a scope and sitting in a safari vehicle. The video zoomed into the man's very pink face.

"Hey, isn't he a member of the US Congress?" Paloma said.

The video continued. A slow and peacefully munching rhino ambled into view less than thirty meters from the car. The man with the rifle raised it and aimed it at the animal. They could hear other people with South African accents urging him to fire. There was a loud report, and the rhino stumbled. Somebody shouted for him to fire again. The man reloaded and fired again. The rhino dropped to his front knees. They drove the car right up to the stricken beast. The man kept firing and reloading until the beast finally rolled over and stopped moving. Someone shouted, "Great shot!" There were high fives. The last clip showed the man on one knee, rifle in hand, in front of the dead rhino.

Paloma spoke up again. "That video could destroy someone online. They are the perfect weapon to use for blackmail."

"Exactly. Thanks Misha," Dr. KV said. "So, we have a lot of things going on that we don't understand, and the only way to find out is for you three to go in and look. You have two places to collect information from: One is the strange film set city ten kilometers away you're your present position. Second, Sidi Haneish one hundred and fifty kilometers away. Don't get caught. Get out fast." Dr. KV finished, letting the last sentence hang.

"Roger that." Alistair responded.

"Any questions or additional information?"

"Yes, before we go on we want to talk to the people in the shacks. It looks like someone has kicked them out of their homes. We believe it is connected."

"Agreed, but be careful. Getting to the film set of the city first is the priority. OK. Let's do it."

They shut the connection. Paloma and Tatiana began packing up.

"Whoa, whoa, whoa. What about supper? I see steak and kidney pie followed by spotted dick and custard on the ration list for tonight. You know what Napoleon said: an army fights on its stomach."

"Alistair, it is only 4:00 p.m."

"Exactly. We head off at 5.30 p.m., it gets dark, we visit the camp—whose inhabitants look like they are starving so we shouldn't go there hungry because tradition says they must offer us food—then off we toddle, driving through the night, picking at oatcakes... and we

166

totally miss supper."

The women looked at each other. They were not hungry, but he was right. They should eat while they could. Alistair smiled. "Sit back, relax and I will prepare a delicious British Army special, the world-renowned steak and kidney pie, served with delicious, freeze-dried mashed potatoes accompanied by peas and carrots. Served on a light bed of sand."

31

Refugee Camp Recon

They packed the car, leaving the drone in the air. Paloma had named it "Biggles," for obvious reasons to the rare followers of Captain W.E. Johns' novels. Alistair and Tatiana put on the billowy Arab clothes Charlie had given them. She had included 'pockets' that fitted UZI submachine guns against their stomachs.

They took one of the emergency bags of rice as the traditional gift. It was 2.5Kgs, so for hungry people it would make a difference. They also bought some tea and sugar, which could be shared while they talked, and a pocketful of lovely bonbons dusted in white confectioners' sugar.

Alistair and Tatiana hid small mikes in their ears, enabling them to communicate with Paloma, who would remain back at base.

It felt good to be walking after so much sitting still. At first they walked at right angles away from their hidden base and then after a thousand meters they turned directly towards the village. They realized that as they got closer; they needed to be seen, so their appearance did not surprise the villagers.

Once they got into the village, there was no one to be seen—everyone was hiding.

The shacks looked even worse close up; most were just rubbish piled up to make some sort of shelter. Even the slightest wind would threaten to destroy them in seconds.

Tatiana spoke in a soft, friendly tone Alistair had never heard from her. In Arabic she said, "My friends, we come in peace. Do not be afraid of us, we are tired and wish to sit with you a while."

"And we bring tea." Alistair clearly thought that tea was the ultimate offering of peace and friendship.

A little girl's dirty face appeared around the side of one shack, and she stared at them with big, dark eyes.

Alistair offered a bonbon in his outstretched, open hand. He knelt down so he was at her height. Her eyes lit up when she saw the bonbon, and she took a tentative step forward, looking into Alistair's pale blue eyes to see if she could trust him.

He smiled, and she stepped forward, carefully picking the bonbon from Alistair's palm like she was handling a fragile object, never taking her big, dark eyes off Alistair's. She smiled up at Alistair, instantly melting his heart. She didn't put the bonbon in her mouth, but held it between her thumb and forefinger.

Alistair and Tatiana said down on a 'bench' made of a scrap of wood balanced on two broken plastic containers. The girl sat down opposite them, a few feet away, cross-legged. Another equally ragged little girl appeared. She was smaller than the first. Alistair gave her a bonbon, and she immediately put it in her mouth, winning a disapproving look from the older girl.

"What are your names? My name is Tatiana, and this is Alistair."

"Yasmin, and my sister is Fatima."

"Yasmin and Fatima, those are lovely names. Is your mother or father here?"

"They are dead." Both girls spoke at once, without emotion.

More children appeared and sat down quietly in a semi-circle around Alistair and Tatiana. Each one got a bonbon. They were all filthy, with matted hair and dressed in rags. There were twelve of them.

The oldest one looked around fifteen, but it was hard to tell her age because she appeared exhausted. Her eyes were those of an old woman who had seen too much. Her name was Almera.

"Who looks after all of you? Where are the adults?" asked Tatiana, once they had all introduced themselves.

"We look after ourselves but sometimes 'The Engineer' comes and brings us food and helps us make our houses."

She said the words 'The Engineer' in English, like it was a movie title she had heard.

"Almera, I'm hungry. when is 'The Engineer' coming again?" asked one of the smallest children.

"Soon, my little moon. Soon." Almera put her arm around the little girl and stroked the hair out of her eyes.

"We have rice for you, and tea and sugar."

Tatiana pulled the bag of rice, tea, and sugar from her backpack.

The children got very excited, their little faces visibly changing. Almera immediately gave instructions to different girls and boys to get a fire started and get the cooking pot ready.

The children all became preoccupied with preparing the food, bustling around with smiles and excited anticipation, too distracted to answer any more questions.

Tatiana and Alistair were feeling ashamed of the machine guns hidden inside their robes, a feeling which disappeared the instant they heard Paloma in their hidden ear pieces.

"Chaps, I have movement heading towards you, range about 2 kilometers. I'll confirm when it gets closer, but it looks like a convoy of five vehicles driving very close together without lights." She was monitoring the area with the drone. With it, she could see approximately ten kilometers, even at night. "It looks like it's coming from another settlement."

Tatiana explained to Almera that there was a group of vehicles coming. Almera shouted something to the rest of the children and they instantly dropped what they were doing and ran into the darkness and disappeared, including Almera.

Alistair and Tatiana, who didn't want to give themselves away by getting into a firefight, also ran and hid amongst a heap of junk. Even through the heap, they could hear the convoy getting closer, or at least they could hear one car, because it seemed not to have a silencer, and was making a noise like a Harley Davidson motorbike inside a long tunnel. As soon as the children heard that noise, they reappeared and ran towards the source.

"Paloma, what on earth is going on?"

She was monitoring the convoy in growing disbelief. "I do not know. It looks like a junkyard on wheels."

They could hear the children shouting, "The Engineer! The Engineer!"

Yasmin ran over to Alistair and Tatiana's hiding place and pulled them both out by their hands, shouting, "The Engineer! The Engineer!"

They had no choice but to go with her.

As the vehicles came into the light of the cooking fire, they could see that the 'convoy' was led by what the Americans call a Dually truck, a Ford F550 with a huge 6-liter engine and dual wheels on the rear. But it had no glass in the windscreen or windows, no door, no bonnet, and looked as if all the paint had been burnt off. It was pulling an assortment of four other cars joined in a line, one behind another, by a short length of chain, all of them in a similar state. Under the open bonnets of the four cars were piles of wood.

The Dually made a wide circle around the fire and the little encampment. When it came to a halt, the rest stopped by simply bumping into the car in front, like a train at a station.

Before the vehicles had even stopped, a dozen children poured out of the doorless cars, dragging out the car seats as they came, and putting them in a semicircle around the fire.

The boys were covered from head to toe in a patina of what looked like old engine oil.

Out of the Dually stepped a short, active-looking man of late middle age. He was wearing short-sleeved overalls with remnants of reflective strips around the ankles and chest. It opened to his belly button, revealing a well-browned, barrel chest. He was missing an eye, and a badly repaired injury ran down one side of his face. He had a full beard and on the back of his head he wore a very greasy navy officer's cap.

The children danced round him, all trying to hold his hand. They pulled him towards the biggest car bench seat near the fire. He had a huge grin on his face, like the one given to Santa Claus on Christmas cards.

Before he sat down, he looked at Alistair and Tatiana and gave them a gesture with his open palm, as if he were inviting them to sit down in his living room somewhere in Soho.

They sat in two empty car seats near his, and half a dozen children piled on the sofa with him, lifting their chins and looked pleased with themselves.

The engineer looked at Tatiana and Alistair. He spoke quietly and in English. "My name is Pieter, they call me 'The Engineer.' I see and hear everything."

Alistair and Tatiana relaxed a bit. If the children trusted this man, they should hear him out.

"I want to tell you what happened here. I know you are not alone. I know you are armed and I judge that you are here to help." He had the kind of accent that comes from living among many cultures and speaking many languages. If he was asked, he probably couldn't say where he came from.

Alistair replied, "The reason we are here is complex. But you are correct, we are here to help. Right now, we're just trying to work out what is going on. We are connected to a bigger organization but not to a government. Can we share what you are saying with our team?" He pulled out a small GoPro. It was hooked up to a satellite phone.

"Yes, I need you to." The Engineer steeled himself. "Six weeks ago, these children lived in a small village near an oasis. They lived in fine mud huts. They had water, shelter. They harvested dates, had goats. There was a small school, a mosque, and medical center shared by all the nearby villages. It was a tough existence, but it was their way of life. Their ancestors had lived there.

"One day, a group of cars filled with men arrived. They told the villagers that they had to leave because the land had been sold. They told them they had to be gone by the same time the next day. They told them they had to go beyond the track marked with red and white posts and they could not come back. When the men left, the elders had a meeting. People came from other villages bearing the same news.

"The elders decided no one could 'sell' the desert: it belonged to everyone. Their ancestors were buried here; they were proud warriors and they would not just walk away from the land.

"They sent all the children off to the nearby hills and since the children all take turns looking after the goats there, they know the land well.

"I know this because I would drive around the villages in my truck fixing small things, like pumps. I was an engineer in the merchant navy almost all my life. The villagers often paid me with food and I have enough money from my pension. Working, fixing things in the villages was a nice nomadic life, and the people are my family.

"For two days I was working in a well, trying to get a submersible pump out. I was down the well when the men came back. The well was on the edge of the village, and they didn't know I was there.

"I heard the cars, some shouting and then a sound I recognized and thought I would never hear again: a 30-cal machine gun. It fired for several minutes. Then I heard pistol shots. Then the cars left. It was all over in 15 minutes.

"When I got out of the well, almost everyone was lying dead in straight lines with horrible wounds, like they had been standing together in a defiant wall. The 30-cal is a terrible weapon at close range. It's too much to describe the scene. A few people had crawled a short distance and been shot by pistols.

"They had set fire to my truck. I managed to put it out, got it running, and dragged all these cars to find the children." He nodded towards the cars. "I walked back to the village in the night and hid to see what would happen. The next morning bulldozers came. They pushed all the bodies in a pile and then blew them up with explosives. By the nightfall the vultures and stray dogs had carried everything away. Nothing was left. These children," he gestured to the ones from the village, "didn't see what happened to their parents; they only heard it. But other children did. I spent the night driving around the villages collecting all the children that had escaped—many had not. The scene was repeated over and over again in each village. This was not an act of anger, it was a calculated removal of people. From what I can work out, this was a massacre of nearly 50 people. We helped them set up camps across this absurd new 'border.'"

They sat watching the fire, each in their own thoughts.

"But why?" Alistair spoke to the fire.

Tatiana's voice was broken. "Surely someone would notice?"

"Sadly, if you look through the back pages of a newspaper, sometimes, and not very often, you will find an article saying an entire village has been wiped out by another village somewhere in North Africa. Livestock rustlers or some religious issue. The sad truth is, because they are brown people in the middle of the desert, nobody really seems to notice.

"I've been watching. In the territory where these indigenous people lived, someone is building villages, streets, shops, but old-fashioned, like back in the 50s. Colonial style. Except one which is like a film set of a city, and that I don't understand. Everything has the 'Nation First' letters on it."

The Engineer continued. "They stick to their roads and tracks, which means if you can stay in the desert you can hide from them. Like Rommel's troops in the war, the SAS could move in the desert because the Germans wouldn't leave the roads."

"You like the desert, I see," The Engineer said, nodding at their outfits.

"Do you have any idea how many people they have?" Alistair asked.

"It's hard to tell because I can't get very close and everyone is in the same uniform. I hear a lot of planes going in towards the North West. That film set city is about ten kilometers from here, really in the middle of nowhere. They have erected tents around it. If you show me a map, I can show you how to drive to it without going through the Erg which is very loose sand."

Alistair pulled out a small iPad and showed The Engineer a map of the area. He traced a route with his finger in a spot in the middle of a very flat piece of desert. "This is where they built the weird city."

"Thank you, we will follow your route."

32

'City' Watch

They thanked the Engineer and said goodbye to the children, who were busy enjoying their rice.

By the time they reached the Landy Paloma, who had been watching Alistair's video feed, had marked out the route and also possible OP (Observation Post) that they could hide up; with Biggles their drone they didn't have to get too close. They would send another winged drone high above the 'city' to get closer footage.

They set off immediately, their mission amplified. Now they were dealing with an act of genocide and the persecution of an endangered species. They were determined to put a stop to it all.

They had talked to Dr. KV and Misha who, after hearing about the massacre of the villagers, had suggested they pull out and hand over to a UN operation. They refused. Something was happening in the next few days and judging from Olenburgh's influence so far, the local police and government channels were most likely compromised. No doubt any international investigation at this point would get tied up in red tape, or worse.

The Land Rover silently made its way across the still, hot sand. The 'city' they were heading towards was on the edge of the Great Sand Sea, with miles of nothing beyond. They drove on, covering the distance in less than twenty minutes using The Engineer's route. The going was flat, fast, and with only a few soft spots. Suddenly, flares blasted into the sky. Popping noises cracked in the distance. Paloma sniffed. "Is that burning petrol?"

Alistair pointed the Landy towards a large rocky outcrop a thousand meters away from the city. Now he was driving on a surface of small pebbles so their tracks would be invisible. Because the Great Sand Sea was behind them, they were confident that nobody would approach from there and it provided an escape route. They knew the Nation First vehicles would never risk driving across the Sand Sea, but they were confident they could do it. At the outcrop, Alistair jumped out and quickly camouflaged the Landy while Tatiana sent Biggles up. Once they started getting the images on their screens, they were even more confused by what they were seeing. Paloma sent up the fixed-wing drone so they could get a view directly above. The drone would fly a grid, taking both still images and film.

The flares, the popping sounds and the smell of petrol were coming from a location that had all the elements of a medium-sized European city. There were shop fronts with French names and apartments above. The street was wide, with cars parked on each side. There was a bus lane and street furniture.

From inside the set it looked like a normal European city street, but that was where normal stopped.

Several of the parked cars were burning. In the center were about fifty riot police with shields, helmets and protective gear. At one end of the street there were over a hundred people in a mixture of military gear, camo, helmets, and several wore respirators. They thrust placards into the air. 'Nation First', 'Immigrés Out', 'Get off our Land'. They marched in a defiant, but disciplined, way toward the police, stamping their feet in unison.

Alistair jabbed his finger on the screen. "Look. That sign says 'NF,' the same logo that was on that border patrol vehicle."

The other end of the street was chaotic. A tangle of people were throwing bits of rubble at the police. Several people were in the process of pulling down the protective plywood from the shop fronts. As soon as the plywood came down, people poured into the shops, grabbing things and running out. Others held up banners that said 'Migration Isn't a Crime' and 'All People are Equal.'

Cameramen darted everywhere, 'PRESS' written on the backs of their bullet-proof vests, and low-flying drones added to the scene of tumult.

Alistair pointed out dark figures in several windows and on rooftops. "Look, these guys just raised silenced rifles at the police and the NF protesters."

Several police and NF marchers fell to the ground as if hit by gunfire.

The cameramen moved into where the fallen figures were and people stepped aside to let them through. Even from the drone image, they could see dark pools of blood appear around the fallen figures.

The pro-migration mob began stampeding away from the scene. Paloma pointed. "Zoom in there. Look, they are dropping their guns." The retreating mob littered weaponry as they ran. Cameramen moved in to film the scattered rifles, pistols and machine guns.

"Holy shit, did pro-migration snipers just take out those police and the NF marchers?"

"What the Dickens is going on? Are they making content for the internet?" Alistair was talking over the secure connection to Misha, Dr. KV and the rest of the team at the Ops center in Gamboa.

Dr. KV replied, "If that is the case, they are trying to portray the NF side as the disciplined victims and the other group as looters and killers."

Then a klaxon siren blared. The 'fallen' stood up and dusted themselves off while the stampeding mob turned and became ordinary.

Everyone stopped what they were doing.

A man appeared on a flat rooftop. He walked forward to a lectern with a microphone. A spotlight illuminated him. Armed guards in black uniforms flanked him and two long red flags unfurled downwards behind him, the letters NF written in black in the center. The people on the streets gathered below him and looked up. A strange mix of police uniforms, ragged looking people and militia were now all united.

Tatiana zoomed into the man's face and gasped. "That is Van Olenburgh, I can see his eyepatch."

Van Olenburgh opened his arms in a general embrace and then applauded the assembled crowd.

"It is time." There was a slight echo, and his words reverberated around the walls, menacing and clear.

"It is time to take back our country. It is time for action. No more talking. What you will do in the next few days will change history. Have courage my brave troopers, do your work well, the rewards will be great. It is TIME!"

The crowd stamped their feet and shouted in unison, "IT IS TIME!" The spotlight went off and Van Olenburgh. The crowds went quiet and then moved as one to the far end of the street.

A convoy of 4x4 trucks arrived and the Nation First, immigrants and police, all piled in together. The trucks disappeared toward the nearby tented encampment they could see at the edge of the drone footage in the distance.

A group of men in fireproof overalls carrying extinguishers drove up in a pickup and began putting out the fires. Another group started cleaning the broken concrete from the street and repairing the shopfront windows.

"Hold tight, let's see what happens next." Dr. KV's voice was patient.

After the cleanup squad swept through, the trucks appeared again, full of more people in costume and armed with fresh props. Tatiana zoomed in. "Hey this is a different group. See that guy in a Union Jack motorbike helmet? Last time there was one with a Swiss flag helmet. And look, they've changed the shop names to British ones. And hey, there's Sainsburys."

"Oh good. I hope they have Marmite, I'm nearly out."

"Alistair, are you always thinking about food?" Paloma shook her head.

"Actually, yes, and I think it's time for a nice cup of tea. This is just too crazy. We need to work out what's going on and the best way to do that is to consider everything over a nice cup of tea and some ginger cake."

He turned away from the drone footage and set-up the camping stove while Tatiana and Paloma continued to survey the crowds. There seemed to be 'handlers' who placed everyone in specific places and gave them instructions.

They drank their tea while the crowds and press cameramen got into place. The klaxon sounded and the riot started again.

Misha came over their comms system. "Guys, I know what this is. Yes, Olenburgh may very well be creating internet content. But to my eye, this is training."

Dr. KV's steady voice came through the line. He was choosing his words carefully, and it sounded grave. "Yes. Misha is right. You will remember Enoch Powell's Rivers of Blood speech? Olenburgh is pushing everyone's natural fear of foreigners. He is choreographing a show that portrays immigrants and foreigners as agents of death and chaos."

Misha added, "Yes, we set this up with the KGB in London in the 60s. Same bloody thing. And it works."

Dr. KV spoke everyone's thoughts aloud. "Yes. This is making sense. We know Olenburgh has already set up the Nation First rallies in every major city. Counter marches will, of course, be organized. Olenburgh's snipers will be standing by to take out police and they will sacrifice a few unwitting NF protestors. It will look to all the world like the migrant protestors are the evil killers."

Dr. KV added, "And looters. Looting takes on a life of its own once it starts. And looting is an emotive issue all on its own. Killing unarmed protestors plus looting. Anti-immigration will move from a right-wing manifesto and unconscious bias to a mainstream crusade."

Misha finished. "And, I imagine, Van Olenburgh will circulate the nighttime close up footage to 'confirm' that migrants and their supporters were the source of all chaos."

"So that means that these trained actors will leave in the next few days to get set up in their European and North American cities. Question is, how are they getting there?" Alistair asked. Then, immediately, he answered his own question. "Wait, didn't you say, Misha, that Sidi Haneish was like a beehive with planes going in but none coming out?" The picture was becoming clearer. "Tatiana, bring up the most recent satellite image of the airfield, please."

The image showed a number of passenger planes parked in lines by the runway.

"Let's see the same shot from six weeks ago."

Tatiana brought it up.

"Yup, only one plane."

She flipped it back to the recent image.

"I think these planes will take the riot trainees to the Nation First rally cities. Let's see—" He counted. "Eight planes. Paloma, how many seats do you think they have on each plane?"

"They look like Fokker 50s, Bombardier CRJs. So, mostly 50 seaters."

"So, if we guess each team is 50, that would be eight cities, right? I see some very shiny targets sitting there on the sand. If we go across the Great Sand Sea, we'll get there faster." Alistair rubbed his hands together.

"Take out their planes just before those thugs arrive from their training camp? But they'll miss their party." Paloma pulled a face.

Dr. KV's voice was very grave, employing the tone he reserved for particular moments when as teenagers they went too far, putting their lives at risk.

"Alistair! The plan was for you to drive around the edge of the Sand Sea using tracks and roads where possible. Then you were going to set up a well-hidden Op and sit and watch. Are you suggesting that you drive over to Sidi Haneish, across the Great Sand Sea Desert—something which only the most experienced Long Range Desert Group or the SAS would even think about—and blow up eight commercial jets in a heavily guarded airfield and then escape into the desert?"

"Exactly, Dr. KV. I know you're worried, but do you have a better plan? We can't drive down the roads because that lot going will spot us as they travel to their planes. These people are planning a series of assassinations. They have already massacred over fifty people. I don't think we have a choice. For the children."

"I am going through the registers of the planes online. It seems they originate from fairly dodgy countries, the spoils of war perhaps?" Misha had been multi-tasking. "It looks like these planes are owned by Unicorn Travel, same as the cruise ships. They are all Van Olenburgh's."

"Remember the Extinct Company's mission? To stop Olenburgh's pursuits, we have to take out all his infrastructure. These planes are part of his infrastructure," Alistair added.

There was a silence from both the Misha and Dr. KV.

Dr. KV was getting more than he bargained for. He had expected them to operate outside the law, but this was extreme, and very perilous. Finally, Dr. KV spoke.

"You are correct. This is why you are Commandos in the Company. Likewise, by your age, I was operating as a lone agent in war torn Vietnam, in the name of good. So, I can't really apply one rule to myself and another to you. Just make sure you come back."

"Thank you. We will return safely, we still have many missions to complete in the future."

"OK, what do you need from us?" Dr. KV was back in command.

They spent the next half hour going over details. During this time, the 'British' riot rehearsal had wrapped up, and the crews were preparing for another one.

"So how do these rehearsals link up with what is happening here? The massacre, the building of towns?" Paloma asked.

Dr. KV answered, "I am now convinced Olenburgh's ultimate pursuit is to create a 'homeland' for fascism, sort of extreme right-wing real estate. Its inhabitants will be 'pure.' That's why they had to take the locals out. It will be ground zero for spreading the fascist gospel across the globe, funded by Rhino horn sales. The eight city NF riots will create an atmosphere where people want somewhere 'safe' to escape to. It already happens across the world. This is just on a bigger scale. Plus, there is always the possibility that they find more oil."

33

Crossing the Great Sand Sea

By cutting across the top corner of the Great Sand Sea, the three would rendezvous with Taboga and the Atlas at an old airstrip 80 kilometers away. She would bring supplies and equipment. Tatiana estimated they should allow 36 hours if all went well. Alistair pointed out that, in World War Two, The Long-Range Desert Group had crossed here in two-wheel drive Chevy trucks using sun compasses. But of course, they had the advantage of very recent satellite images and accurate GPS. They also had their four-wheel drive electric Land Rover, which meant that their load was much lighter than a conventional vehicle, as they didn't need to carry fuel.

Paloma paraphrased from the internet. "The Great Sand Sea is exactly like a sea. It has massive waves of dunes that stretch over 500 kilometers. The individual dunes can be huge, over 60 meters high, some with a sheer drop on the other side. Like soft sanded cliffs. The Great Sand Sea presents a formidable challenge for a vehicle."

Undaunted, Alistair let their tires down to 10psi to give them a floatation effect on the soft sand.

The sky was packed full of stars, and the heat from the day had vanished beyond the horizon. Alistair was driving in his battered duffle coat, and over his head he had arranged a Shemagh, the traditional Arab scarf, held in place by his night goggles. He had suede desert boots on his feet.

Paloma had found a poncho made of camel hair and she pulled its worn and patched hood over her hair. Charlie had thrown it in as something to lie on when working under the car on rough surfaces. Paloma looked like a mix between a goat farmer and a futuristic warrior. Tatiana admired the look as Paloma performed a cat walk fashion show, flicking the Poncho over her shoulder and then laying her hand on the World War Two Webley Scott pistol in a holster on her right hip. Tatiana provided a Russian song to accompany the performance. They had reduced each other to a heap of giggles.

The caramel dunes looked like the windblown manes of horses, sailors slang for wild seas, and like an ocean they were constantly in motion. They set off riding the dunes like night surfers in their Land Rover, the three of them trying to read the 'waves' of the sand dunes stretched out in front of them.

Once they got over their initial fear of driving up and over such tremendous dunes, it became addictive. The most thrilling part was when they crested a towering dune, driving up the hard sand on a windward side. Then there was a split second to decide whether to sail straight over the top and down the other side, which was sometimes too steep, even for them, or to bank right and drive down the ridge until they found a spot where they could drop into the next valley.

When they went straight over the ridge and straight down, they felt like snowboarders. The dive was often so sudden they couldn't help screaming, both from fear and the thrill. More than once Paloma screamed out, "Enjoy the ride!" just as they went from pointing straight up into the sky to straight down a very steep slope. Screams notwithstanding, the Landy had become a silent roller coaster.

If Alistair braked at the crest, the car would belly out on the soft ridge, which would sometimes simply collapse and they would go down in a mini avalanche of sand. Or they would be stuck with all four wheels spinning in the air, like a crawling baby picked up from the floor by its midriff. This meant they had to dig, which they soon discovered to be a miserable job.

After several hours, they were feeling decidedly tripped out, and they stopped for a quick brew of tea at 3am and a much-needed rest. They were exhausted. Digging sand had been especially draining. McDonnell had made them home made 'energy bars' and they recovered quickly. In fact, they were wondering what he had put in them they had such a remarkably restorative effect.

By 6.30 am the sun was coming up and they had covered 65 kilometers. Stopping in the lee of a dune where the sand was hard, they put the Arab tent over the car and then covered that in the desert camo netting. The combination worked remarkably well; they had become a small dune. In the deep shade of the Arab tent it was refreshingly cool, even with the sun becoming a furnace as the day went on. A few fixed wing planes flew overhead, high in the sky.

As soon as they were settled in, Tatiana sent Biggles up, and they could see nothing but rolling dunes for 10 kilometers in any direction. With Biggles they were back in communication with the Ops Center, and Paloma gave them their SITREP. Alistair took first watch, while the other two fell into a deep sleep in their bedrolls on the sand. Every two hours they switched. They didn't expect any visitors, but caution was essential.

At midday, they received a report from Misha. She said they had got the latest satellite images of the fake city set and it looked as though the whole place had been set on fire and destroyed. This probably meant Van Olenburgh's Nation First acting troupe had finished their rally rehearsals. She was trying to see if they were now heading towards Sidi Haneish and their planes. If they were, time was running out.

Misha explained it was hard to tell what was happening at the airport because the satellite only passed over the area every 12 hours. She had, though, identified all the airport guards from communications they were intercepting in the factory in California that Tatiana had hacked into. There were 48 including technicians. If they had thought the ones in California were an unsavory bunch, these guys were pure evil. All of them were on the INTERPOL Red Notice list, and their crimes were all violent and often sexual assaults. The crew shuddered to think about what they were up against.

They resumed their journey at 4:00 p.m. The lengthening shadows would help them negotiate the sand dunes and they were confident they wouldn't meet anyone who would challenge them.

As they threaded their way across the desert, the evening light turned the dunes into exquisite soft folds of caramel that were so beautiful they stopped on a flat plateau formed of rock to take a picture.

"I need to pee," Alistair announced, rather spoiling the moment. "Hey, that's strange."

"What, did you just find out you were a boy?"

"Look, Paloma, over here on the ground." He pointed to a sizeable chunk of greenish, glittering, translucent stone. All around them, the ground shimmered with verdant light.

"I do not know what this is," came an uncharacteristic, defeated comment from Tatiana.

Paloma decided it was fossilized pee. "See Alistair, people have probably peeing here for millions of years. Maybe it's some kind of gravitational pull that's making you want to go?"

"Thank you, Paloma, for your great wisdom. However, I think we can attribute that to the large quantity of liquid I drank two hours ago."

They got back in the Landy, each collecting a small souvenir of the green glass on the way. Alistair's was shaped like an arrowhead.

The sun grew bigger and heavier when it touched the distant hills before disappearing. The show was over as darkness fell. They continued into the night, and the heat of the day was rapidly replaced with cooler air. At first, this was a relief, like someone turning on the AC in a hot car, but soon it was biting cold. Without a windscreen or doors and often traveling over 50 kilometers per hour, the draught they created doubled the chill factor. One negative of an electric vehicle was that they didn't have a great big lump of hot steel to give them warmth.

They stopped every couple of hours to thaw out with a cup of tea. At these times they took off their night vision goggles and stared at the stars. Once, they all saw a shooting star burning to its spectacular end. The team decided that must be good luck.

As they travelled through the desert and closer to their battle, they talked candidly. Alistair and Paloma agreed they felt tiny and humbled by the sheer vastness of nature. Tatiana said she understood why some people had found religion here—it felt like there was another, much bigger being, watching them from the dark, studded sky.

They stopped and made camp 10 kilometers from the edge of the Sand Sea. The rendezvous with Taboga's resupply team was just another 20 kilometers away. They hoped they would have no other company when they crossed the flat desert and track beyond the Sea of Sand.

Once Biggles had been launched, and comms reconnected, they gave their SITREP to Misha.

She told them what she had sent on the Atlas with Taboga and her team.

"You have some goodies as you requested: Twenty-five individual magnetic limpet bombs with timers, those are for the planes and any other equipment you can find. One Javelin anti-tank missile with four shots; Alistair knows how to use it. VSS Vintorex suppressed sniper rifle. That is the Russian baby Tatiana requested, silenced, and goes through body armor. M3A1 Demolition charge. Three intelligent target lock drone bombs. Fifty liters of water. And a pleasant surprise for

Paloma."

Dr. KV added, "You haven't used any ammo for the weapons you have, so your supplies are good. I am sure you will spend this evening cleaning the dust and sand out of them."

Misha said, "Now I am sending you the latest satellite image of Sidi Haneish. We have spent several hours doing a detailed analysis."

They opened up the image on their screen. Labels popped out as they moved the curser across the image.

"So, as we decided, priority targets to stop their operation are the planes and the main administrative building where we believe the vile internet traffic is originating from. There is also the control tower, the fuel dump, and if you can make a big hole in the middle of the runway with the Demo charge that would be super.

But you are also going to need to deal with three guard towers along the perimeter fence, barracks with—we are thinking—30 armed guards, plus 18 technicians who may be armed, six pickups with 30-cals mounted on the back and two Panhard VBL light-armored vehicles.

Plus, there is a reinforced concrete hanger with steel doors and we have no idea what's inside. That's your bonus target, with 20 extra points for taking it out!"

"Thanks Misha, sounds like a piece of cake. Our aim is to get in, do as much damage as we can and then get out before everyone can mobilize and mount a counterattack against us." Alistair looked at the other two to see if they had anything to add.

"Then drink our 50 liters of water?" Paloma quipped.

"Any other questions?"

"Yeah, when can I open my surprise?"

"You'll see."

34

RV

The rendezvous with Taboga was an abandoned airfield 20 kilometers away. Ahead was a track that had some traffic on it. They had seen roughly one vehicle pass every half hour, mostly construction vehicles, but twice they had seen pickups with 30-cals known as a 'technicals,' full of armed men.

They had covered the Land Rover's sides and bonnet in desert camouflage netting, breaking up the shape. Paloma said it looked like a bath sponge, but they were pleased with the effect from a distance.

They set off at 21:00 ahead of their RV at 23:00.

Leaving the safety of the Sand Sea increased their anxiety. They pulled on their bulletproof Kevlar vests. Charlie had found female body armor for Tatiana and Paloma.

Paloma was driving, Alistair was manning the twin GPMGs in the back, and Tatiana was in the front with the other GPMG.

They waited and listened beside an abandoned hut on the side of the track.

"All clear. Go." Alistair had the best view from his elevated position. It was pitch black, and Paloma was driving with her night goggles.

As they crossed the road, Alistair noticed an overgrown irrigation ditch running parallel to the track.

"Stop. Irrigation ditch ahead. Damn."

Tatiana jumped out, grabbed a stick and poked it into the overgrown ditch. "It's too deep, and two meters across we'll get stuck. Back up."

She jumped in as Paloma was reversing.

"I'm going to drive along the track until we find a crossing point."

"OK. Go."

The track felt like driving a motorway after being off-road for so long.

"Paloma, slow down. We can't see well enough."

"Sorry, had my rally boots on. Hang on, something coming. Head-lights ahead. 1000 meters: closing fast."

"Quick, cross the track, pull off and head in the same direction as them. Look, the side of the road is much lower there."

There was nothing to hide behind, but they hoped they wouldn't be spotted below the track.

Tatiana and Alistair cocked their weapons and flipped off the safety, preparing for the worst.

"If it's a construction vehicle, let it go; hopefully the driver will think he's imagining stuff. And if it's a technical, we'll take it out."

"Paloma, keep moving. Let the vehicle pass us so we can have a look."

If it was a technical, the gunner in the rear the pickup would literally have to climb on the roof of the cab to fire backwards once they were driving behind it.

As the vehicle approached, it came into clear focus. It was a pickup with a guy manning a 30-cal in the rear bed.

The gunman saw the camouflaged Land Rover in the headlights a split second before passing it. The last thing they saw him do was to bang madly on the roof of the cab to get the driver to stop.

Alistair and Tatiana lit up the night sky, firing their guns upward through the body of the pickup. The rear gunner was thrown into the air by the force of lead. The pickup swerved sideways and disappeared. Smashing glass, thump, then a grinding screech and glass again. They were the sounds of a vehicle doing a sideways roll at high speed.

Paloma maneuvered back up onto the track. A mangled figure dressed in battle fatigues lay pasted on the dirt, dark blood pooling out around him.

"Paloma, watch the front. I'll cover the rear. Tatiana, can you check him and pull him off the road? Where's the bloody truck?"

"He's dead." She pulled him across to the ditch and pushed him in.

"Found the truck, it's here in the ditch and the driver is…"

The truck was lying neatly tucked upside down in the drainage ditch, cab and presumably driver completely flattened.

Tatiana kicked sand over the bloody pool in the middle of the track.

"I've got more lights coming. Two kilometers… moving fairly slowly."

"That must be a big lorry, we need to find a place to cross this ditch now."

Tatiana was standing on the underside of the upturned pickup. Two wheels were still turning slowly.

"We have a bridge!" she shouted

"Oh yes, the shooting star worked! Let's go." Tatiana jumped in and Paloma guided the Landy over the chassis of the pickup between the four upturned wheels.

"Nice job, Miss P."

She drove up a bank on the other side and stopped the Landy behind a small cliff.

The lorry was an open truck full of armed men, but they rode past without noticing a thing.

"Phew. Right, we have ten kilometers and fifteen minutes before our rendezvous, let's move."

Tatiana gave Paloma the bearings, and they set off across the stony desert floor.

A few minutes later, they hit the flat sand of the wartime airfield.

They drove down the entire 1,000 meters of dirt landing strip, checking carefully for holes or rocks with their goggles. All was clear.

Paloma pulled into what she figured was the 'parking' apron. Immediately they could see the rusted remains of what looked like an old Chevy truck. It had settled into the sand and was gradually disintegrating.

"That's the type of truck the Long-Range Desert group used. Well, at least they got home. This was an allied airbase." Alistair was trying to decipher the logo on the back, which looked like a scorpion. He had been studying the LRDG since he was ten. That was their symbol.

A dark shape roared over their heads like a dragon in the night. It dipped its wings before carving a neat half circle in the sky and dropping to the airstrip. A great plume of dust clouded the air as it hit the dirt and the wonderful smell of burnt avgas filled their nostrils, reminding them of airports. For Alistair and Paloma, it told of distant childhood journeys and excitement—not that they were in short supply of adventure right now.

They had been washing in a cup of water for several days, and it occurred to Alistair that he was about to see all the girls on Taboga's team. He certainly hadn't looked in a mirror, and he was pretty sure he smelt fairly ripe. On top of that, he'd just come out of a firefight, so he was still bouncing off the walls with adrenaline.

The massive plane landed and spun around, facing back down the runway for a fast exit. The three continued to scan the surroundings while the plane came to a halt. They were in enemy territory.

The rear ramp of the plane began to drop, showing red light from the inside. Taboga's team descended the ramp, aliens coming into their empty desert. The girls from the aircraft were all fully kitted for combat and armed, completing the tableau.

Paloma backed the Landy up next to the ramp and Tatiana organized the equipment for a quick transfer.

Then Paloma and Alistair went into the belly of the plane to wait for Taboga. She was going to give them a quick briefing.

Paloma's eyes lit up, and she partly opened her mouth in an expression of delighted discovery. "Ooooh I am going to have a pee in a real loo…" she held up her finger, spun on her heels and disappeared into the very respectable toilet next to the cabin. Alistair could hear her humming happily as she closed the door.

Alistair waited, sitting on the bench. The cabin door opened and Taboga and her copilot stepped forward, fully kitted out in flight suits, helmets and gloves. They removed their headgear and shook out their hair.

Alistair was transfixed.

"Um, hi Taboga. How are you? Did you have a pleasant flight?" Alistair stammered.

She smiled and introduced her companion.

"Perfect, thank you. This is Klara, my copilot."

They sat down next to him. Paloma stepped out of the loo.

"Oooh heaven, I just had a sit-down pee. Lovely. I even washed my hands with soap and water. I see you found my brother. You'll agree he smells like a camel."

"Right," he said, before he lost the plot completely, "we've got some planes to blow up."

Taboga popped up. "No changes from Misha, everything is go. Oh, gosh, I nearly forgot—" She dashed out the door, which was pushed opened seconds later by a large black nose.

'Jeeves' buried his head in Paloma's lap, and she squealed with delight. He was wearing a Kevlar coat and tactical harness.

"Misha has been working him. She says he is actually a highly trained combat dog who responds well to the right handler. They flew him to

Gibraltar with the rest of the gear. She said he is brave and intelligent, a compliment she doesn't hand out to many humans. They also loaded his rations."

They stepped back out into a wall of noise and fuel smells in the loading bay. Taboga put her helmet back on, and the other two put on their ear protectors.

The Land Rover was loaded and ready. Jeeves obediently jumped in the rear and was clipped in by a beaming Paloma. She updated the delighted dog on the mission.

The other two got in the Land Rover as the ramp of the plane closed.

Two minutes later it was hurtling down the runway and disappearing into the black night sky.

"Wow," Alistair said to himself.

35

Battle

They drove on for the next four hours with brief breaks, arriving one kilometer from Sidi Haneish at 2 am. By the time they stopped, they looked like ghosts. The Land Rover, equipment and their bodies were covered in a fine layer of desert dust.

Alistair brewed a pot of tea while the girls unwrapped the weapons from their protective covers: cleaning, checking, and arming each one as they did so.

The plan was to approach from the South end of the runway and farthest away from the airport terminals. At this section, there was only one sentry tower. The airfield was surrounded by a three-meter-high fence topped with razor wire, except at the very end of the runway where it was only two meters high and without razor wire, to allow for any low-flying planes on approach or takeoff.

The lights for the airstrip were off and the guard had only a rather ancient looking searchlight, which he left pointing at the fence near his tower. He was looking at his cell phone and smoking.

Alistair and Tatiana crept forward. They needed to cut a hole in the fence big enough to get the Landy through. They realized they had no choice but to take out the guard, so, when they were 200 meters away from him, they got behind a rock and Tatiana flicked the safety catch off the silenced sniper rifle. Two clicks, like somebody playing with a ball-point pen, sounded and the guard crumpled. One more click and the glass of the searchlight exploded, summoning darkness all around them.

They were counting on the guard in the next tower, not noticing them as they ran forward and started clipping a line down the center of the fence. When they reached the ground, they folded the fence back like a banana peel and radioed Paloma to come forward. As the silent car crossed the folded fence, they jumped in.

They had stacked the magnetic limpet mines with timers in a canvas bag in the rear. The timers were all set at slightly different times between 1 and 20 minutes to cause maximum confusion.

With Alistair and Tatiana in the rear, Paloma drove down the edge of the strip until she reached a taxiway to the side. All eight aircraft were stationed in a neat line, noses pointing out along the parking just off the taxiway.

The first plane they came to was an Embraer 145 with its two jet engines mounted on the rear. Paloma drove under one of the rear jets. Tatiana activated a limpet mine and handed it to Alistair, who was perched on the roll cage. The limpet mine was set to twenty minutes. The engine cowling made a low ringing sound as the magnet clamped on. Alistair had put the mine inside the cowling where it couldn't be seen.

"Sorry, sweetie," Paloma whispered to the sleek-looking aircraft.

They moved to the next aircraft and repeated the process, but this time putting the mine on the undercarriage.

When they had set four mines, they found themselves near the center of the 2,000 meter runway, where they were planning to set an M3A1 Demolition Charge that would blast an enormous crater.

Just as they were headed to their target, a burst of automatic fire coming from the tower on the other side of the parked planes shattered the silence.

Several rounds pinged the tarmac around the vehicle and Alistair swung the twin GPMG, blasting the tower and guard, which disintegrated and crashed to the ground. But the game was up, the airfield lights came on and a Klaxon sounded.

The remaining tower searchlight swept around looking for them. The Land Rover came to a halt in the center of the runway and Tatiana fired off several rounds from her silent weapon, taking out both the third guard and the light.

"I'm setting the demo charge for ten seconds."

He placed it on the tarmac and jumped in. They headed back to the parked planes, where there were deep shadows for cover. They eased under the fifth jet, and Alistair threw the charge on top of the wing. It had a five-minute timer set.

A technical with a 30-cal and six men came screaming down the center of the runway. They spotted the demolition charge a fraction of a second before it went off, lifting the pickup and everyone in it into a backwards somersault; bits of asphalt pattered down to earth. A 7-meter-wide crater had appeared in the middle of the airfield. The pickup finally stopped rolling and skidded off the runway on its roof.

Paloma floored it, and they reached the fuel tanks. Tatiana threw two mines with short fuses and they stuck to the 10,000-gallon tanks with their magnets.

They could hear shouting, tires screeching, and sporadic gunfire.

Nobody knew where they were. The combination of keeping to the shadows, the silence of the car and the camouflage net made them a fleeting dark shadow.

Tatiana sat up front with her mute weapon and every time someone appeared in the distance ahead, she sprayed them with silent fire. She was an incredible shot, hitting moving targets over 200 meters away.

They reached the main administration building, where the computer hub was located. Alistair jumped down, kicked open the door and threw in three M14 incendiary grenades in quick succession, then jumped back on the Landy. The grenades exploded with three loud *crumps* and flames lit up the windows.

They moved on without a sound to the next cluster of buildings, setting limpet mines as they went. They found the generators chugging away and belching black smoke. Alistair pulled the main switch, and they fell silent. As the airfield lights turned dark, he clamped a limpet mine to the back of it.

The charges on the Avgas fuel tanks went off with a massive *crack*, followed instantly by a rolling ball of fire that filled the sky.

"Let's go home. Nobody is flying out of here for months!" Alistair shouted above the sound of debris thudding to earth. "Back the way we came."

The fireball lit up the scene, and they saw a dozen men running towards them, firing AKs from their hips as they ran. Rounds peppered the Landy's steel plate.

Hand over hand, Paloma was trying to turn the vehicle away from the oncoming men. Alistair opened up from the rear, picking off several running figures. But one unarmed man reached the car, grabbing Paloma and pinning her to the ground in front of the vehicle with his knees. He drew a knife from his belt and was raising it when the dark shape of Jeeves leapt over the bonnet, grabbed his wrist and yanked him to the ground. He screamed in pain. Paloma drew out her Webley .445 service revolver and shot the man in the chest. The shot pushed him right off her.

Paloma and Jeeves jumped back in the Landy. As more men poured out of the barracks, both Tatiana and Alistair opened fire as Paloma steered straight at them. There was no other way around the flames from the fuel tanks, which were blocking their retreat.

These men had been asleep when the first explosion went off and many were not fully dressed. The silent Land Rover covered in camo net must have looked like a ghost to them until the guns opened up. The surprise earned them precious seconds, and they went straight through the crowd, knocking over one confused guard without a shirt on. As they went, Alistair pulled several fragmentation grenades from his belt and dropped them off at the back like depth charges. The men chasing the Landy ran straight over them just as they went off.

Then the real show began: the mines on the planes started to go off, sending fireworks into the sky.

Alistair shouted above the gunfire. "Paloma, drive around the back by that hanger—we need to hide!" Chaos reigned. Multiple explosions were going off all over the place and the defenders had begun shooting at everything that moved, thinking a much larger force was attacking them.

But the escape route was blocked.

Paloma guided the silent Landy to the back of the hanger, which was closed. They were in a dark shadow of the building, the flickering fires creating an orange glow around them. The hanger was built of reinforced concrete buried halfway in the sand. Blast proof doors sealed the front.

They could see a slit of light coming under the door.

"Damn. They must have backup generators inside. What the hell is in there?"

They knew there were only seconds before their assailants found them. Technical pickups were racing around with searchlights mounted on their roll cages. They could see them bobbing up and down on the sand around the main runway. Every now and again they would 'find' something and everyone would open fire. They were massively outnumbered.

'We need a diversion—what have we got left?"

"Four limpet mines, the Javelin anti-tank weapon, the drone bombs, and a couple thousand rounds of GPMG ammo. Plus, my silent friend," Tatiana said, patting her Russian sniper's rifle.

"Brilliant. Tatiana, see if you can pick off some of those guys in the pickup. All we need to do is get them to run for cover. They won't know where the shots are coming from. I am going to send the drones over to blow the top off the control tower. Paloma, get ready to get us out of here if they find us."

Tatiana's fingers moved fast. The consequence was silent and deadly—two men flopped out of a pickup and survivors started firing wildly in the wrong direction.

Alistair sent the drones up, clicking on the control tower with the cross hairs in the little green screen, and they zipped off like angry insects.

Seconds later, the top of the control appeared to pop open and a fraction of a second later, the sound carried three very satisfying explosions to their ears. Then the top of the tower burst into flames, making a wonderful impression of an Olympic torch.

"Armored cars 10 o'clock!" Paloma shouted. The stubby little French cars were equipped with thermal imaging and were heading straight towards them.

"Go! Go down the runway. I'm going to get the Javelin out." The anti-tank missile was loaded in a huge plastic case and not designed to be set up in a fast-moving vehicle.

"Don't forget our bloody crater. Stop 200 meters beyond it! I can't fire while we're moving."

A pickup popped up onto the runway at the other end, heading toward them at high speed. Tatiana was firing controlled short bursts from her machine gun and the driver, fearing for his life, was swerving wildly. Her bullets had turned his windscreen into a spider's web. They were now coming under attack from both directions.

"Just before they get to the crater, flick on all your lights." They hadn't used them, but the Land Rover was equipped with more LED driving lights than a rally car.

Paloma flooded the tarmac with light, blinding the driver in the pickup and forcing it to sail straight over the edge of the crater. For a split second it looked as if it would actually jump the whole thing but the wheels hit just before the lip and, as if in slow motion, the bumper compressed and the whole thing pitched tail over nose without touching the ground.

Paloma flipped off the lights and did a perfect chicane around the sliding car and the gaping crater. The Land Rover had fast outpaced the armored cars, who had stopped firing to avoid hitting the pickup. Paloma pulled to a stop just off the main runway.

Tatiana climbed in the back to help Alistair, but he had already got the weapon up and she took the controls while he prepared to fire.

Just before the first armored car reached the crater, the missile shot out of its casing and locked onto the stubby French vehicle. The car was only lightly armored and as the weapon was designed for tanks, the explosion effectively disintegrated the car and knocked the other armored right over on its roof like a flipped tortoise. The two crew crawled out just before it exploded.

Alistair reloaded. Paloma headed towards their cut in the fence. They could have driven through any part of the fence, but the mess of dragging broken fence would have been too easy to follow.

As they left the end of the runway, another one of their limpet mines went off, filling the sky with orange light. It must have been on the fuel tank of a plane because a second, much bigger explosion followed the first.

They whooped in celebration as it went off, but their joy was short-lived. They heard it first. Out of the flames, rising like a deadly Phoenix, came a heavily armed Huey attack helicopter.

It was on them in seconds, firing its side-mounted M60D machine gun from an open door. Van Olenburgh's demonic face appeared behind the gun. He was screaming and laughing while he fired. The rounds ripped through the Land Rover, hitting Paloma and Tatiana in the legs. Paloma screamed out in pain but kept driving. She knew to stop would be the end of them. She could feel the warm blood running into her boot.

Alistair rolled out the back onto the ground with the Javelin Missile. "Keep going! Get to those rocks! I'll nail the bastard."

The helicopter swung around for a second run. Tatiana had pulled herself up into the rear gunner's seat and was firing a solid wall of lead in front of the helicopter so it flew straight into it. Rounds sparked off the belly of the aircraft and it swerved madly, so the storm of Olenburgh's bullets only made holes in the sand.

As Olenburgh's helicopter flew over, Alistair aimed. And as it started to loop back, the Javelin locked on. The missile streaked out of its tube and the pilot, recognizing a missile lock, heaved the aircraft over, throwing the Van Olenburgh out the door so he was hanging by his harness like a puppet on a string. The missile narrowly missed the aircraft. But the Javelin was a highly sophisticated weapon, and it simply pulled a tight loop and came back on target, slamming straight into the helicopter engine and creating an enormous ball of explosion. It dropped out of the sky like a burning log and rained red hail down on the ground around Alistair. The main body of the aircraft exploded as it hit the sand, leaving nothing but hot debris and a column of smoke.

Paloma looped back to pick up Alistair. She was looking pale from loss of blood, and they could hear another pickup coming towards them from between the remaining planes.

Alistair lifted her out of her seat. He took over driving while the girls ripped open trauma kits and patched each other up as best they could. As he accelerated across the bumpy sand, he pulled their last limpet mine from the bag, set it on a short fuse and dropped it out the open doorway as he drove. He did the same with a white phosphorous and fragmentation grenade.

The pickup had hesitated at the helicopter crash site to see if there were any survivors, and was now back in pursuit. But the team was already being swallowed by the darkness. The phosphorous grenade went off first, exploding right in front of the pickup and completely blinding the driver and gunner for several seconds. Next, the frag grenade went off, missing the pickup but giving the impression that they were under heavy fire.

The pickup and its crew fled back to the airport, having imagined that they had met a huge attack force in the dark expanse of desert—not chasing a lone and badly damaged Land Rover with one guy, two women and a dog.

As Alistair drove on, he heard the last mine go off, and wondered if it had hit the pickup. He realized he was having trouble breathing and there was increasing pain rising from his chest. He checked for warm blood and then remembered he had been hit several times in his body armor and his ribs may have been broken.

"How are you doing in the back?"

"We are having a trauma kit party. I'd ask you to join us but Tatiana says it's girls and dogs only."

"We have stopped the bleeding, but we both lost a lot of blood so we are going to need to get on a drip pretty soon. We were also hit in our vests, so we think we may have broken ribs. Nothing you can do about that." Tatiana had realized he wasn't asking out of niceness, but to assess if he needed to stop and help.

"Alistair, was that Olenburgh in the Huey, did you get him?" Paloma gasped as the pain grew.

"He was in the Huey but when the missile hit he was hanging out by his harness, he may have been blown clear. It was pretty low when I hit it so he could have survived. Let me call Taboga."

"Seco, this is Whisky. Our ETA is ten minutes."

"We are not under pursuit."

"We need emergency medical help."

"Roger that—we are coming in."

Taboga had been making lazy circles at 3,000 meters above another abandoned airstrip 20 kilometers from Sidi Haneish. If they were under close pursuit, they would abandon the rendezvous and keep going until they lost their pursuers.

"The plane should land as we arrive at the rendezvous. You guys OK to keep going? We are ten minutes out."

"Yeah, don't stop, we're having fun."

The Land Rover was a complete mess, riddled with holes, everything inside seemed to have been smashed, there were empty cartridge cases all over the place, the seats looked like execution chairs full of holes and splattered in blood. Jeeves seemed to be the only one who had come out unharmed. He had fixed his eyes on Paloma.

"I hope Charlie remembered to get the comprehensive insurance for The Pink Panther—third party would be useless."

Alistair reckoned they were driving with only one functioning electric motor instead of four. In fact, he was amazed they were driving at all. The noise coming from the car after the helicopter attack was awful: grinding, screeching and bumping as they went along.

The Atlas swept over them. An incredible roar of its four engines felt like it would shake the Land Rover to pieces. The sound reminded Alistair of airshows when the last remaining Lancaster bomber would do a low pass.

He smiled at the memory and the feeling of safety the aircraft brought.

It landed neatly, presenting its tail end to them and dropping the rear ramp, the warm glow spreading out across the sand.

They screeched and bumped their way up the ramp, and the Atlas team swarmed over them, pulling them out and securing the Land Rover.

The ramp shut, and the engines wound themselves back up to full speed.

The faint first light of dawn came through the cabin windows.

Alistair said, trying to lighten the mood. "So, what's for breakfast?"

36

Gibraltar

hree hours later, the Atlas crossed the deliciously blue Mediterranean Sea and touched down at Gibraltar airport. The Rock loomed above the three wounded Extinct Company team members who hobbled out into the warming sunshine. Both Paloma and Tatiana had refused the indignity and fuss of a stretcher, much to the annoyance of the Queen Alexandra's Royal Army Nursing Corps sister. They got into two army ambulances and were taken over to the Gibraltar regiment barracks where there was a small hospital wing.

The nurses cleaned the wounds. Luckily, the rounds had gone straight through without hitting any bone. X-rays showed multiple cracked ribs. Their torsos were black and blue from the bullets hitting their body armor. But they were fortunate. Nothing would leave permanent damage, only scars.

Alistair and Jeeves were given the unusual permission of being allowed to sit in the room where the girls were laid up.

At 3:00 p.m. The Earl came in. They were surprised to see him in full Blue's and Royals regiment General's warm weather barrack dress. The nurses were dismissed.

"Good afternoon. Apologies for the kit. This is my old regiment, and

I thought it would be good cover. There are army officers coming out the walls here."

They greeted him warmly.

"I just received a new satellite image from Sidi Haneish. You chaps certainly made a nice mess. I have had a brief review of the footage from the vehicle cameras, and it looks like it was a pretty hot party. My informal assessment is that it will be unusable for months, if not longer. Plus, if you look at the planes, they are all clearly severely damaged. The filthy rubbish they were feeding into the Internet has come to a complete stop. We are sending a team in to see the actual situation on the ground. Importantly we need to see if Van Olenburgh was killed. The video footage is inconclusive.

"Sister Maclean tells me you have no injuries that will be permanent, although you will be in pain for a while. Now, I would like you to give me a blow by blow account of what happened. I'll record it and have it transcribed, then you can revise it later but better get it out while it's still fresh."

They told their adventure, pausing briefly when the sister brought them tea: Marmite and cucumber sandwiches. Two hours later, the details and their minds were exhausted.

"Excellent, thank you. Let us meet at 0900 tomorrow and go over the next steps."

The Earl excused himself. He was off to have supper with the commanding officer, an old friend.

Sister Maclean led Alistair to an officer's room down the hallway from the hospital wing. Alistair was exhausted, but his mind was still buzzing like a beehive, so he took Jeeves for a walk around the famous rock, which was nice until the Barbary apes started swearing at Jeeves. He ended up having fish and chips with beer at the Angry Frier.

Next morning, The Earl was ebullient. They connected with both the Ops room in Gamboa and with Deirdre in California, who had been updated the night before. The Earl kicked off. "Good morning everyone. Excellent news—thanks to your show, the Nation First marches went off like damp squibs. Just a few people showed up and nobody was hurt. So, let's review what still needs to be addressed: Nation First owns the equivalent of a small country in North Africa. It seems the organization bought the land through corrupt officials and then eliminated the local inhabitants, leaving hundreds of orphaned children without a home.

"There is a network of spas worldwide which are a front for the sale of rhino horn online. These spas are also the conduit for Nation First recruitment. Smuggling of Rhino horns using retirees on the Unicorn cruise ships.

"The laboratory in California is used for the illegal production and use of rhino horn based medicines.

"Finally, and importantly, we think that the big hunting meet in Tanzania at Risasi Nzuri ranch I talked about earlier is actually a secret society meeting. Remember how we hypothesized that every sector of the upper echelons of government and global security had been infiltrated, including INTERPOL? We now believe this is their annual meeting. We think it is being disguised as some kind of charity auction."

"Damn, and we thought blowing up a few planes would solve the problem." Paloma looked disappointed, and her leg was hurting.

"So, what is going to happen if we killed Van Olenburgh? Who will be in charge?" Alistair asked The Earl.

"Good question. With all these influential people involved, several in very high leadership roles, it's hard to tell who would take over. From what you said yesterday, he may still be alive. However much infrastructure we destroy, as long as NF connects powerful people in this way, it will just bounce back. For now, all we have done is slow its progress. For us to destroy the organization we have to get inside it and break it from the heart."

"What are you suggesting? I imagine a secret club like that is almost impossible to join?" Alistair continued.

"Well, you probably don't know it but I am actually a very voluble member of the House of Lords. My position is always strongly anti immigration. This is a cover and not my genuine belief. I am also an avid hunter, not of big game, but of grouse in Scotland where I have an estate."

"So, my team has successfully secured an invitation to Risasi Nzuri Ranch in Tanzania for me. I suspect NF wishes to recruit me."

"Wow, amazing, when do you go?"

"Tomorrow morning, but I am missing something essential."

"Gosh, do you have your rifles with you?"

"It's not that. I do. However, I need a batman."

Knowing the definition of a batman, an officer's servant, a sort of gentleman's valet, Alistair's eyes grew wider.

"At least I need someone who is highly capable, who knows their way around guns and who can do things like plant bugs while I am being jolly charming. They just need to pretend to be a batman. Perhaps with a slight Scot's accent?"

"Aye, understood my Lord, anything else?" Alistair did a very good Scot's accent and a crisp salute.

"He needs a mustache, a nice bushy one, like a Sergeant major—and sideburns!" She was always trying to get him to grow 'Victorian Style' facial hair and dress up to match some portraits in their Scottish home. This might be the closest she'd ever get.

37

Safari

The following morning, in an army staff car, Alistair, Paloma, Jeeves and Tatiana traveled back to Gibraltar airport with The Earl. The guard at the gate saluted and ushered them towards the tarmac to a very smart-looking hanger where Sebastian, The Earl's pilot, was waiting with the Citation jet.

Both Paloma and Tatiana were limping badly, and the QARANC nurse, Sister Maclean, had protested when they insisted on going to see Alistair and The Earl off.

Alistair was now 'James Morgan' from Durness in the North of Scotland. He had a passport and a complete history online, created by Misha. He wore a magnificent mustache and positively agricultural sideburns, created this morning by Paloma. They had given Alistair lessons on how to remove and reapply.

Paloma was thrilled. "Alistair, you have to grow those for real. You look magnificent! Doesn't he, my Lord?"

"Paloma, you are too overly soaked in Victorian Romance novels to make sound judgements about my facial hair," Alistair pointed out.

"I really want to go on safari with you guys. Alistair, you are going to miss all my wise advice."

The Earl put his hand on Paloma's shoulder "Paloma, my dear, when this is over, I promise I will take The Extinct Company team on a lovely safari. I have some excellent friends who love to entertain and they have a sprawling lodge on an island in Kenya."

"I don't speak Swahili." Tatiana was making a joke about herself.

"Yeah, but I bet you'd pick it up in a week." Paloma replied, laughing.

"Be careful. It's a jungle out there," was Paloma's farewell as she stood there resting in her crutches, Jeeves sitting neatly beside her.

Alistair and The Earl stepped on board the Citation.

Sebastian's French co-pilot and assistant, Pascale, who served gourmet meals and lovely wines, made the twelve-hour flight to Arusha very comfortable.

Sister Maclean had given Alistair some powerful painkillers.

"Only one every six hours, or you'll be hooked."

In between eating and sleeping, they worked on their cover story.

The plane descended early the following morning and the mighty Mt Kilimanjaro filled the windows. Once snowcapped, and now naked, a bleak reminder of climate change, even in Alistair's lifetime.

When they landed at Arusha and the door of the plane opened, it was like a homecoming for Alistair, who had gone to prep school at Pembroke House in Kenya. He breathed deeply: wood smoke, diesel fumes, avgas, sweat, burning plastic, the rich smell of an African city. He loved it. From here, they were told they would need to take a smaller plane that could land at the rough airstrip by the lodge. This plane would wait for them.

Alistair and Sebastian unloaded The Earl's leather Globe Trotter suitcases and his pair of Purdeys in their elegantly battered gun case with the Godolphin two-headed eagle crest embossed on the front. Plus, Dr. KV had generously lent them his .375 Purdey hunting rifle with a silencer, lovingly packed inside a dusty, waterproof Pelican case.

Alistair put the gear in a cart with a wooden bottom, loaded his own battered, green canvas bag on top and pushed it towards the small customs and immigrations building on the tarmac. The Earl walking slightly ahead.

A young blonde man in short shorts and suede Bata boots intercepted them. "Good morning. My name is Kevin. There is no need to go through the formalities if you give this gentleman your passports, he will deal with it." As he spoke, a Tanzanian official came out of the building. He was wearing a blue uniform. Alistair handed over the passports.

"I will be your pilot to Risasi Nzuri lodge. I hope you had a pleasant flight?" He had a South African accent. He ignored Alistair.

"Good Morning, Kevin. Thank you. This is my man, James." The Earl's attitude was offhand.

"Follow me, please." They walked across the hot tarmac to a Beechcraft King Air. 'Pamwe Chete Safari Company,' was written in green letters under the round windows.

Kevin opened the aircraft door and bowed slightly to The Earl, who marched up the steps. The Earl then said dismissively, "Be a good chap and help James with the bags," and sat down in the plane.

Alistair grinned inwardly as Kevin reluctantly picked up a bag, he already disliked Kevin.

With the luggage on board, Kevin started pulling up the stairs. Alistair, who had just finished belting the Purdeys into their own seats, walked back to the door of the plane.

"Kevin, we have not got our passports." Alistair was looking towards the immigration building nobody was coming with passports for them.

"Ack man, don't fuss, they'll bring them to the lodge on the next plane, it always takes ages for them to put all their little bloody stamps." Kevin slammed the door shut and pushed his way past Alistair to the pilot's seat.

Alistair sat down and belted in, feeling like something was not quite right.

They taxied out to the main runway and took off North East towards the vast open savannah of the Serengeti and beyond.

Tanzania was one of the twelve countries in Africa where you could still hunt big game. Risasi Nzuri existed solely for that purpose.

After an hour's flying, most of the time spent over the private lands of Risasi Nzuri, the plane began to descend toward the ochre haze. Below them, the landscape came into focus. A patchwork of kopjes, umbrella shaped Acacia trees and, as they got lower, thousands and thousands of gazelle scattered about the dry grassland, little puffs of red dust exploding behind the ones nearest the plane.

Kevin turned around. "Sorry Sir, we have to circle around. There is another plane taking off." He pulled the plane up from its slow descent.

As they made a long loop, Alistair and The Earl could see the airstrip from the window. It wasn't what they had expected; it was a full-length concrete runway and the plane taking off was a Citation jet, just like The Earl's.

"Interesting. I wonder why they made me land at Arusha and then take their plane?"

On the approach, their eyes followed a large river winding its way through the dry landscape, flanked by green trees. On a distant bank, they glimpsed a large stone building and several others dotted beyond.

Taxiing, parking and then killing the engine, Kevin looked back and said, "Welcome to Risasi Nzuri Lodge. You have arrived."

Kevin dropped the stairs and a smart green Land Cruiser drove forward to meet them. Instead of windows or a windscreen for protection, it was equipped with a simple canvas roof. A tough-looking man in a green, well-pressed uniform parked near the plane and walked towards them.

"Good Morning, my name is Chulu. Kindly get into the vehicle? The crew will unload and take your bags to your rooms shortly."

Alistair spoke respectfully but firmly. "Good Morning Chulu. My name is James, and this is Lord Godolphin. We would like to keep our bags with us, please. I will unpack for his Lordship."

The bags were full of bugging equipment. Although well-hidden and disguised, it wouldn't be too difficult to unearth. Alistair walked over to the plane and ferried the bags to the Land Cruiser.

Setting out towards the lodge, they were escorted by a herd of springing Thompsons Gazelles. Further on, Alistair was sure he heard the rumbling stomachs of two elephants, massive boulders on four legs, as they pulled a small tree to pieces. A confusion of Guineafowl scrabbled about with their comical helmets in the sparse grass along the roadside. Impala and hundreds of zebra seemed to welcome them with their strange laughing sounds as they arrived at their destination.

The lodge was an impressive stone building. Cool verandas wider than tennis courts were punctuated by impressive columns.

At the front entrance, a young, energetic looking couple came out to meet them. Chulu and James carried the bags.

The Earl marched towards the couple like he owned the place. The man met The Earl's enthusiasm and extended his hand.

"Good Morning, Lord Godolphin. Welcome to Risasi Nzuri lodge. My name is Rory, and this is my wife, Ursula. We are your hosts and want to make your stay as comfortable and as enjoyable as possible." They gave a little bow in unison. Rory had a strong Afrikaans accent.

"Good Morning, Rory, Ursula. The pleasure is mine, I am sure. This is my man, James."

Alistair nodded, feeling a bit strange. He was shown The Earl's rooms where he was left to unpack the distinguished collection of The Earl's luggage.

The suite had wonderfully high ceilings and massive French doors that opened onto the veranda. A stack of wood stood in a stone fireplace, ready for the evening fire. Trophies adorned the walls. Heads of magnificent animals with huge horns and tusks glared down at Alistair. On one wall was a collection of black and white photos depicting tough-looking men, dressed in old-fashioned safari gear, holding rifles and standing next to the beasts they had slain.

An attendant disrupted Alistair's self-guided tour and escorted him to the 'Guide Quarters' in a decidedly less salubrious part of the compound. He was shown to his own small room and given a key. He felt a bit like a sprog back at prep school. Alistair found his way to the staff area for breakfast and served himself from large pots on the stove. Ugali, eggs and Chai tea.

"Excuse me, laddie, please can I also have some toast and butter. A morning's not a morning without Marmite." a smiling Alistair asked the young cook in a thick Scots accent.

The cook smiled knowingly and made him several thick pieces of toast from the bread that had come out of the oven that morning.

The staff came from many tribes with different languages, but their common one was Swahili and they talked freely. From his years in a Kenyan Prep school Alistair was fluent in Swahili, so he could listen in while the staff assumed he was a soldier from Scotland who only spoke English.

Meanwhile, The Earl was being served the full Monty on the verandah: Eggs Benedict, fresh fruit, croissants and lovely coffee. After breakfast he requested a game drive, not to hunt, just to soak up Africa—and to talk to Alistair.

Rory organized the safari car. Chulu was their driver, and they had a bushman tracker Rory called 'Henry'. Rory said Henry's actual name was "too bloody complicated" so they called him Henry instead. Rory seemed to find this very funny. 'Henry', perched on a specially designed seat attached to the front of the vehicle, would read the animal tracks as they drove along.

Alistair and The Earl sat in the back row of seats so they could talk in private. The staff busied about, loading the vehicle with provisions for a full day including wicker baskets, a cooler, and canvas safari chairs.

As they sat waiting, a figure appeared at the entrance. A massive man stood there with his feet apart, like a statue of Cesar. Above polished boots and long socks, his calf muscles bulged like those of an international rugby player. He wore khaki shorts below a safari jacket, fastened with a wide leather Sam Brown belt. On his hip was a Webley .445 revolver. Sleeves rolled up, he crossed his massive forearms and fists over his barrel chest.

His face was weathered and battered, and wore a black patch over his left eye. Standing there, he looked like he was ready to stop a charging lion and pull it apart with his huge hands. If this man had any fears, he had conquered them long ago, beaten the shit out of them, and left them bleeding in the dirt.

Alistair shivered at the sight of him. He was pretty sure the last time he'd seen this man it was through the sight of a Javelin missile. "Chulu, who is that?"

"That, Mr. James, is the boss. Piete Van Olenburgh."

"Bugger," said The Earl to Alistair under his breath, "he survived," and began polishing his glasses nonchalantly.

"Carry on Chulu, thank you."

Below the sound of the engine, Alistair reflected on the man they'd just seen. "Bloody hell, not a scratch on him by the look of it. Not sure if I'm going to arm wrestle with him. He looks like he just fought a Cape Buffalo and had it for breakfast."

"Do you think he'll recognize you, A—" The Earl hesitated, "James?"

"Not with these whiskers, m'lord. Seriously though, he saw me from a fast-moving helicopter, under fire, at night and I was wearing helmet and goggles."

After an hour, they stopped under an acacia tree with a perfect view out across the plains.

The Earl turned out to know a great deal about animal behavior, enough to impress their trackers, Henry and Chulu.

The four of them spent a very happy morning discussing what the vast herds of animals were doing and why: it was a soap opera on hooves. The Earl had them in peals of laughter with his very ribald description of a male impala attempting to seduce the females.

Alistair could see he had been a great commanding officer.

They watched a cheetah explode from behind a clump of grass, missing a Thompsons gazelle by a micro-second.

Alistair and The Earl slipped questions into the conversation with Chulu and Henry. *What was it was like to work at the lodge? How long they had worked there? Where were they from? Did they see their families often? Etc.*

The Earl was an expert at mining for information without appearing to. At first, the two were very reticent, not used to talking about themselves, but they soon opened up. After the picnic, Henry even told them his actual name, which Alistair could pronounce, but The Earl struggled.

"Chulu, what kind of guests do they have here?" The Earl continued.

"Very important ones, like you, Sir."

"Can you remember their names? I might know a few."

"We must never speak the names of our guests, Sir."

"What happens if you do Chulu?"

"Sir, we cannot. My cousin, who worked here, spoke the name of a guest when he drank too much beer one night in a bar in Arusha. He made jokes about that person being a very bad shot. Then, one day, he was gone."

"What do you mean by 'gone', Chulu?"

"He and his family disappeared from the staff quarters one night. Everything disappeared that belonged to him. Sir, we are very afraid."

By the time they headed back to the lodge in the late afternoon,

Alistair and The Earl had a pretty good picture of what was going on.

38

Old Friends

As they passed the airstrip on the way back to the lodge, Alistair nudged The Earl. It had filled up. They counted at least twelve small jets and planes parked on the taxiway. At the lodge, newcomers filled the wicker seats on the verandahs, and dozens of people were at the bar and milling about the lounge area.

They went off and got changed. Walking towards The Earl's room, they noticed an armed escort waiting outside the door. Inside the room they stayed in character, Alistair dutifully helping The Earl with his dinner jacket and tie, realizing there may be hidden cameras and microphones. Alistair was wearing a Gordon Highlanders kilt, white shirt, tie, and a tweed jacket. In his sock he had tucked his Sgian Dubh knife. Charlie had decided this was the appropriate costume for a batman from a Scots regiment.

Misha had sent them tiny cameras that they could hide in their clothes. The cameras would film everything and burst encrypted uploads using the satellite phone in their pockets, or in Alistair's case, his sporran.

The Earl swept into the middle of the throng of people with the air of a man befitting his position. From the greetings and the vigorous handshakes, clearly The Earl already knew half the people there.

Alistair, however, would have been much happier back in the desert, with a rifle in his lap and a mug of tea in his hand. The collar of his shirt stuck into his neck and his ribs were killing him as they knotted themselves back together. Apart from the staff, he surmised he was by far the youngest person there.

But, standing across the room, he saw the toned and tanned shoulders of a young woman in an open backed, black silk dress. She had caramel hair that she kept pushing up with her hand so that it was sticking out in all directions. In her other hand, she held the fire poker, and she was jabbing the fire angrily so that it made little fireworks of sparks. It was clear she was not at all happy to be there. Although her back was turned to the room, Alistair felt a twinge of familiarity.

She turned around and glared at the room in fury. Alistair recognized her immediately, and felt a tremendous surge of relief and happiness. Sandy Kelly looked devastatingly beautiful.

As she renewed her attack on the fire, Alistair walked up behind her and said into her ear in a thick Scots accent, "Would madam be needin' some towels?"

She spun around and looked like she might bash him with the poker. Then, recognizing him, she suppressed a grin. She made sure no one was listening and, noting his whiskers, said between her teeth, "And who might you be today, some agricultural version of 'The Highlander'?"

Alistair held out his hand. "James, James Morgan. I am The Earl's batman," he said, indicating The Earl, who was talking animatedly to a German Duchess.

She put her fingers up to her mouth in an attempt to stop the Champagne coming out.

"Show me your wings, Batman."

Alistair explained the meaning of an officer's batman, but she wasn't having it.

"Last time I saw you, you were flying off the back of a ship, carrying an injured, old black man."

"As you know, that was actually my grandfather. Would you mind if we stepped out on the veranda for a minute?"

The air outside was cool, and they could smell the wood smoke from the fires being lit.

She looked at him. "What happened to you? I never heard from you again."

"I'm sorry, Sandy, things just went crazier from there."

"Crazier than dragging an Admiral and a CIA man bleeding into your room then finding your towel steward dressed in combat gear who then shoots his way out and disappears in a helicopter, leaving a pile of broken furniture?"

"Yes, well, as you put it like that, it does sound rather mad. I apologize. Are you OK?"

"I'm eighteen now," she said, as if she had been waiting to tell him. She looked into Alistair's pale blue eyes.

"Which means in Texas you can buy a gun, but not a beer?" Alistair took a sip of his beer.

She chuckled.

"Well, actually I did." She pulled her dress aside, which was slit up one side to the top of her thigh, revealing a long, very athletic leg and a few millimeters of delicate black lace at the top. Strapped to her leg was a small Walter PPK pistol.

Alistair leaned against a column to steady himself. She knew exactly what effect she was having on him, and she giggled with delight.

"You OK there, batman?" she said in a manly voice, slapping a reassuring hand on his shoulder. "Sooo, James Morgan, what do you have under *your* kilt?"

"Um, actually I'm not armed."

"Really, or maybe disarmed?" She looked out across the dark

savannah. "What it means is, now that I'm eighteen, I can finally get away from my parents. You know they adopted me from Bosnia. For years they used me as a sort of unpaid maid. I think I was a trophy to put on the wall. They paid $45,000 for me."

"Wow, they got a bargain," Alistair blurted out.

She squeezed his hand and kissed him on the cheek.

"You are adorable, despite your facial hair! Nobody else knows that story."

"I guess this means you can legally breed ponies on Dartmoor?"

"You remembered, and I found the perfect farm so we don't have to live with my grandmother."

"So, Sandy, what *are* you doing here?"

"My 'parents' tricked me. They said we were going on holiday in Madagascar but we had a short layover in Tanzania."

"When we landed here, I realized what they were up to. It's The Last Club's annual auction tomorrow. That's why I am so furious. It's so despicable."

"What is The Last Club Auction?"

"The Last Club Auction is Van Olenburgh's filthy show, which he spends the entire year preparing for. Tomorrow he bids out the hunting of the last remaining animals of select species that are going extinct. The fewer the number of surviving animals, the higher the bidding. Last year the highest bid went to the last remaining male Northern White Rhino, it was $27 million. My 'parents' shot some obscure goat in the Himalayas: its head is now sticking out of the wall above the fireplace at home. It cost more than me. So what are YOU doing here? Last time I heard you were trying to save animals?" She didn't wait for an answer. Alistair could tell she was furious.

"As soon as you win your bid you rush off, get into a jet and go and shoot it, then you bring back the body and they have a huge, bloody party.

"They even put some animals on the spit to roast. They start with the cheaper, more abundant animals. This year they're starting with four Grevy's Zebras and then they'll work their way up to the ones closest to extinction. The last animal is always a surprise.

"Everyone gets an encrypted iPad, and they stream each kill online. There is a prize of a week's free hunting here for the best shot of the auction.

"Wait. I know why you're here. There's talk about a member of the British aristocracy on the list of 'an almost extinct species of the human race.'

"So—you are here to stop this madness." Her voice was hard and desperate.

39

The Game's Up

Alistair and The Earl had both learnt about The Last Auction happening the next day and had come to the same conclusion—their cover had been blown. The Earl was a quarry. They were under guard. They went for a walk in the garden to talk to their team and decide what to do. Their escort watched them from the veranda.

"Damn it, our cover is blown. How the blazes do they know what I do?" The Earl put his hand to his ear.

Misha responded from California. "It's Sebastian, your pilot. Pascale, the co-pilot just called from Arusha. Sebastian just took off from Arusha without her. She said a man came with a briefcase, Sebastian took the case and then took off stranding her there. Don't worry—he won't get far. They probably knew you worked for INTERPOL the moment you landed in Arusha. The key thing is to pretend you don't know your cover has been blown or they will lock you up."

"Bugger him. I'll wring his bloody neck. He came from the RAF. I thought I could trust him."

"We don't think he knows much about your actual operations but he seems to have been reporting your movements."

"Gentlemen, we suggest you slip quietly away tonight, pretend you are looking forward to the auction tomorrow." Dr. KV was looking at a map. "Go due North and you will eventually hit the Mara River. Follow that West until you get to the Maasai Mara.

"You should be aware that at 0700 GMT, which would be 1000 tomorrow in Tanzania, we are going to release the press pack. All hell will break loose. It includes Footage of high-ranking government officials shooting rhinos; scenes of rhino horns being cut away with chainsaws; labels naming each criminal and his or her position; film of the horns being planted inside the hideous dolls; a step-by-step description of rhino horns being transported to California in the arms of retirees on the Unicorn Cruise ships. Every person who has smuggled a doll; how much they got paid and their addresses, are listed. You need to leave as soon as you can."

"Damn it, we need to nail Van Olenburgh." The Earl was furious.

"No way to get him now. He must have thirty armed men around him. If we could get him alone, we could do it." It surprised Alistair to find himself in the voice of restrained action.

They returned to the party. The Earl did an excellent impression of drinking large quantities and getting squiffy.

Alistair had the hard task of telling Sandy that, once again, it would be much safer if she didn't come with him.

He actually could think of nothing better in the universe than running away with her into the African bush. But he realized that to take her with him would put her in danger that she didn't need to be in.

He explained this to her, but she was livid. He asked her if she would help them by stealing one iPad that they were using to live stream the kills. If she could get one, he was sure Misha could hack into it and it would be the window into the Last Club.

"Listen, when I was putting The Earl's kit in his room, I noticed a ladder. It looked like it went up to an attic. Could you go up there and monitor the iPad? You could also communicate with our team using this?" He handed her a secure satellite phone.

"You mean, I could get my so-called parents arrested in the act of shooting some poor, almost extinct creature? And hunting down The Earl? Oh God."

"That's part of the idea."

"I like it. But you aren't really giving me a choice here. You go off and have your boys' adventure."

"Thanks Sandy, you are a truly amazing woman."

"I get the 'woman' title now I am eighteen? Good. I like it. I was tired of being a girl in a woman's body." She gave a twirl. She was definitely a woman, Alistair thought to himself.

"But here is the deal: when this mess is over, we get to know each other?"

"I promise, I really do. Time will go fast."

"Well, don't go getting killed."

"You too."

40

The Hunt Begins

The Earl was carried to his room at 11:00 p.m. by his faithful batman, James, in a 'drunken stupor.' Alistair wanted to make sure they implicated none of the African staff in their escape. That had turned out to be easy, as they were all busy with the party or preparing for tomorrow's big day.

With their escort fast asleep in a chair outside the door, Alistair snuck out to the safari vehicle compound via the verandah. The ruse had worked well. Nobody expected The Earl to be moving for a very long time.

It turned out that they would hold several trophy competitions on the ranch. He found eleven Land Cruisers fully loaded with supplies for three-day safari hunts, and he took the keys of one of those nearest the exit from a row of hooks on the wall. He then collected the keys for the rest of the vehicles and dumped them into the staff long-drop. Next, he strode to the kitchen, got a jug of water and poured the contents into the fuel tank of each of the remaining Land Cruisers, a trick French resistance fighters used to incapacitate Nazi vehicles. It wouldn't have an immediate effect, which was even better.

The party was still going strong. Music and lights filtered onto the lawns. Alistair casually strode past windows and darted through the shadows with supplies. He loaded up his chosen vehicle with their two shotguns, Dr. KV's pelican case, as many cans of food that he could find, several gallons of water, and a water filter. He found a machete, axe, shovels and a sizable piece of green canvas. Then he added several jerry cans of diesel.

He raced back to his tiny room and stuffed his bed with pillows. He and The Earl did the same in the suite and, together, crept out to the car.

The Earl had replaced his dinner jacket with a well-worn suede safari jacket that looked like it had seen some action. The right shoulder pad was polished from repeated firing. He wore boots that were laced halfway up his calf and a very battered Akubra hat with a Maasai bead band.

Alistair hadn't had time to change. He threw a heavy cotton shirt in the car and had put on his brown Israeli defense force boots. For his head, he just had his khaki shemagh. He still had his kilt on, which he enjoyed wearing.

Alistair carried an iPad for navigating, which he tethered to a GPS, but they also found a collection of good old maps and an old British army prism compass. The Earl was much happier reading those.

The car compound was on a slight hill so they rolled silently into the night without disturbing the Askari watchmen who were stationed near the lodge.

Alistair had wanted to destroy the planes, but knowing they were well-guarded, they left them.

"Pity, I've rather got hooked on blasting planes to pieces."

They felt confident as they headed out into the bush. Alistair missed the quiet electric motors of the Pink Panther.

They stuck to the existing track as long as they could. These were already well crisscrossed with Land Cruiser tires, and thus made their direction hard to follow. Alistair had his night sights with him. This had the unexpected effect of confusing the animals, who had grown used to the combination of engine noise and headlights. Several times he had to swerve around bewildered antelopes standing in the track.

Dawn broke. The lodge woke up slowly, with many guests nursing mighty hangovers. Though normal breakfasts at hunting lodges were predawn, at 9:50 a.m. most were feasting on eggs and bacon, and there were a few jokes at the expense of The Earl and his inability to absorb alcohol.

At 10:00 a.m. Tanzania time, The Extinct Company sent out 500 emails across the world, spreading information so inflammatory that it would cause governments to collapse, corporations to disappear, and many years of trials and imprisonments.

By 10.30 a.m., CNN was running the story, including a segment about 'The Last Club Auction.'

Sandy, who was looking at the news on her phone, took the unconventional step of wheeling into the dining room and switching on the huge TV that was normally used for the lodge's live streamed hunts. She flicked the channel to CNN.

At first, people were confused and thought it was a joke. They saw bouncy images of themselves the night before, talking about how they wanted to 'take out' the last Forest Elephant or be the person whose made the rhinos extinct. They were clearly drunk, and the images were sickening. But the CNN logo didn't go away.

People were getting angry and asking where the Van Olenburgh was.

He appeared in the doorway with the sun behind him, feet apart. He had a pump shotgun in one massive fist—it looked like a toy. In the other hand, he held a huge wooden staff with a carved lion's head at the top.

"This is the work of The Earl of Godolphin. It is he who has betrayed you. He wants to take over our First Nation, he wants to destroy its founder and father. You will never be safe while he lives. He must be DESTROYED."

One guest, dressed in a corduroy jacket and lizard skin cowboy boots said, in a rather timid voice, "Actually Van Olenburgh, Maisie and I have decided its time we went home."

Several other people nodded their agreement and said, "Yes, we have too."

Van Olenburgh slammed his wooden staff against the slate floor, and the noise reverberated around the room.

"ENOUGH." His voice silenced the room instantly. "You came here for a hunt, and I have one for you. A rare species on the brink of extinction. A member of the British Aristocracy. It is he who brought this down on you; it is he who has exposed you. Now hunt him and his Scots batman down. I want them back here, dead or alive. You are not to go after any other quarry. They are your only target."

A very large bald man wearing a voluminous safari jacket stood up. Breathing heavily, he said in a Texas accent, "I'm sorry Van Olenburgh, but we'd rather go home. We have lawyers who can sort this out." He looked to the others for support.

It was Sandy's 'father'. She was trying to be inconspicuous behind the fruit salad bar.

"Mr. Kelly, you misunderstand me. I am not asking you, I am ordering you. You cannot leave until one of you gets that filthy English Earl and his batman."

To his credit, Mr. Kelly pulled out his stag horn handled Colt.45 pistol, the very one that used to belong to General Patton. He pointed it at the Van Olenburgh. His hand was shaking. "You can't stop us."

The Van Olenburgh laughed, his great chest heaving with mirth. Around several of the columns guards appeared, dressed in black fatigues. They cocked their weapons and aimed them at Mr. Kelly. His wife started sobbing.

"Your planes are under armed guard, the perimeters of the ranch are patrolled and guarded, and anyone attempting to cross it will be shot."

"The faster you bring me The Earl, the faster you can go home to your slobbering lawyers. Rory here will collect your phones. Do not try to keep one—I will find it. You will use your iPads to communicate with us here. We will know where you are and what you are doing. Rory, get the staff to bring the cars to the front. Enjoy the hunt." With that, he turned on his heels and marched out, laughing as he left.

Five minutes later, a terrified Chulu came running up to the Van Olenburgh. "Boss, all the keys are gone."

Van Olenburgh swore and then added, "Those are crafty blighters. Get the spares from my office, then check the cars, check the fuel tanks. Rory, get Kevin to take you up in the Piper Cub. Sit in the back with a rifle."

"Wait,—you just fitted GPS trackers to all the vehicles so we could find them if they got in trouble."

"Yes," Rory was grinning, "brand new and—" he tapped for a minute on his phone and held it up, "—here they are."

"OK, go, monitor them while these 'hunters' get ready. I want to film them in a manhunt. Don't shoot unless they are getting away."

Alistair and The Earl were over 50 kilometers from the lodge.

Rory and Kevin ran over to the hanger where the Piper was stored, Rory grabbing a Lee Enfield Rifle on the way. This one was designed for tank crews with a short barrel, perfect for the Piper Cub where the passenger sat behind the pilot. There were no doors or windows, so he could shoot either side.

The little yellow plane popped up off the runway and began chasing the flashing dot on Rory's phone.

Meanwhile, the staff had found the water in the fuel tanks and were busy flushing them out, while Van Olenburgh stood in the middle of the workshop, bellowing at them to work faster.

41

Moonshot

Alistair and The Earl were still feeling pretty confident. They were very near to the Mara River and there was no sign of anyone in pursuit. As they neared a muddy water hole, they saw a group of highly agitated elephants.

Alistair turned and approached cautiously, hoping he wouldn't find an elephant that had been shot. But what he saw was a young calf stuck deep in a mud hole. The mother was too big to get in and push the baby out, and the sides were too steep and wet for the baby to climb out by itself. She looked exhausted.

The mother heard their vehicle, turned and looked at them. It was a look of panic and pleading. Alistair had never seen an animal so plainly begging for help.

The Earl knew what Alistair was thinking.

"Alistair, we cannot stop. If we stop and try to help, they will catch up with us. Think of all the animals we will save by escaping."

Alistair turned the engine off.

"Paloma would never forgive me if I left a baby elephant to die in a mudhole."

Then they heard the distinct sound of a plane. They stood still, hoping their ears were deceiving them, but the roar of the plane's engine got louder—it was heading their way.

"Quick, get the car under that Acacia and let's run up the kopje. If they are armed, the first thing they will do is shoot up the car and we don't want to be in it."

For now, at least, the elephant was forgotten. Alistair positioned the car under the umbrella of the tree as best he could and, together, they threw the dirty canvas tarp over the top. It was actually pretty well camouflaged. They grabbed their gun cases and some water and raced up the kopje, which was strewn with enormous boulders, offering the perfect hiding place. They tucked themselves into a deep crevasse near the top.

The plane was flying in a dead straight line towards the car at a low level. It was so close they could see the silhouettes of two figures in the cockpit against the sky.

"Let's see what Dr. Kitts-Vincent has got in here." The Earl opened up the Pelican case, revealing the Purdey silencer, cleaning kit, and several boxes of .378 ammo. "Tracer, dumdum, standard, and, yes, armor-piercing. Perfect." He handed the rifle to Alistair with the box of armor-piercing rounds.

Meanwhile, the plane had looped around and was doing a low pass. The shape of a stubby Lee Enfield was sticking out one side. Swooping close, the passenger fired, and the bullet disappeared into canvas with no apparent effect.

"They are going to stick around until the rest arrive. We need to get rid of them." The Earl pointed at the rifle in Alistair's hand.

Alistair pushed an armored piercing round into the breech.

"You need to get him to fly right at us so you can send a round straight into his engine block. It's the only way we can stop them."

"OK, so let's give them a wave?"

The plane was just coming around in a loop. It was almost level with them on their kopje. The Earl ran out from his hiding place and started waving both arms at the plane as it whipped passed them. "Come on, you silly blighters! Come and play!"

They didn't notice him.

"Bugger, we are both dressed in clothes they can't see. We need something that stands out."

The plane was doing another lazy loop, searching for the passengers of the car.

"Alistair, my boy, you need to do something for Queen and Country." The Earl had a wicked grin on his face. "Are you traditionally attired under your kilt?"

"Oh no—I am not doing *that*."

"How many men could claim to have shot down an aeroplane by mooning it?"

"OK. I'll do it. But I hold you responsible if I get shot in the arse. Hand me the rifle as soon as they see me."

As the plane continued its loop, Alistair ran out onto a big flat rock, turned his back on them and gave them the traditional highland war greeting by lifting his kilt and bending over.

"Feast yer eyes on that, yeh wee Rock Spiders!"

He could hear The Earl hooting with laughter.

The plane changed direction and headed directly towards them.

Alistair grabbed the rifle from The Earl, spun around and went down on one knee. The plane was coming straight at him; so straight that Rory could no longer see Alistair. The Purdey kicked like a mule and the plane disappeared over their heads and the top of the kopje.

They ran out to watch it start another arc.

"Wait for it...Wait for it..."

There was a loud bang, and the noise of the engine simply stopped. The propellor bounced to a halt and black smoke poured from the front of the aircraft as it immediately started to lose altitude.

They watched the plane as it glided, silently belching black smoke as it went down in the distant path of the Mara River.

Finally, it hit the water with an almighty splash, rolling and falling apart, yellow fragments bobbing. The river was running fast. Two heads popped briefly above the brown wash, arms flailing.

"Nasty... a lot of crocs in there."

"Yup, lots of crocs."

The Earl smiled and nodded his head at Alistair in a silent 'good job'.

"You've done that before, haven't you, Sir?"

"Aye, laddie, but not with the kilt lifting part. That will go down in history."

"That plane was headed straight for our car, like it was being guided by a wire." Alistair reloaded the rifle and flicked on the safety.

"Or —a GPS tracker?"

They hurried back to the Land Cruiser and started searching. Alistair found it in the engine compartment. It was held into place by powerful magnets on each side of the car body. He pried them off with his knife and was about to smash the tracker with a rock—

"Wait, don't do that. If we can attach it to something else that moves, it will lead them away from us."

"Alright, you go and catch a vulture and I will wait here."

"Well, that's not such a bad idea. We need an animal that will move long distances."

"You mean like a baby elephant that has just escaped from a mud hole?"

"Alistair! You, Sir, are brilliant. Let's go and rescue an elephant. Paloma will be proud of you."

They drove carefully towards the still-bellowing elephants and reversed the car close to the hole. The rest of the herd moved away, but the mother hung right beside the car, not letting her calf out of her sights. Just feeling the presence of such a massive, ancient beast was humbling. Alistair could see the hairs on her cracked muddy skin and hear her stomach.

"She knows what we are doing. She won't hurt us. I suspect this has happened before in her life." The Earl said, sensing Alistair was nervous.

They grabbed some tow straps and The Earl started talking to the baby in soft tones. Alistair had never seen this side of him but then he remembered that The Earl had dedicated his life to saving animals.

Alistair took one look at the deep, muddy, pit and shook his head. "Twice in a day." He took off his kilt and jumped in.

He heard The Earl chortling, startling the elephant.

He fashioned a harness around the backside of the baby. The poor thing was so exhausted that she hardly moved and let Alistair do whatever he needed to. Once he had got it in place, he called up. "Pass me the tracker, please. I'll stick it on her ear using the magnets, one on each side. She won't feel it."

"OK, ready." Alistair put his arms around the back end of the beast to keep the straps in place. He could feel her breathing with his hands.

The Earl put the Land Cruiser in low range and eased forward. The baby seemed to realize what was happening and as she rose up the steep bank; she began using her legs. Finally, they got high enough for her to get some purchase on the bank. The mother put her trunk around the back of the baby and pulled too. Alistair could feel the soft tip against his arm.

Once they all got onto the top, Alistair pulled the straps away from the baby. The mother touched Alistair's face with the tip of her trunk and then lay it on the back of her baby, and they walked off.

Tears were streaming down Alistair's muddy face, making tracks. He put his kilt back on and they set off.

42

Poaching the Poachers

"Do you remember what you said when we first met?"

"I do. We need to become poachers of poachers. We need to make them extinct."

"I believe we need to start hunting now, Alistair."

"I agree. Let's head back to the lodge and put a stop to that awful man. My guess is that everyone will be out hunting us. Coming back to the lodge will be the last thing Van Olenburgh will expect." Alistair slotted the Land Cruiser into gear.

Back at the lodge, Sandy had stolen one of the encrypted iPads and had been working with Misha. Now the team could watch the hunt being live streamed. She was hiding in the lodge's attic, burrowed in amongst trunks of old safari kit, clothes, photo albums, and press clippings with a basket of buffet food, and two bottles of champagne. Despite the seriousness of the situation, she felt like she was finally free. Her parents had gone 'hunting' at gunpoint, which pleased her immensely. She was a critical element of the team, relaying information and giving Misha and Dr. KV direct access through the iPad.

Eyes glued to the screen, The Extinct Company watched the hunt for Alistair and The Earl unfold.

Ten Land Cruisers, filled with some very rich and very influential people, armed with the most expensive hunting rifles money could buy, were reluctantly following two men whom they needed to either capture or kill. It was hot; it was dusty; and the blinking target on their iPads was moving in very peculiar ways for a vehicle.

'Henry', the tracker who had always been so brilliant before, seemed unable to pick up the tracks of the prey—the men— they were after. He tried to explain to the group.

"Actually, this is very strange. Even me, I am confused. If they are in a vehicle they are moving very slowly. If they are walking they are moving very fast. And for the first time I cannot see any tracks."

The armed guards, hailing from highly organized military back-grounds, by the looks on their faces, resented having become million-aires' babysitters with no structure, no plan and no leader. One guard pulled 'Henry' roughly out of the car, stuck a pistol in his belly and told him what to do.

"Look, you little moron, they have a GPS tracker. Just bloody follow that. Forget trying to find the spoor."

Tempers were fraying. Amongst the hunters there were many people who were used to being in command, and none of them had any genuine experience of surviving in the harsh environment of the African bush.

The sun was lighting up the underside of the few clouds in sky and turning them deep orange.

Within half an hour it would be pitch black—the time the real predators started their bloody work.

Back in Panama, they were enjoying the reality show.

"Pretty soon, all those very wealthy people are going to find out what the law of the jungle really means and no lawyer in the world will be there to help them,"

Paloma said to the team who were sitting around the screens drinking tea.

From the information they gleaned from their own GPS and the live streaming of the hunters, Alistair and The Earl now knew exactly where the people hunting them were, and simply gave them a wide birth and headed back to Risasi Nzuri Lodge.

Alistair stopped a suitable distance away. Through binoculars, he scanned the savanna and saw the staff on foot, without uniforms and with bundles on their heads. They looked like wartime refugees. They were making a run for it.

"No movement at the lodge that I can see. But let's do a recce." They retrieved their weapons and loaded small backpacks of equipment.

The small kopje they'd seen when they had arrived provided perfect cover. It overlooked the lodge and river. They carefully made their way towards it. On the way, they had to skirt around a *boma*, an enclosure made of thorns.

"Wait—lion." The Earl had remarkable hearing. They froze.

The last thing they wanted to do was to tackle a charging lion.

By standing still, Alistair could now hear the grunts and growls coming in quick surges. "There are two. Adult males together. That is strange," The Earl whispered.

He put a pair of fat-nosed bullets into the breach of the Purdey. "Insurance. I'm going to look."

He came striding back seconds later, shaking his head, and motioned for Alistair to enter the boma.

Inside were two pickups, and in the back of each were very heavy-duty looking cages with solid sliding doors. Pacing angrily within were two magnificent male lions. They glared at Alistair and The Earl with such hatred and ferocity it made them shiver.

"What on earth are they doing in there?"

"This, my boy, is the soft underbelly of big game hunting: known as *Canned Hunting*. Not all wealthy clients want to spend their days exposing themselves to danger and getting sweaty by tromping round the bush looking for lions.

So, the lodge stages a 'hunting experience'. The lodge driver will park one of these pickups behind a suitable rock. The 'tracker' pretends to spot 'fresh spoor *bwana*, quick, big male lion.'

The cage is opened and suddenly the client has a mature male lion to shoot, with of course two back up Big Game Hunters in case the client misses in the excitement of the moment and they need to 'finish-him-off.'"

"Are you serious?"

"Fairly common practice, I am afraid. In fact, sometimes they even give the lions a mild sedative to ensure a slower moving target."

"But, but that's not cricket!"

"Exactly, but to be honest with you, the people who pay to do something like that probably have no idea what cricket is. These animals were probably for today's hunt but now the staff have gone, there's no one to feed them."

The Earl was pouring water from a jerrycan into the animals' empty bowls through the bars and talking to them like they were domestic cats on his living room carpet. The lions noisily lapped up the water and stopped snarling.

"Let's let them out."

"Not on your Nelly. Sorry Alistair, but I doubt you have seen a caged lion charge. And these chaps are angry and hungry. We'll see to them later. They'll be fine."

Alistair reluctantly followed The Earl, crouch-walking towards the kopje.

They scrambled up the enormous stones and tucked themselves under a deep overhanging rock, near the top of the pile of boulders. There was a small whistling thorn bush in front of the entrance, which hid them perfectly. The floor was flat, sandy and covered in droppings. "Thompsons Gazelle," The Earl said, inspecting one between his finger and thumb.

They were a good 500 meters from the lodge, and even in the fading light they had a view of the driveway and most of one side of the principal building, including the entrance.

They called Misha on their encrypted phone and gave her a situation report. She told them she was talking to Sandy, who was hidden in the attic. Sandy peeked out of the dusty dormer windows at the top of the building toward the kopje. Alistair, from his position, scanned the attic windows and could see nothing except for an old 'widow's walk' and noted that, if she needed to, she could exit by the flat part of the roof.

Misha told them that their press release was making waves across the world and had galvanized forces. There had already been high-profile arrests by INTERPOL. Footage of several well-known politicians were breaking the internet, exhibiting them in handcuffs and through police car windows. They had also raided the spas and the lab.

From tracking the 'hunters', and their armed escorts, and from Sandy's reporting, Misha told them she calculated there were six armed guards left at the lodge. Clearly the guards had one job: to protect the Van Olenburgh. From the cameras inside the lodge which Misha now had control of, she and Dr. KV had identified the guards. They were all on the INTERPOL wanted list. She didn't, however, know where the pilots for the client's planes were.

According to the live stream, all the African trackers and guides had 'disappeared' from the hunting vehicles so now it was just the guards and their charges. It looked like they were completely lost and appeared to be driving around in random circles. One hunter, Mr. Goldberger, had stomped off in a temper, probably not realizing what the darkness would bring.

Alistair and The Earl were chuckling through this last description.

"So, what will be the P of A?" Misha said, pleased with her new phrase.

"Silently remove the guards and then get the Van Olenburgh?"

Alistair offered.

"Love it."

"Misha, please tell Sandy to stay where she is and not come out until we get her."

The Earl grinned at Alistair. "I've been behind a desk too long," he said, patting his belly. "This is the most fun I've had in a decade. Now, let's decide on our game plan." He drew a plan of the lodge in the sand and then used the Tommy droppings as the guards. "This," he broke off a whistling thorn and stuck it into a piece of dung, "is Van Olenburgh."

"So, they posted four guards at each corner, two spares inside. They don't seem to walk around much, which is good."

"Yes, but I'm worried that even if we shoot one of them with the silenced rifle, he might cry out before he goes down. This will alert the other guards and Van Olenburgh our goal is to take out the Van Olenburgh, and he may make a run for it if he hears us before we reach him."

"Looks like we have to do it the old-fashioned way then." Alistair drew his finger across his throat.

The Earl nodded.

Alistair descended the kopje and crept forward towards the nearest guard, who was standing with one leg propped up on a flower bed wall. He was running his palm across his unshaven face.

The Earl was covering with the silenced Purdey as Alistair maneuvered quietly along the building wall behind the guard. Alistair kept his eyes on the unkempt hairs on the guard's neck and slipped his Sgian Dubh into his hand.

The guard straightened up and spat into the flower bed. Alistair used the moment to step forward, put his left hand over the guard's mouth, and pull his head back. He drew his knife across the man's exposed throat.

Alistair put both his arms around him and lowered him to the ground as the guard silently thrashed and gurgled. Alistair pushed him into the dust covered bougainvillea bed, speckling the purple leaves with bright red blood.

The Earl joined him and pointed to the corner where the next guard stood watching. They moved forward along the wall of the building, keeping ten meters between them.

"Karl, have you got a light, mate?"

The other guard was walking in a wide arc back to where the now very dead Karl was lying.

He had an unlit cigarette in his fingers. Alistair and The Earl tried to sink slowly down behind a low wall that surrounded the house. But they had stepped on gravel.

"Oy, who's there?" the guard raised his MP5 and flicked on the flashlight attached to it.

Seeing the crouching figures, he opened fire immediately, spraying the side of the building with lead. They hunkered down behind the low garden wall, which was disintegrating around them. Just as the guard finished his magazine, The Earl popped up and put an armor piercing right through the center of his Kevlar jacket. As he fell, another guard appeared. The Earl was trying to load another round into the breech as the guard walked forward, weapon raised.

They were trapped.

Somebody turned on the floodlights, and it brought the entire scene into sharp relief, blinding the guard for a second.

A massive explosion went off above their heads and it threw the man backwards with such force it looked like an invisible bus had hit him.

He didn't get up.

Alistair and The Earl took the chance to run around the corner and into the side entrance of the building, grabbing the dropped MP5 as they went. They padded softly through the darkened, empty kitchens that looked like the staff had abandoned it halfway through cleaning up breakfast.

Coming from the main lounge were sounds of muffled audio and maniacal laughing. Working their way towards the noise, they heard footsteps.

"Lock all the doors. They are outside. They got Karl and Jan." The guard was talking on his radio, trying to work out who was left in his team as he walked unknowingly towards the enemy.

The Earl twisted the knob of a nearby door and slipped in, followed by Alistair. The tiny closet was full of boxes of tins. They waited thirty seconds.

"Let's even the odds a bit more, shall we?" The Earl said as he opened the door again and followed the receding steps.

The guard came through the kitchen door, closed it, and was turning around as The Earl's rifle issued a barely audible 'therwp'. The bullet drove the guard against the door and he slid down it in a bloody smear.

"Capital, these armor-piercing rounds."

"Three guards and the Colonel remaining."

As they grabbed the dead man's radio, they heard a second massive blast outside. From the window, they saw another guard sprawled out on the lawn.

"I think your friend Sandy has found herself a rifle, and it sounds to me like a 600 Nitro Express. The most powerful gun available to civilians. It can stop a charging bull elephant."

Alistair could not suppress a smile of pride. "She is going to have one hell of a sore shoulder."

They heard a door slam, a Land Cruiser start, and then it flashed by the window. They caught sight of two figures, both remaining guards, in the front seats, gunning it down the road.

Another tremendous crack came from the rooftop widow's walk, and the driver slumped forward into the steering wheel. The vehicle careened off the road and into a ditch, with the last guard sprinting off as fast as he could.

"Well, looks like we have an appointment."

They moved forward towards the lounge again. Muffled screaming, arguing, swearing, things being smashed and in one instance loud crunching, were issuing from a TV somewhere inside the room.

They crept forward to look. All the furniture had been dragged, thrown, and smashed to the peripheries. A castle of sandbags occupied the center of the room, like a child's playhouse. Gun slits all around. Flickers of light emanated from inside the castle. The Van Olenburgh had holed himself up with a big screen TV which was filled with the live streamed hunt for The Earl and his batman.

"I can see you, you miserable insects," and with that, the room filled with heavy machine gun fire. The walls, paintings, windows disintegrated around them. Alistair and The Earl dropped to the floor, rolling sideways into a hallway. They covered their heads as heavy rounds exploded in all directions. Bits of masonry and stone stung their faces as they crawled further down the hallway.

When the firing stopped, they heard the Van Olenburgh laughing again. "Come in and join me. I am having a drink, you filthy rooi nekkes!"

"Lovely. Such a charming chap. You realize he has a Vickers machine gun in there? And goodness knows what else." The Earl was shaking his head.

"How the dickens are we going to get the blighter out?"

"Perhaps something needs to jump in from a window, move at lighting speed, climb a twelve-foot sandbag wall and then leap down and tear him apart?"

The Earl turned around and looked at Alistair with complete admiration. "You really are a genius. Let's get the cats, poor things. They must be starving by now."

They crawled down the rest of the hallway, and they left by the kitchen door. As they walked around the building, they heard a light thump, someone jumping to the ground.

"Hello Chaps."

"Sandy, how did you...?"

"Fire escape." She had raided the trunks in the attic. Knee height lace up riding boots, full khaki pleated skirt, silk white shirt with a very narrow tie, khaki safari jacket complete with ammunition tucked into the pockets and wide brown leather belt with Webley Revolver in a holster, pith helmet with silk scarf wrapped around and a 600 Nitro Express rifle under her arm. She struck a pose, cocking her head to one side and her eyes blazing with adrenaline.

Alistair stared at her, "You look amazing. You are amazing. Thank you for saving our lives."

He was still filthy from the mud-hole, still wearing his kilt and carrying an MP5 machine gun.

"You don't look so bad yourself..."

"OK, Karen Blixen and Dennis Finch Hatton— if you don't mind, we have to feed the cats."

When they explained their plan, she was incredulous.

"So, you guys have a couple of lions tucked into cages just ready to leap into action, right?"

Nearing the boma, the lions roared, like two massive steam trains firing up.

"Shit, are you sure this is a good idea?" Sandy exclaimed.

"Trust us, we have no idea what we are doing." The Earl chuckled.

"We need you to entice a completely mad and heavily armed Van Olenburgh to fire his Vickers machine gun at 700 rounds per minute through what remains of the front door. Just don't get hit. You can hide behind the columns. In the meantime, we will reverse the pickups with the lion cages up to and through the veranda doors that lead to the lounge where the Van Olenburgh has barricaded himself."

"We will open the cages and release the hungry lions who, after getting a whiff of slightly rotten Van Olenburgh meat inside the sandbag fortress, will leap over the parapet. And—well—you know the rest."

"Someone has been poking them with a sharp stick all week. Van Olenburgh obviously wanted them furious when he released them."

"Once you've got him firing in the direction away from the lions, we suggest you go back up your fire escape and wait until the lions have decided to go back to the bush to digest their delicious supper."

Alistair was quite matter-of-fact.

"So, you think it is better that the Van Olenburgh fires his Vickers machine gun at me rather than the lions?"

"Correct," they both answered.

"OK, got it."

She got into the pickup with Alistair. Her smell filled the cab, and he lent across to her, reaching for her hand. The vehicle rocked as the lion moved inside his cage. He straightened up and started the car.

"You know, that weapon you have might actually go all the way through a sandbag."

"Thank you, Alistair. You always say the sweetest things. My sore shoulder supports that opinion," she said, stroking his cheekbone with the tips of her fingers.

They drove the pickups around to the veranda. Sandy jumped out, keeping close to the wall. Her shots would signal the other two to ram the veranda doors.

After waiting a few second for the pickups to get into position, Sandy leaned around the column by the front entrance and shouted, "Come out you yellow-bellied Rock Spider!" she punctuated her summons by firing one barrel of the Nitro express into the Van Olenburgh's barricade.

The bullet went straight through the sandbag as Alistair had predicted, but missed Van Olenburgh. Instead, it turned the screen in his hiding place into a thousand pieces of glass. He swung around in fury and the rapid exploding, *clang, clang, clang* of the Vickers filled the building. Everything around Sandy was raining down on top of her. She could hear Van Olenburgh shouting as he fired.

"Get out of my house, you miserable rooi nekkes!"

There was a slight pause, and Sandy poked her weapon around the riddled column and fired again and hissed, "You missed, you crazy bastard."

He opened fire again, but she heard the veranda doors at the back smashing open, and then the deep growl of a lion on the attack. The firing kept going for only a couple of seconds before the sound of grunts and moans, ripping and cracking, replaced it.

Sandy leapt back to the bottom of the fire escape, replacing the two cartridges as she did, and then pulled herself up onto the lower rungs.

Halfway up the ladder, the remains of the doors she had just fired through burst open and the pair of bloody-mouthed lions ran into the floodlights.

They hesitated, looked up at her, and then trotted into the darkness beyond.

Alistair and The Earl came running around the front. The Earl cautiously stepped through the doors and Alistair looked up at Sandy. She jumped down, and he walked across to her. She was shaking violently. Alistair took the rifle from her and put his arms around her.

"So, is this your real job?" she asked.

The Earl appeared. "Van Olenburgh is dead. Not too much left of him in one piece."

"I believe our work here is complete."

They walked down the drive.

"Let's go and get our car," The Earl said.

She put her wrists first through Alistair's, and then The Earl's arms and the three headed back to the Land Cruiser.

"I'm gasping for a cup of tea," Alistair said to the gradually dawning sky.

In the distance they heard the unmistakable whine of a turbocharged rally car. It was approaching very fast, displaying a massive rooster tail of dust. As it got closer, Alistair recognized his old Toyota Celica rally car.—his mate from school, Leboo, had arrived.

43

R&R

Misha had her waterproof laptop open on the worn wooden bar. Above were twenty hurricane lamps suspended from hooks in the sprawling acacia tree. A fire crackled beside the pool, throwing reflections in the water.

The Earl had come through on his promise of a team safari. The Extinct Company was at Harry's Island on Lake Baringo in Northern Kenya.

The island was thick with Acacia trees with twenty thatched bandas tucked around the rocky hill that rose out of the lake.

They each had their banda, with a well-appointed bathroom and deep, private verandah with sweeping views of the lake and the mountains beyond.

From the island they could watch the hippos happily bobbing under the water, giving out deep, contented grunts that sounded like slow motion chuckling.

Everyone had spent a very happy few days together. Charlie and Tatiana had found a very well equipped 'safari' boat, and they had been exploring the lake—water-skiing, drinking bloody Marys and having blowout picnics while fishing.

Alistair and Sandy had been taking long walks together. Sandy was passionate about the navigational aptitude of the dung beetle, insisting that they follow the beetles rolling their precious balls of dung for hours, with Alistair recording their journeys on his GPS. He was just happy to be near her. She told him dung beetles make bond pairs. Dartmoor pony breeding was also mentioned on several occasions.

The Admiral and Georgina Rowena were avid bird watchers and had spent many hours watching the fish eagles dive bombing fish and the weaver birds working on their nests.

Misha, it turned out, was a serious water-color painter, and she enthusiastically joined whoever was going somewhere that had painting potential. She also persuaded the staff to sit for her individually and charmed them by giving them their portraits once she had completed them.

The Earl and Deirdre hit it off immediately and engaged in a series of long poolside chess battles accompanied by large quantities of Champagne.

Paloma, Jeeves, and Dr. Kitts Vincent had been taken under the wing of Leboo, Alistair's Maasai friend from school. They went on long game walks in the surrounding hills and came back at the end of each day exhausted but full of tales of wildlife, ancient Maasai legends and medicinal plants.

Every evening they all gathered for sundowners on a cliff overlooking the lake and then returned to the bar for more drinks and supper around a vast table.

Right now, they were huddled around the laptop watching the BBC News. The images were of a very bedraggled group of people being led away for questioning. The newsreader was showing edited footage of the previous year's 'The Last Club Auction.'

"That's my adoptive dad," Sandy announced, as a very large man with a bloody face and without a shirt wobbled toward a waiting

Tanzanian Police Land Rover.

There were people with the words INTERPOL written in bold letters on their backs working with the police.

Misha shut the laptop, and The Earl cleared his throat.

"I understand that the government land that was 'bought' by Nation First has been reclaimed, the people involved in the sales are going to trial and the villagers are being returned to their homes.

"The land in Southern Africa has become a National Park.

"As you know, Taboga and her extended team including volunteers from Panama, and McDonnell are now helping The Engineer create an orphanage. They have plans for a school, boarding rooms, gardens, kitchens, medical center and mosque."

"Our team eliminated most of the people that carried out the massacres. The rest are now are in prison and will remain there."

"Hey, what happened to the dolls in our plane?" Paloma asked.

"You led us to the Kenyan Army Captain Githanga. It made little sense that he arrived at the scene so quickly—unless he knew what was going to happen beforehand so he could grab the dolls."

"He now is awaiting trial in Nairobi."

"The Nation First and their rhino horn operation have been eliminated. It is now extinct. The poachers have been poached."

He raised his glass, and the others followed

"The Extinct Company. Nobis Non Est. We don't exist."

#

The End

About the Author

British-born author A. J. Coates has spent his life working, living and exploring Africa and Central America. His exploits have included crossing the Sahara Desert and North Africa in an old Range Rover named Fifi, entering the World Rally Championships and expeditions through the depths of the forests in Central Africa and Central America.

A. J. Coates and his wife run Cresolus, a company that specializes in creating sustainable infrastructure in National Parks around the Tropical world. Cresolus often works closely with antipoaching units. They live on the side of the Panama Canal in Gamboa with their two children.

https://www.theextinctcompany.com

https://twitter.com/TheExtinctCo

https://www.facebook.com/historicalwildlifeprotection

* * *

Printed in Great Britain
by Amazon

65938788R00158